No Thanks to the Duke

By Alastair Dunnett

Fiction

NO THANKS TO THE DUKE
TREASURE AT SONNACH
HEARD TELL
THE DUKE'S DAY

Non-Fiction

THE HIGHLANDS AND ISLANDS OF SCOTLAND
QUEST BY CANOE
THE DONALDSON LINE
LAND OF SCOTCH
ALISTAIR MACLEAN INTRODUCES SCOTLAND (EDITOR)

No Thanks to the Duke

ALASTAIR DUNNETT

PUBLISHED FOR THE CRIME CLUB BY

DOUBLEDAY & COMPANY, INC.

GARDEN CITY, NEW YORK

1981

2518057

All of the characters in this book
are fictitious, and any resemblance
to actual persons, living or dead,
is purely coincidental.

To Dorothy

3.17.81 Creme S.00
Club

Library of Congress Cataloging in Publication Data

Dunnett, Alastair MacTavish, 1908–
No thanks to the Duke.

I. Title.
PR6054.U557N6   1981   823'.914
ISBN 0-385-17389-X
Library of Congress Catalog Card Number 80–1984

CHAPTER 1

This time, the doctor came personally to the front door to show Raeburn out. On the earlier visits it had been a receptionist who had led him to the street, but today she was not to be seen, and the doctor, a hand on Raeburn's elbow, steered him up the oak stairway from the carpeted basement. No doubt it was part of their long and decent tradition, the patient thought to himself—an extra courtesy after the death sentence.

The door was already opened upon the pavements and trees and looming circumference of Moray Place. "Well, I'll be hearing regularly from your own doctor, but keep in touch." Raeburn made an effort to concentrate on what was being said. This was Torrie, the specialist, the whole force of his lifetime's renown narrowed at this moment to the diagnostic searching of Raeburn's face. "Let me know if you want to talk —you know. Well . . ." and he shook hands firmly, nodding with the same direct gaze, until Raeburn turned away to walk down the steps, and the door softly closed.

A chill wind moved in the massive circle of the terrace, striking up from the cobbled roadway and pushing at the black spring twigs of the trees. The man stood looking at the familiar place, wondering if he might find any perspective of reality for the little time that lay ahead. He caught himself staring at the doorway he had just left. Nearly everybody he knew in Edinburgh had gone through it at some time, burdened by some hint of mortality. A double column of discreet small brass plates carried the individual names of a score and a half of the famous who consulted here. From attic to cellar of a mighty earlier town house, they perched with their apparatus and presided over hearts, kidneys, livers, stomachs, lungs, throats, ears, knees, necks, brains—everything. He noted that his own man was second top of the right-hand column. Much further down was the chap who had done his cartilage, when he was still playing.

I'll really need, he was saying to himself, to remember what he told me. And then he thought that Torrie might be watching him from behind the milky lozens of the door pane, so that it would be better to move. Anyway, one or two cars among those passing had passengers who waved to him, or pointed. It was always happening, requiring him to adopt his expression of agreeable vacuity by way of acknowledgment.

What was it, that long last summing-up of Torrie's? What exactly had he said? That was one of the irritating things about doctors—you never could remember what the devil they had been talking about. For one thing, Torrie had never once mentioned the name of the disease, and it had taken Raeburn a long time to discover what it was. He had had to look up books to trace some of these obscure names. Cancer was a word they seemed to avoid. And for that last interview he had stored carefully the word "terminal." Torrie would have to use that, surely, and then things would be clear-cut. But no. It wasn't there. And Raeburn, walking the streets, struggled to remember the sequences of words that built up unmistakably to his death.

All the time Torrie had held his eye. Probably this was something they all did, to see how much you could take as they adapted the words. Raeburn had found it embarrassing, and once or twice had strayed away to look towards the window top and the remote high chimneys of some further terrace. Ainslie Place, maybe—Doune Terrace?—where were they facing? It seemed to matter . . .

". . . of course, you know, we have to remember this. Mother Nature has some tricks of her own we know nothing about. Things could turn out quite differently—can assure you I've seen it happen in cases like yours—my duty to tell you what I have said. You ought to know now . . . you realise, I think, that what I've been trying to do for the last few weeks has been to stop it—even to hold it up . . . to some extent we had a little success. But . . ."

Torrie had paused then. This was where the questions came. Often the protests.

Raeburn let the silence run a little, and said: "I don't think that so far I feel any particular one thing about this . . . Thanks, incidentally, for the way you put it. It must be one of the least pleasant aspects of your job."

". . . Yes—well . . . I'll be giving a full report to your own doctor. You are in good hands with John Grant. He'll be keeping an eye on you, and I shall be in touch."

Inevitably: "How long have I got?"

The grey eye fixed unobtrusively on him again. "It's likely to be as much as a year. For at least half of that you can count on being as active as you are now."

Raeburn wondered if this might be even partly true. Certainly the thing had moved fast since his first visit hardly four months ago, and the scene in the consulting room was far from what it had been then. Stripping for that examination, he had been aware of Torrie's cool eye sizing him up:

". . . Yes—John Grant told me about these symptoms—quite right to have a check-up. We all need one from time to time . . . I must say, you look in as good condition as you were when you were playing. It seems only the other day that you retired. That Calcutta Cup try at Murrayfield—none of us will ever forget that. How long since . . . ?"

"Eighteen years. I got my knee the next season and was never sound enough."

"Is it really? Eighteen years! Time passes . . . Well, let's have a look at you."

It was always the same familiar dialogue, from which he never could escape. At times it bored him, especially when newer ploys were afoot, but he never resented it, for the people who spoke to him knew he was part of their own history. For all his twenty-seven caps, the two tours with the Lions, his nine-times captaincy of Scotland, the glorious Welsh trips, the almost always impossible odds at Twickenham—in spite of all these and more, it was that try against England that they remembered. He had taken a good ball direct from the scrum and made a beeline for his opposite, the marking stand-off, for he had spotted a thinning of the field beyond the man, left by the English backs as they herded to run the attack out of play. Their flank forwards lost him, too, and as he came up to the grabbing Fuller he punted the ball briefly over the stand-off's head, took it one-handed five yards beyond him, where a swerve and a lean with the free hand on the shoulder tumbled the converging inside three-quarter.

And there was the line, and he could be there in four seconds. The noise was not voices but an ocean wave of surfing emotion, lifting him. He held on straight, although he could see the white blaze of Mallinson, their wing man, going for the corner flag to cut him off; Mallinson with the flying tackle that had disheartened many a good man. The crowd moaned enormously as the dive started, aiming for the knees. But Raeburn put in the swerve again, this time to the inside, and again his timing held, so that Mallinson was flat out and knee high and in front of him as he leaped, hurdling above the taut airborne figure of the tackler, and then clear to the touchdown.

In later years it would perhaps have become less memorable if there had not been, behind the English goal, a photographer who took the famous picture. It was perfectly in focus. There was no blurring, no straining of neck muscles, no cut-off features, no grotesque tongue-out distortions. The lens had been low, and Raeburn seemed to stride the upper air, invulnerable, not gasping but triumphant, with the start of a smile, and beneath him, half a yard from the ground, stretched the lithe and baffled Mallinson, hands clawing the air, the puzzled look reaching to follow the scorer. It was a picture constantly republished

—one of the great sporting photographs—and Raeburn, whenever he saw it and remembered, knew again that unquenchable zest.

"Yes, I was saying to somebody the other day, 'We could do with Barry Raeburn back in the Scottish team these days' . . ." (Everybody said that.) Then Torrie with the stethoscope had become detached and professional, and soon the time had passed for offhand reassurances. There had been two more visits only, and then the twenty-four-hour stay in the clinic. And now this was it. The finish.

He remembered now more clearly another part of the earlier dialogue, when he had taken a small bottle from his pocket and put it on the desk in front of Torrie. "Perhaps I'd better show you these. They're sleeping pills I got from Dr Grant. He prescribed them because I wasn't able to sleep on the overnight south trains when I go to these conferences. There were fifty in the bottle and I've only had two or three—"

"Have you trouble sleeping?" Torrie took the bottle remotely, watching. "At home?"

"Not really. I only needed them for the train. I suppose, though, later on . . . I'll need . . . drugs and things." He held his hand out for the bottle.

Torrie, gently ignoring the hand, opened a drawer and slid the bottle within. "Better just leave these here. They're really not at all suitable at this stage. You can be absolutely certain, Mr Raeburn, that everything you need will be available long before the time comes. As I say, I'll be in constant touch with Dr Grant . . ."

That had been a bad mistake of his, about the sleeping pills. Torrie had seen the danger at once, of course. They were the sensible way out. It was intolerable that Torrie and Grant and many another decent medical should have to put up with his dwindling frailty and corruption as the disease encroached upon him for all that time ahead. He wasn't going to be one of these lingerers.

The simple idea that would allow him to master his own future grew clear in Raeburn's mind. He wondered, as he walked, why he should be so little moved by the enormity of it. Occasional pedestrians were noticing him now, and some waved boldly or diffidently, or, rarely, with the friendly understanding that did not impel them to be seen making up to a celebrity.

There was one shambling figure, in tweeds and with a stick, who lurched to a stop, clearly glad for the excuse to cease the effort to make one laborious step after another. The ancient fellow lifted his tremulous walking stick and squeaked: "Barry!"

Raeburn flourished a return wave full of courtesy and deference, with that motion towards his wrist that told of how the time pressed upon him, or otherwise he would stay and talk away an hour or two.

It was "Beaky" Dobson, well into his nineties now and refusing to die. Perhaps, it occurred to Raeburn for the first time, long anxious to be gone and resentful at the Lord's reluctance to take him. Dobson was one of the immortals of Scottish rugby, scrum half and captain for a handful of successful seasons away at the beginning of the century, a hero of tales, although hardly a living soul had seen him play. Already then an old man, he had been chairman of the selection committee which had awarded Raeburn his first cap, and had kept in touch, inoffensively patronising. Now the younger man found it impossible to encounter him, finding no tolerance left in him for the pitiful bag of frailty Dobson was.

Not that way—Not that way! Raeburn was saying to himself almost audibly as he hurried, and he felt elated and even healthier for what was now a decision already taken.

By this time the steps of his purpose had taken him to the Dean Bridge.

Thomas Telford had built the Dean Bridge some time in the 1830s to carry the main road from the West End of Edinburgh to Queensferry, and it was still the main route to the road bridge across the River Forth. On the level it seemed like a part of the ordinary highway crammed with the traffic in and out of the capital. The high parapets concealed the immense arched drop to the Water of Leith, which here has torn a canyon out of the rock so that the river runs a hundred and twenty feet or more below the road.

It would do, thought Raeburn, as he strolled the pavement of the bridge on the side that looked to the east through the New Town. There were few pedestrians, but already the cars were numerous. Beside one of the first lamp-posts he found a spot where a section of the small parapet spikes had been broken away, leaving a span of a foot or two where the stonework was clear. He stopped here, craning over to see the river below, and the tops of the trees.

It would be easy. He needed first to see where the direct drop would take him, and this meant a clear view straight down over the parapet. He waited for a long break in the traffic, until the bridge was practically empty. There was no stir at any of the windows of the overlooking terrace houses. So he put his hands on the cleared portion of parapet and jumped in a checked vault, several times, so that his easy lifting showed him successive glimpses of the immediate target of the plunge. When he finally came back to rest on the pavement, and took his hands from the wall, he found that he was nodding in approval. Moreover, the effort had not touched his breathing or waist muscles, in spite of the rot within.

Then he went round by Bell's Brae and the Miller Row that led the thoroughfare down to the riverside and under the bridge. Here, although the roadway would be wide enough to allow the mortuary van to come in, it had a barricade of padlocked posts to keep out the sight-seeing cars. Immensely high above, the bridge road dropped its graceful arches to the slabbed bed of the river, now murmuring into quiet after the turmoil of the mill waterfalls upstream. He stood for a time at the clear-domed barrier of the low, irregular wall bounding the river, the stones almost painted smooth with a close green fungus. At this place the bed of the Water of Leith spread in shallow stone steps where the flow streamed and quickened towards the sea. Above the small rock walls that formed the glen, the high house terraces crowded solid, like cliffs themselves with their stone faces, and there were plentiful trees, brushed with early green.

From further along the path, looking up to the bridge, he could read-ily identify the lamp-post which would be his mark, and fancied he even saw the cleared top wall where the length of three-inch iron spikes was stripped away. The whole place was, of course, ideal. It would have to be at night—that night; and a letter or two delivered by daylight would ensure that everything was cleared up before the town was stirring.

The few details left were already resolved in his mind by the time he had walked back to his flat in Marchmont. The main items would be the letters, but first he tidied and packed and sorted, although little of that needed to be done, since his housekeeping had been for many a year a low-pitched system of simplicity. He had enjoyed this austerity, with only an occasional pang of yearning for some close companionship that had never come.

In the first hour or two he was tempted to linger over the small tasks; to sort and fondle the familiar books, remembering where he had bought them, their midnight intimacy, the enlargement they had given to a life which had perhaps had too much fame, too soon. To many of them, or to the mixture of them, he owed the peace that held him now.

It was time, now, to write the letters. Although he was a man used to words and to being heard, he had still thought this part would be difficult. But it came easy and flowing. First there was the letter to the lawyer—brief and only mildly apologetic. These were realistic chaps, and in fact there wouldn't be much to do. They had the will and the other papers. They knew quite well the next-of-kin—his stepsister in Perthshire. There wasn't much, but everything would go to her two boys, who were shy of him but who spoke of him elsewhere. Next, a letter to her. She would understand. There had been good friendship between them—nothing like blind family affection, but a gentle matur-ing regard of which this, the last intimation, would be one more revealing fold.

He had then, of course, to do a note for his own doctor, John Grant

—the decent man, a friend even in the remoteness of his attentions when Raeburn, embarrassed, had gone to him with the trifling twinges of early middle age. Grant had almost stopped playing rugby by the time Raeburn was into the senior scene, but they had met occasionally on the field and thereafter, and this made for timely pleasantries, although Grant had never got beyond club games, and seemed content with that. His letter asked Grant to advise Torrie of the final stages before it made the newspapers. Thank God it wouldn't make much in the newspapers, anyway. No coroner's court and that wallow in amateur dramatics. A senior police officer would intimate that there was no suspicion of foul play, and so they would dispose of him . . . One or two other letters. The headmaster, to whom he had already hinted of a health crisis. One or two of the teachers—good fellows who had taken boys on climbing and ski-ing trips with him, refereed games, made up parties for the big matches—all the essential trivia he had always thought so important because they conditioned people who were to be men, but trivia still, now growing remote.

The letter to the police was going to be the difficulty. It would have to be in their hands by about four the next morning: no earlier, and for decency's sake not much later. It would go to Jimmy Paterson, the night superintendent who would be on duty between midnight and morning, and who would get everything cleared up before the city got started the next day. He had played with Jimmy and they had kept in touch. Raeburn's problem was how to ensure that the letter got there at the right time, when he himself would be gone. He pondered this one. There was still time.

It occurred to him at last to phone to the home of *The Scotsman*'s rugby writer, to find out if any late-night editorial worker on the paper could hand in the letter to Jimmy at 4 a.m. And this was easy, for the late-night sub-editor would be going home at that time and the car could drop him off for a moment in the High Street while he went in with the letter for Jimmy personally. A few telephone calls were necessary to make this arrangement, for the rugby reporter was an outside man and didn't know much about the late-night working of the production side:

"If you like, Barry, I could get our late chaps to phone a message for Paterson to get immediately he comes on duty. Eh?"

"Thanks, Angus—No, I don't want it that way. The letter in at four in the morning. No sooner."

"OK. You go in and see the late man—Peter Morrison—and he'll do what you want. I've spoken to him. Incidentally, is there a story somewhere in this? I don't want to miss anything. Can't you give me a line for tomorrow's paper?"

"No—sorry—too soon. There may be something of a story for the paper the next day."

"Bloody mysterious, eh?"

"Don't worry, Angus. You won't miss anything."

They finished at that, and Raeburn wrote the letter straightforwardly to the police officer. A letter, too, he thought, to the rugby writer, who had been helpful on many an occasion. He could be told in confidence what lay behind the whole procedure, and the time might even come, in the years ahead, when he might write something of this. Many another future victim, Raeburn thought, might be glad to learn of this simple way out.

It seemed to Raeburn, as he sealed the envelopes, that he had never known such freedom. Tomorrow, there would be no petty smallness, no fearful looking out for symptoms, no groping for cures, no regrets, no guilt, no forethoughts. This was the way to do it, when the time came. The future fell from him like a drear burden.

Soon after midnight he gathered the letters together, and sealed them in a plastic bag, enclosing them with his passport, which as an afterthought he added by way of identification, and then put the packet upside-down inside another plastic bag, and sealed that. He had already looked out his newest track suit, thinking of its suitability for the purpose with the elastic at wrists and ankles. By daybreak, after some hours in the threshing water, he should be reasonably tidy and assembled.

He had left from the package the letter for the police official, which he had marked "Urgent. Immediate." The others, in their bundle, he pouched in the inner pocket of the track suit, and as he pulled shut and locked the door of his flat, he put the key in the trouser pocket. That was all he took.

He walked to the Old Town, and at the back entrance to *The Scotsman* in Fleshmarket Close, Peter Morrison was summoned from inside to come and meet him.

"Hullo!—Yes, I know about this, Mr Raeburn. You want me to hand it in about four when I am on the way home. Right?"

"Right! Glad if you can try to give it to the Superintendent personally. He's an old friend. It's a wee personal thing."

"Fine! Yes, I'll do that. OK, then. Good night. Pleasure. What sort of team will we have next season?"

"Oh, well—you know . . . Good night. Thanks again."

As he walked to the other end of the town, it was pleasant not to find any nostalgia bearing upon him. The castle was floodlit, not dazzling but a subdued gold, and the streets were thronged with people and wheels. He went by Rose Street and the lanes, not to be recognised nor to have the oddity of his gear remarked. The St George's West bell rang one in the morning as he passed it, and two minutes later he was on the Dean Bridge.

At the part of the parapet he had selected, beside the lamp-post, he had to wait briefly for a car or two to enter the bridge and pass. Now it was empty. It was time.

He placed his open palms strongly upon the bald parapet, flexed his knees and waist briefly, and vaulted over, lifting his legs high, the ankles together, as they carried him out from the stonework to let him fall flat and face downward into the void.

Momentarily, in the preparations of the evening, he had even thought about his posture as he went down. It would be best to turn face-down to the river, legs and arms spread. But as he now fell he stretched his arms involuntarily below him, seeking the first impact with his fingers. It was in his mind that, before the smashing of his belly and pelvis, with the rest to follow, his fingers might encounter the trees at the end of the hundred-foot fall and more, and he had wondered how long this might take, and whether there would be time for his mind to signal that the earth and the stones awaited him.

Now, as he fell, almost at once his fingers seemed to be meshed in the twigs, and there was a check rather than a blow. He waited for the crushing, ruinous battering of his body at the middle. But instead, there was nothing—and then it was his head, at the back, that felt the impact, the eliminating blow. And again. And he was lifeless.

CHAPTER 2

Men who awaken from a deep and normal sleep know readily where they are. There is a long habit in the mind that quickly reassures the stirring brain, reminding it of where it lay down last and of the slow, conscious certainty of finding itself there again. If for any reason in the night the mind has strayed unanchored, there is a small period of quiet nightmare when the sleeper reaches for his soul, to tell him again how he is placed in the world of life.

When it is not sleep but insensibility that carries the man into the night, it takes longer. In such a case an unnatural oblivion has been inserted between the man and his mind, so that he will be inert for a time, even with most of his senses back, and not know how he fares, nor where he is—nor even care greatly. After violent unconsciousness, or surgery, however gentle the anaesthesia, there is always this suspended awareness, a kind of floating indifference, with not even a human curiosity which would help the mind to force itself back into play.

How much longer then will that pause be for the mind which is expecting death. As he lay, wherever it was, Raeburn knew he had been in space for a long time; and for a long time after that he had swum as he now was, suspended, not knowing if he suffered or not, saw or not; or even existed. In his frequent lifetime thoughts about the matter he had felt convinced there was indeed a hereafter, but could not persuade himself that in its early stages it would be spectacular and full of revelation. All that would take time—adjustment—and of course this was as it should be.

There was no telling where he was. He could see nothing, and imagined this might be because his eyes, if they remained, were probably shut, and that in any case the new dimension of his existence would need to prepare him for some visual experience immensely more profound than mere human sight. With the growing wakefulness of his reason, it occurred to him that, even detached as he was, he ought to be able, if still in life, to feel the sodden cold of the river. But there seemed something like a dry warmth about him. And it might even be comfortable.

But this must be death. There was no pulp of pain, so the healing, that some had so long to wait for, had fallen upon him. Once over that parapet and nothing mortal could have borne him up.

It seemed that the thoughts, flooding from somewhere, started to run through him almost as if he were in life. He waited for what was to happen next: ready to test if there were mortal comparisons. He not only saw and heard nothing, but there was no awareness of a mouth and eyes.

What would come back first, if it were to be a normal return to living consciousness? Of course, the hearing. There was nothing to hear. Not merely a silence—a nothing. But he was able now to compass such a thinking—to bring back some order from the remoteness of his mind. To put questions to what he remembered of his life.

How much of him was left? Hands? Fingers? These must be gone. And he was able now to send out, from what might be his mind, questing messengers to what might be his body. This was a long, inert groping into the dark.

He was not broken. There had to be some effort now from him to link one world and the other, because he was between them. This he knew, if only because he knew he was able to make some enquiry of the darkness. Then he remembered more. He remembered that he had long ago invented for himself an invariable test, in the several times he had experienced senselessness—say after anaesthesia, or finding himself senseless on the field of play. It was simple. You simply twitched your toes. If they moved at your will, this could be the start of the return of nerve and muscle control.

Gently, within himself, he searched out the faraway sinews of his toes, and curled them. They twitched in movement—and again at his bidding. It was real, because he felt them touch familiarly at the linings of his shoes. The same training shoes, and he was wearing them. He made larger movements now, and frictioned against the wrinkle on the left side little toe where he always blistered during a run, but had never felt sufficiently discomfited to get the lining fixed.

Normal! By God, normal!

Now his tongue moved easily round the inside walls of his teeth, and they were all there. His mouth intact. Another curtain lifted, and he sought out his hands, which were laid folded gently in front of him, as they usually were when he slept. Consciousness now came fast. He was lying on his side. He was unhurt. He was not dead.

"That's right, Barry—Barry Raeburn. Take your time. No hurry."

There was nothing alien even about the voice. Suddenly the whole situation became trifling, shrunk to his own small predicament. What other world existed which used these comforting banalities? Wise—reassuring . . .

He had to see.

"Open your eyes."

A pause, and he opened them. He was looking into a known face—a man with greying tufts at the temples and a half-smile of professional encouragement. It was the face of John Grant, his own doctor, and he spoke again in an approving banter:

". . . a practically classical case of recovery from unconsciousness."

The two pairs of eyes stayed upon each other. Raeburn at last heaved out an articulation.

"Hullo!" he said, but it was a sideways mumble. He ran his tongue again round the inside of his mouth, remembering faintly the difficult start of vocalising after insensibility—even after ordinary sleep. Tried again.

"Where am I . . . ? Where's this?" He had made a strong effort, but again it was a slurred nothing.

Grant was brisk in the reply, leaning forward from some large chair. "You may well ask." That well-known, slightly nasal Speyside rumble in the voice. "It's a long story. You're all right. Just be quiet and do what you're told. I'm going to"—his fingers were already searching as Raeburn's eyes fell shut—"see if you've come to any harm."

He took seconds only to reach the wincing spot behind the ear that had distantly ached, and that now stabbed Raeburn to the brain as the fingers probed. At last the touching moved on, seemingly contented. He moved his limbs to the routine command, and they moved. The two men went through the familiar doctor routines, the voice quietly taking the confident authority that made one lift this and bend that, while Raeburn's only thought grew and prevailed that, but for this lethargy that seemed all his hurt, he was also in control. The shattered body, drained and washing in the stream, was a planned dream which had not come true. There was nothing in his mind that could compass this change, nor could he arouse enough to question the events. All he realised, unmoved, was that the death he had arranged had not come about, and would at another time have to be met again. He was alive somewhere. He could not recognise whether he cared.

The hands stopped roving over him. "Are you there?"

It was still Grant's voice, so he forced his eyes open to look at the physician, who was still looking down, quizzing, sizing up.

There was to be no escape from this long struggle back to the small scale of life. "I'm here . . ." Raeburn managed. It was clearer now, although slow. "But where?"

"You're in good hands." Grant was preparing something. "Now I'm going to give you a real sleep." The knowing fingers took Raeburn's arm, and he felt the sting of the needle and the cold mingling with his blood.

There was a distant dialogue:

"How long will that take?"

"Five hours—six maybe—not more." This was Grant.

"His Grace will see him immediately."

It didn't mean anything. "Time?" Raeburn grunted. No use, it seemed, asking where.

"About half-past three in the morning," said Grant briskly, and he appeared to be shutting his bag. "Hell of a time to get me up."

That must be right, Raeburn thought, as he felt the drug dropping between himself and his awareness. Of course, it must be the middle of the night. That was what was different about Grant. He wasn't shaved. Raeburn had seen a lot of him in one setting or another for the last twenty years, and he had never seen him with this grey stubble. It was an aspect of him reserved for childbed women, or the dying, and others with no sense of time.

As the drug took him, Raeburn had a sudden clear sense of a ridiculous failure.

There was no clouding of his mind when he came to life the next time. He was aware of a sweet, soaring sweep upwards from some benign depth, and felt his mind clearing with it. He was in the same place, relaxed, limp, ready. Deliberately he set to a session of stretching, pushing out each limb and tensing the sinews. Then he opened his eyes.

It was a bedroom, quite large, expensively and quietly furnished; the most stylish he had ever lain in. A youngish man was seated in an armchair, meeting his eyes across the room, and speaking:

"That's fine! That's very good! How do you feel?" The last words came through a sudden smile that might have had no more emotion than ingratiating efficiency.

"I'm fine—I think." Raeburn had started to sit upright, and found he could. "Would you mind telling me . . ."

"Dr Grant said you would come out of that last lot without a hangup—and my goodness, he was right!" The stranger nodded, approving a minor phenomenon. "My name's George Dale, by the way. Now, can I tell you—"

"Yes, for God's sake tell me!" Raeburn had stepped to the floor, and stood there. In his sleep he had been stripped of his track suit. All he wore now was a shirt. Someone else's.

The other man stood at the window, looking out. "I'm not the one to tell you the whole story, but I can say this much. You were trying to commit suicide, and we stopped you. We had a damn good reason for stopping you." Again the smile, fixed to please. "Will that be enough for now?" He pointed downwards from the window. "See there—"

Raeburn stepped to the glass. The view looked down on to the Dean

Bridge, where the morning traffic was strung close, starting and stopping as it jerked forward in groups on the congested parapet. Away below, far out of sight of the drivers, was the gorge of the Water of Leith streaming harmlessly in the sun. The building which commanded this view was one among those piled terraces he had studied earlier, below which he was to come to rest in the recent darkness. There was his parapet—he could even see the break, smoothing the top, where the small spikes had been broken away and which had been the resting place for his open hands.

Seething with questions, he turned to this George Dale. But the fellow was shaking his head:

"First things first." It was a diffident but firm instruction. He pointed to a door. "That's a bathroom. Some of your clothes are in there. After a shower and change there will be something to eat. Plenty of time then for talking—"

"A minute though. How did—"

Dale's head shook again, and the smile came back, like a perpetual salesman. "His Grace will tell you everything."

"His Grace? Who's he?"

The other was holding out a card in his hand; a photograph, which might have formed part of a passport or some such document of authority. The likeness was of a man Raeburn instantly recognised, for it had looked at him for years from the pages of newspapers, usually the pages he did not feel able to read closely. It was a Duke, not royal, but powerful. Not one of those who showed the public renowned gardens, but a man in business, owning and influencing things, buying and selling, mastering the movements of fleets of ships and aircraft, making shares rise and fall, demolishing buildings and raising others, making banks ponder and hold meetings. The face had been in the financial pages only yesterday morning—had it been yesterday?—in connection with some story about amalgamating half the breweries of Europe. He hadn't read it attentively.

"Oh, I see. *That* Duke."

Even Raeburn knew that this Duke was the sort of man whose answers to questions would be worth hearing. Moreover, his clearing head was telling him that from now on there appeared to be very little need to be troubled with aspects of events that were no more than incidentals. It was large answers he wanted.

But whatever happened, Torrie's words still remained. This was only a lengthened breathing space. A shower seemed desirable. He nodded back at Dale.

A chair in the bathroom had some of his familiar underwear, his second best tweed suit, and the shirt and shoes he would have chosen himself.

He enjoyed the shower, and stopped guessing. Every minute he now lived was filched from the future. As he dried off, he watched himself in a full-length mirror. The flat, muscled belly seemed unimpaired, and suddenly he did what he had not dared to do for many weeks. His tensed fingers went to the spot where first Grant and then Torrie had found and delineated the pain, and he pressed hard.

It was less than he had expected, so that he kept the pressure up. He had grown used to probings, but there seemed to be less sign than before of the disaster that bloated there; less hint of the eventual pain.

"That's your grub ready—any time." Dale's face was looking at him in the mirror as he leaned through the door at Raeburn's back. He had perhaps been there for some time.

"Yes," he said, pointing to the searching fingers that Raeburn still thrust inwards, "your doctor said a funny thing. He said that things like an extreme shock might abate the development of whatever is going on in there. You know—sort of waves of adrenalin. Well," he broke it off chattily, "you never know your luck. Certainly you've had a shock or two."

He closed the door in front of himself. Opened it almost at once, sagely informative: "More to come," and was away. Raeburn locked the door and dressed.

He slid into the familiar pockets a collection of his personal things that were lying on a dressing-table top; pocket book, cheque book, note case with his driving licence and other things; keys, car keys, pens, comb, scribbling memo pad, pocket-knife—you needed some of these things when you had to do with kids. Whoever had made the selection hadn't brought the lucky Irish penny a referee had given him at his first captain's game at Cardiff Arms Park. But he felt dressed now—assembled.

The bathroom door opened on to a freshly laid table with coffee things and plates of hot sandwich rolls, marmalade and cold meat. Dale set a chair for him, poured the first cup of coffee.

"One thing," Dale said. "Dr Grant said you were to phone him at once if there was anything he could explain. You know, if you wanted to talk to him—to see him."

Raeburn's mouth was full. He found it satisfying. "I've seen him."

"Very good." Dale was at the door, on his face the smile that made him look like a salesman. "Now I'll go and tell him you're ready. He wants to talk to you." For all Dale's schooled informality, as he went out closing the door there was an undoubted sibilant hint of capital letters on "Him" and "He."

Raeburn ate on, and did not pause when the Duke came in. Dale rushed an armchair into the window space. The Duke rearranged it, and sat at ease. He was clearly not a person to be impeded by greetings or handshakes.

"Please go on with your food," he said. ". . . I see you are. Good."

He was not as tall as Raeburn had expected, but more sallow. The elbows resting on the chair arms allowed him to prop his temples with two fingers on each side, while the black hair fell lank and straight. There was a jet ring on a finger.

"The time is twenty minutes short of midday," he stated. "Good progress, I should say. You must have many questions to ask."

Raeburn drank coffee, swallowing. "Not yet."

The Duke's nod was fully approving. "There are two chief elements to the narrative—mainly—indeed only. The first is how you come to be here." He faintly raised an eyebrow. "The second is why."

"Quite right." A fragment of ham hung from Raeburn's lip. He pushed it into his mouth with his thumb.

"I should say by way of preliminary that this house belongs to me."

"Never knew you lived in Edinburgh."

"I do not, except occasionally. The house is in another name."

After a pause: "It would in fact be difficult to say exactly where I do live, but I have a foothold in one or two other parts of Scotland."

He felt no need to look towards Raeburn while these words were spoken. After a pause, he let a hand fall over in the direction of Dale:

"Yesterday afternoon, he and I saw your performance on the Dean Bridge below us. I may say I was the one who recognised you. The behaviour, however, as you will recall, was unusual, and eloquent. By the time you had ceased your, shall I say, unmistakable jumping actions, it was all too clear what your purpose was.

"I do not think we need to examine motives and reasonings at this stage. I have no objection whatever to anyone disposing of himself in any way he pleases, provided I have no continuing interest. It happened that I was moved to investigate and probably to abort the decision."

"Why?"

"Ah, well." The Duke was tolerant of the interruption. "That belongs to the second part of our discourse. I think you may be more interested in the first place in how it was possible to suspend your plans."

He waited for Raeburn's query, but there was none. The Duke continued:

"Some necessary deduction led to the thought that the attempt would be made at a late hour. Accordingly we had some time to prepare plans. A servant of mine, MacFarlane, had accompanied me from the north of Scotland. He is a man of some resource, employed primarily as a gamekeeper, but available for a variety of duties.

"If you will now step to the window you will see that there is a lamp-post on the pavement at the spot which you had selected. After dark at this time of year it lights the roadway and leaves the outside of the bridge in darkness. Using, as you did yourself, some fortuitous gaps in the traffic and pedestrian flow, MacFarlane climbed the lamp-post—it should be mentioned that he had and still enjoys a reputation as a Commando trainer, as do some other of my estate workers. He fixed thin lines to the bracket of the lamp and brought them unobtrusively to pavement level. He then crossed the wall with some climbing apparatus and fixed a series of cleats below the parapet on the outside. To these he hooked a large net like a curtain, making a bag of it by attaching the ends of the lines from the top of the lamp-post to the outside edge of the net. I may say that the lines were not visible in the lamplight, and of course no one of ordinary height could see the net. Thereafter MacFarlane spent some hours of last night—"

The Duke turned suddenly to Dale. "Has he met MacFarlane?"

"No, sir."

"He shall. They will travel together to Kintalla. This afternoon. Raeburn will drive." The Duke held up a limp hand to ward off any questions. "I was saying that MacFarlane spent some hours in the net, waiting for you. He had an arrangement with two fishing rods which thrust the tied ends outwards. We gave him a bleep radio signal about 1 a.m. when you arrived, so that all was ready. You leaped into the net. I am afraid it was necessary for MacFarlane to give you a brief blow at the back of the head."

Standing at the window, Raeburn pushed the last bite of sandwich into his mouth and rubbed the back of his ear:

"I see. Then you carried me round here."

"Mm?—not quite. We brought you by car. MacFarlane stayed behind briefly to dismantle the trap."

Raeburn sat again, finishing his coffee. "I suppose you know that a lot of people will know by now. What about them?"

The Duke spread his hands. "Now, there, I am afraid we took some liberties. You had the letters in your pocket. There was no problem involved in intercepting them, and you can have them to retain or destroy as you will. The letter to Dr Grant was particularly helpful, and he came round, as I think you apprehended, to see you.

"The letter to the police proved to be the most difficult, as the journalist who was to deliver it would not hand it back except to you personally. It was necessary to snatch it from him at the entrance to police headquarters. He did not come to any harm, and the only trace of embarrassment will arise out of a telephone call you must make to Superintendent Paterson, who will no doubt be looking for you, to learn why a letter from you to be delivered personally was stolen in the middle of the night on his official doorstep."

"Yes, he'll be after it by now." Raeburn rubbed his ear. "I suppose I can think of something. The main item now is . . ."

"If your imagination fails, Dale here has sketched out a credible script."

Raeburn was again aware of that sloughing of the small things; astonished that he cared little how the record was closed. Only one single thing now.

"Only one single thing now interests me," he told them. "We know how it was done. Now—*why?*"

The man in the armchair did not bend any responsive look upon him. For a long time he didn't say anything, resting his fingertips at his temples where the hair dangled straight. Then:

"I have employment for you," said the Duke.

CHAPTER 3

Raeburn let the responsive phrase move loosely through his head for many seconds before he even began to guess at what it might mean. Then he conned it more closely.

What did the fellow mean by this studied pedantry? He waited for the expansion of the theme, but the Duke had lapsed again into incommunication, as if what he had said explained all. Having spoken, the arrogance of generations came through, and he would have regarded explanation as a menial requirement.

Raeburn was benefited by being in no hurry himself. "Well," he said casually, lounging, "you'd better tell me what that means. As it happens, I have a job."

"So?" The Duke stirred mildly. "I thought that you had given that up. There was a letter, addressed to your employer."

"Perhaps it's just as well he didn't get it. There is now a basic misstatement in the letter."

Again the Duke was not silent, but absent. Raeburn went on:

"Anyway, I can't take odd jobs—I'm a schoolmaster, a teacher—I'm head of our junior school nowadays but I still teach. It's all I've been trained for . . . Sport's out. In fact, as you know by now, I'm on the way out myself."

This time the Duke nodded sideways, speaking. "That is what you have been told by experts. I do not trust experts or specialists in any field, least of all in matters of life and death. If we are to have an association, you will permit me to pursue this health matter in my own way."

He gave Raeburn a pause. Took his silence. Removed then his fingers from the temples to allow himself to nod his head, not in any spirit of agreement, but so as to alter the course of the conversation. He had the kind of voice which changed agendas.

"Tell me," he asked Raeburn, "do you know where Kintalla is?"

The other worked it in his head, hearing it chime with half-remembered items of information which had no special meaning:

"Kintalla . . . ? Yes . . . I've heard of it. A castle—an estate—

somewhere in the south of Scotland . . . Galloway. Eh? In fact, it's yours, isn't it?"

"Correct. Now, another question, if you will be so good. What do you know about Markland? Markland School?" He looked directly at Raeburn.

Raeburn dragged this one out of official snippets, minor gossip from common-rooms. "Well—I've heard of it . . . It's one of the newer boarding schools . . . country-based . . . broad principles . . . free and easy . . . no old tradition. You know, talk your way to education. Pretty good, I hear. They can afford to be progressive—much in fashion these days—mixed bag of boneheads and sprigs of nobility—That's probably unfair—there is a royal prince on the roll, one of ours, isn't there . . . ?"

The Duke's posture might have suggested assent.

"You may say," he said, "that the last item is the whole point of our current interest," and he began to talk as if giving an instruction, a briefing:

"I have, as you perhaps know, much to do with the managing of affairs in many parts of the world. Consequently, information comes the way of my organisation, and indeed may be said to form an important part of our assets. Some of this information comes from reliable if unorthodox sources, and may be worth passing on to suitable recipients provided we ourselves have nothing to lose thereby. In this context, although it has no bearing on the present topic, we have lately intercepted two distinct and separate aircraft hi-jacking attempts, one on a formidable diplomatic scale. I mention this only as a measure of the weight to be attached to the information which has now come to hand and on which we—that is, including you—are planning to act. The facts are as follows:

"Within the next ten days a highly competent attempt will be made to kidnap the schoolboy prince and hold him to ransom. The coup is already minutely planned. It is the work of an unobtrusively efficient group of operatives, some of whom we have already encountered. A few of them are already to be identified in the neighbourhood of Markland, which is within a few miles of Kintalla. I take some interest in the school already, but of course they know nothing of what is afoot, and I do not propose that they should. Nor should any other authority. It is essential that the attempt should come near to success. Only in that way may we be certain that the kidnapping group can be completely eliminated. This is a prime opportunity for sharp and unforgettable justice in what has become one of the most troublesome crimes of modern times . . . At this point you may want to offer some comment."

"But the Royal Family—princes and so on"—even Raeburn's new

shape of priorities could not abate his staring intent—"they're guarded, even at school. There are people watching them . . . all the time . . ."

Again the controlled nod: "There is a single detective, in residence at the school. He has the prince under his surveillance for about half of the daytime, or less. The local constabulary is also alerted—to use the improbable official word—when the personage is engaged in outside occupations. Meaningless arrangements—useless, all of them."

"But if you are sure this attempt is to be made, why not get the forces out now? They'd turn out the whole damned army—"

"So obvious, is it not, what would happen then. The attempt would trickle away out of sight and be mounted at another time and place. No —can we hold, please, to the plan, which is settled in general principle. We are dealing with not more than ten individuals. I can base on Kintalla at once at least that number of stalkers, gillies, gamekeepers—men who can kill. Others are in place around the parish, not recognisable as strangers. I shall have a small house party at Kintalla—close and reliable personal friends to whom hunting is a serious matter, and patriotism an even larger issue. Various transport and destructive equipment are also at disposition. This has been the work of the past two weeks or so; that is, since the kidnap intention became irrefutably declared. Since this is the end of the Easter term holiday the boys are not yet in residence at the school. They will be arriving on the afternoon and evening of two days from now—Thursday.

"Now"—again that imperceptible change of tone, signalling a new theme: also the pause which would allow Raeburn to insert a query: he could not at that moment think of one that would not sound a miniature irrelevance—"there is one significant element missing from these preparations. We have no unit actually installed in the school premises. I need someone there day and night, thoroughly acquainted with the entire purpose of our planning and the proposed attack; trustworthy; of proved character and integrity; prepared to take physical risks, if necessary—if I may be allowed a crudity for the sake of speed and compression—to the point of his own elimination.

"I am, therefore, thinking of you. You have the requisites. It will be simple to install you as a teacher, vigilant and informed."

Raeburn took his turn at the pause-making. Expendable, that's me. Well, I had already declared that. Everything else seemed minor in style.

"Obvious question," he told the Duke, "but how do you get me in?"

"By arrangement with the headmaster."

It was too simple. There was something wrong, something missing; and Raeburn strained to assemble in his mind some of the prudent considerations he ought to be putting forward. But a great deal of his perspectives had gone with the decision to jump the bridge. All that he could seize hold of seemed to be small things, such as this kind of man would long since have balanced and dismissed.

"So nobody else in the school would know?"

"Nobody. Not the headmaster, not the teachers or staff, not the prince, not the detective. Nor the Royal Family—nor any authority. No alerting. No alarms."

"Well . . . look. You'll have a team of well over a dozen in your outfit. What guarantee have you that none of them will leak out the whole purpose of the exercise?"

"That is truly a relevant question. I have a fair experience of treachery and unreliability, having bought loyalties which were believed to be pledged elsewhere. Except for yourself, every man is bound to my causes in firm ways. Many of the estate and business elements are individuals whose service to me and my house goes back for generations. He"—the hand again drooped to indicate Dale—"is the most recent of my employees. Six years ago he joined me direct from Cambridge, where he qualified acceptably. Since that time he has represented us in Kenya, Libya, Chicago, London, Singapore, and now again at headquarters. I have satisfied myself that his record is proved. Moreover, none of my employees at any level is permitted to engage in outside activities of a formal character—no radio or television interviews, no magazine articles, no writing of books, no charitable committees, and what not. Any such activities of that kind as are required—and they are rare —are undertaken by myself, or they are not done. We are not, on the whole, an organisation disposed to explain itself in public."

"Still, there's me."

The Duke dismissed it. "None better than you knows the answer to that. You are not likely, after recent events, to be about to embark on a course of immediate deviousness. When and if you feel a profound character change coming on it would be wise to let me know. I should think your attitude is one of substantial simplification. This probability allowed me to assume that you would take part." He brooded absently for a time, as if the outcome carried no significance.

"OK," said Raeburn. "I'll do it. I have some doubts about how the whole scheme would work out. I have to think . . . But in any case, if there are kidnappers, let's get after them. When do we start?"

"Immediately."

"First of all," Raeburn said, rising, "I'll need to go back to my place. Have to collect my things . . ."

The Duke motioned him down:

"I hope we have spared you some trouble." To Dale: "Tell him."

Dale said: "We've been to your flat. No trouble—the key was in your pocket. Two of your largest suitcases have been packed with the clothes you were most likely to need for the next few weeks. We have them here. Included is your track suit, which you were wearing when —Also books."

"Naturally, you can send for any other things needed—or purchase them as required. This will not be a long-drawn-out undertaking." The Duke signalled again to Dale: "The documents."

Dale handed a brief package to his master, who dispensed them, still from his chair:

"Here is your passport. Most unlikely you will require it on this mission, but it ought to be with you. This"—in a transparent sheath, the match of the one Dale had shown him at the beginning—"is one of our organisation's internal passes, made out in your name, and with your picture for identification. Again, an unlikely item for immediate use, but it may save time later. Here are some sheets of your own addressed stationery, for any letters which are necessary to send at this time, even to cover your removal from your usual scenes. These next two items are detailed contour maps of the land adjacent to Markland, including the moor hinterland; also the grounds and farther policies of Kintalla; study them when you have an opportunity. Finally, cash. Here is a thousand pounds, for which you can give some reasonable accounting later."

Raeburn had never handled a thousand pounds—had not even been aware of seeing a handful like that. It was a flat package in a buff envelope, in twenty-pound notes, bound with paper strips in fives. He plunged the pack deep into his pocket, tapping repeatedly.

"Don't tap," said Dale. "It only draws attention to something valuable. They won't fall out."

There were only two remaining tail-end pieces of his old life to get rid of. In an internal cubicle off some hall, Dale showed him a telephone. He spoke to Jimmy Paterson, the night police superintendent, at his home. Dale's contrived story had been useless—something about a practical joke to alert the police for a bet in the middle of the night. He found himself telling Jimmy about a worry he had developed; a suspicion that someone was distributing drugs among the senior schoolboys. "But I just got word late last night from our chemistry head teacher, who got an analysis done, that the stuff isn't drugs. Not quite sure yet what it is. I'll let you know, though. So no panic. Don't worry that the letter's lost. It doesn't mean anything now. The snatcher probably thought he had some deadly document. Sorry, Jimmy, but you can't take risks with the welfare of youngsters . . . Looking for me? Yes, that must have been a nuisance. Spent the night with friends. Sorry, Jimmy. Ah, that's good of you. Thanks. See you soon . . ."

Then the letter to the headmaster. Short—not too difficult. Doctor had insisted he take that sabbatical that had been mentioned. ". . . hope for the best . . . might get something to do in our own field to keep me out of mischief . . . will keep you informed . . . thanks for understanding."

That was all. If there was anything to be said for an essentially solitary life, it was that you owed so few explanations.

He came into the hall, where the Duke waited.

"Ready?"

"Ready."

"MacFarlane will go with you. You'll drive the car—an Italian Iglietti—quite straightforward. We'll meet at Kintalla in the evening."

"What about Markland? When do I go there?"

"Not until I have made firm arrangements with the headmaster, Dr Coulson."

"How? Letter? Phone?"

"No. I should have a personal talk with him. I shall see him tonight. I have to be in Belgium tomorrow." He went through a heavy oak door to a room with glimpses of library furnishings.

"That's it," said Dale. "Right? I'll take you to the car."

Immediately the library door opened again and the Duke's head came to the aperture. He said to Raeburn:

"What is it you teach?"

"English and history. French and Latin up to second year, if necessary. Bit of geography."

With an upward nod, more of dismissal than acknowledgment, the head was gone, and the door closed.

Dale took him to the street door, down outside steps where a low, long red car waited. There was a man in heather-flecked tweeds there. Raeburn saw his two bags, and what was doubtless the carton of his books, piled into the narrow back seat.

"This is MacFarlane."

The man, leather-faced from the open air, touched his tweed hat perfunctorily, and said: "Yes, sir."

"That's everything," said Dale. "Keys in. Manage?"

Trying the low lever from the street level where he stood, Raeburn said: "I suppose so," and got in. The stalker followed.

"MacFarlane will navigate. I suppose His Grace and I will be leaving in half an hour, after he does some telephoning. But we're not likely to catch up. See you later."

The Iglietti boomed quietly into life. Raeburn edged it out to the cobbled road, cannily at first, then confident and surging. They turned towards Lothian Road and the south-west.

"You're best," said MacFarlane, with a guarded Highland hint of approval, "to make for Dumfries first. I would say, sir. That's the way we usually go."

"You don't drive?"

"Not the private cars. There's rules—we do the jeeps and the likes of that. This is one of his own." Raeburn's ear strained, not in vain, for the capital letter on the "His."

Soon they were skirting the meagre upland Clyde, picking up fragments of a motorway or two, but holding to the remote and distant west. Near Thornhill, MacFarlane was ready with a directing hand, but Raeburn had remembered the route and swept off from the Dumfries line down to the near border of Galloway.

They talked, but briefly, as they went. Neither man was an early-stage imparter of confidences, but there were some matters that seemed to require wary scrutiny. So their exchanges came in small gusts, and died soon.

"Interesting job you have," Raeburn said. "Have you been long with the Duke?"

"Oh, aye—long enough." (It was that Highland idiom which meant "a fairly long time"; not "Too long.")

"Where is your base? Kintalla?"

"No—at least not often. We move about—sir. There's a lot of estate sport—shootings, fishings—for His Grace and the friends of the house."

"Hence the net, eh? I never heard of a trick like that. I must have looked an ass, coming over the wall there." They looked at each other and agreed to laugh briefly. MacFarlane had a cold depth to him. The laugh had little meaning.

After a few gambits, Raeburn let the talk die, except for reference to the route. Driving this superb car was enjoyable. He learned that the other knew every river and knoll and hilltop, like an intimate. He seemed a man who could look after himself in any kind of country, and was at ease in the Scottish wild.

MacFarlane opened a theme bluntly, smoothing his words to an offhand comment rather than a question:

"You don't look to me," he said slowly, ". . . like one who would want to do away with himself."

"True enough. I daresay, though, you know by now what was in my mind."

"Aye, right enough—His Grace told me something . . . enough—"

"What would you do—in a case like that?"

"Me? Indeed and I'm not sure. It's not a thing I would be thinking about beforehand . . . God, though—I think there's better ways than the long drop."

"Still—a town chap doesn't have much choice. I ought to thank you anyway, especially for the whack on the ear. That could have been a lot worse, if you had wanted."

"Ach—I had another ploy to use. I gave you a silencer."

"A silencer? What's that?"

"Well, we've things we use . . . I have a wee sort of gun that fires slugs with dope in them. Different sizes for different animals, big and small. My trouble was that I didn't know what strength to give you."

"You're not serious, are you? Not joking—really? Listen, I must learn what I was worth. What about a stag? Was that the size?"

"Goodness, no. That would have put you away for a week. You can say that I gave you a double badger—in the hip."

"So that's why I'm not sitting too comfortably!" This was good for a few laughs as they went on their way, with the Galloway hills coming nearer. But MacFarlane was not much of a communicator, so that when, once, Raeburn tried to be expansive, saying: "Tell me exactly what it's like to be a gamekeeper and stalker on estates like that. What is a typical week like?" MacFarlane was long silent; then:

"Well, you know, it's just a matter of what His Grace wants done. We do whatever he wants. Sometimes it's one thing and another day it will be different. Oh, he's a great man, the Duke."

They were in the pale sunlight of the moor where the boundary starts well beyond Moniaive, when MacFarlane started to sniff deeply at the rushing air.

"Burning," said he. "Burning—something near . . . Have you matches in your pocket?"

"No. I don't carry them."

"Then it's not the heather—they're doing no muirburn in this neighbourhood. What's on fire?"

Checking the car, Raeburn looked behind even as MacFarlane craned over the back of his seat. From the stacking of the suitcases and the bundle of books there wisped a lace of dark smoke—a chemical smoke, reaching and searching.

"Stop!" shouted MacFarlane. "Right away! Out!"

Immediately on the left, where a former bend of the road had been straightened, the old section ran off behind a hillock to emerge curving sixty yards on. It was marked as a parking lay-by. Raeburn flung the car in there, skidding to a stop among the old loosened stones. Before he was halted MacFarlane was out, throwing the bags and the parcel far to the turf.

The smoke belched in a snake form out of the back crevice of the rear cushions. Raeburn's hands dived to part the leather. There was a glimpse of a red plastic sheath, zipped shut and flat, with wires.

"Run!" went MacFarlane's ready bellow.

The two of them turned and stretched to it. A dry stone wall of dyking four feet high marked off the old road from the moor; they were at it even as the hiss and whoosh started. MacFarlane, his steel-shod boots scattering the copings, which battered his knees, dived beyond. Raeburn leaped, the front leg bent and clearing the top, the second trailing. They fell together into the dry tussocks beyond, while another stone or two came after them, and the explosion resounded.

It was more a roaring rush of flame and air, for the first impact, tearing open the back of the car frame, split also the petrol connections and tank. The spirit went up in a clear spout of fire that swallowed the smoke, firing their faces as they peered through the top dislodgments of the dyke. Sodden drips of flame fell away from the car and seethed among the short grass. Then came the smells, of rubber, leather, varnish, metals, wool, oils, the melting of glass, plastics. The smoke came back again, while the fire swallowed the car from end to end. They watched. There was nothing to do. Almost nothing to say. The road was quiet, and no one came by.

After a time the fire subsided to the persistent flicker along the rims and edges of the chassis and round the wheels.

"Man," said MacFarlane at last. "They said you could jump, and by God and they were right!"

They crossed the wall now to inspect what had happened, pulling the baggage back beyond the heat.

"I wouldn't go too near. She might have a bit of a bang left in her yet." MacFarlane poked gently with his stick, to which he had held, but they couldn't find a piece of the red plastic container.

"I'm not so sure about being out in the open here," said Raeburn. "If we go on to the main road at this point we can be seen from all round the moor."

"Right enough, sir. Aye, you're right." MacFarlane pointed to a farmhouse half a mile further on the road. "Indeed we don't want to attract any attention. His Grace would want it that way. I'll go over there and use their phone. Now you keep out of sight behind the dyke again—for safety like—until the Duke's car comes along. Maybe half an hour or less. It's a big green estate wagon—there's the number—I'll write it for you. I'll not be long myself."

The hill man swung himself on his curved shoes over the dyke and away across the intervening moorland, pacing in easy strides as if he rocked on snow-shoes, with never a backward look. The lope took him swiftly away, diminishing like a heath beetle. Raeburn noticed how he held to the low furrows of the land, sometimes half running in a stoop. It seemed only a short time until the outward walls and fences of the farm absorbed him, with dog voices signalling his presence.

Dropping to the back of his lay-by dyke, Raeburn waited for some movement or menace. Some explosive danger might still come out of the endless roll and sweep of the Galloway upland moor, or even from the road itself. A spasm of traffic was suddenly coming; a lorry struggled northward with a heaped trailer, tarpaulin-wrapped. He saw the driver and another in the cab, but they had no eye for the smoke trails rising from the ruined and hidden car. Perhaps eight cars went past in all, and there was only one which checked slightly on brakes at the hidden source of smoke, then lifted on again, curiosity readily quelled.

Through the chinks of the dyke rampart he saw the Duke's estate car on a bend three football park lengths away, so he was over the stones and signalling by the time they could first notice him. Dale, driving, pulled the big vehicle round on to the old road, and they were out, leaving their doors open and the engine running.

The Duke walked round the Iglietti twice; signed then to Dale to cut the estate-car engine.

"Explosion?" he assumed in a question.

"We saw smoke—smelt it—had time to—"

"MacFarlane?"

Pointing in the direction of the distant farm, it didn't take Raeburn more than three or four sentences to tell the whole story. He thought he might have expected a rush of questions, but not a word from the Duke, who walked swiftly to the back of the estate wagon and came back with a wheel brace. Dale was on the top of the knoll, looking around.

"I've got the feeling," Raeburn told him, "that it might be a good idea to keep off the skyline. Those who put the bomb in might have thought of a follow-up . . ."

"Unlikely." Dale finished his survey, and came to watch the Duke stirring into the charred shreds of the back-seat leathers.

"That red plastic," said the Duke "—even a shred of it—or a piece of the wiring . . ." He fingered gingerly among the choking debris, seeming to find nothing.

"Very well." He wiped his hands on the short grass. "We'd better go," signing Dale and Raeburn towards the bags. He himself took the bundle of books and slung them into the back space of the estate wagon, sitting then in front.

"MacFarlane . . . ?" It was Raeburn's turn.

"A very resourceful fellow. He will probably be making suitable arrangements. Please do not worry about MacFarlane."

"And this?"—Raeburn held a hand towards the wrecked Iglietti—"We just leave it here?"

"Exactly."

The baggage in the back, and Dale in the driving seat, they were on their way. Half a mile on, MacFarlane, his back against the stone gate-pillar of the farm buildings, waited for them at the roadside, raising his tweed hat to the Duke as he got in. On again.

As they went, the Duke pondered in silence, his hand with the black finger ring to his chin. A few more miles, and he turned to Mac-Farlane, head lifted in a nod of enquiry.

"Your Grace, I got Reid on the phone. You know about his cousin being the deputy chief constable. The police will tidy up there, quick. My own statement will likely be enough. Reid will come to meet us in the jeep, to see if he's needed."

Some movement of the Duke's head acknowledged the arrangement, but did not seem to elicit further conversation. The journey went on, down towards the south-western sea inlets. A dozen more miles, and the Duke turned sharply to Dale:

"Yes! What made you so sure there was unlikely to be anyone looking out for us on the open moor?"

The younger man, no doubt well used to the sudden investigation, was ready enough; confidently offhand with it: "Not much chance, sir. Bomb delivered in Edinburgh—I should say at the garage rather than outside the house. How could they even guess roughly at our speed and location. There's plenty of moor. I don't see them covering much of it. Not that much."

For a time it seemed that the Duke would again do no speaking, but he did make a musing footnote: "All this is target area. 'They' are here." Thereafter no one broke in on his hooded thoughts.

As they charged at a straight of the Glenluce road, "Reid coming," MacFarlane said. Dale edged the wagon off the road while the nearing jeep buzzed and pecked to them. The man who stepped from it was in the same category as MacFarlane—the heather-flecked tweed suit, limp check shirt, narrow knitted tie, the hose and brogues. Lifting a cloth cap to the Duke as he came forward, he showed a balding skull wisped with thin shreds of hair.

"Your Grace—none the worse . . . ?"

"Quite all right, Reid. Thank you. Arrangements?"

"Aye—all covered. A bad wee accidental fire—nobody's fault. The police will be content with MacFarlane's statement. They might want one later from Mr Raeburn." Reid raised a hand not more than half-way in Raeburn's direction in what hinted a cap-touching gesture. "Their own truck will bring in the car to Kintalla. I don't think we'll hear much more, Your Grace."

The Duke was making gestures: to Raeburn, seemingly motioning him to get aboard the jeep: to Reid, to take aboard the baggage. They set about this, while the Duke spoke as he got back in beside Dale: "Markland first. I have to see the headmaster, and then Mr Raeburn

will stay there. We shall all reassemble at Kintalla tomorrow night."
The two cars turned to the south again.

Markland School was a mile from the sea, where it had virtually its
own harbour. The main building was a very ordinary Victorian block,
with adapted outhouses and ranges of timbered structures more recently
put up. The cars swept strongly to the front steps. The Duke pushed
himself out and moved up towards the front door, where a thin, dried
man waited for him. They shook hands and went together into the hall
behind them. Fragments of speech lingered after them: ". . . your
kind telephone call, Duke . . . pleasant surprise . . . a matter suitable
only for personal discussion . . . naturally, sir, in such a case I am
at your disposal . . ." To the people sitting in silence outside in the
cars, the formal grammaticals drifted inwards out of their hearing.

Fifteen minutes later, when the Duke came striding alone from the
front door, he was beckoning to Raeburn on the way down the steps:
"All right. All arranged. Dr Coulson is waiting for you."

MacFarlane and Reid were out, humping the bags and books to the
top of the steps. They turned there, grinding their way on steel-studded
hill shoes to the gravel. The vehicle doors slammed, leaving Raeburn
behind, the Duke saying: "Kintalla." The cortège spurted round the
drive and out through the pillared gates.

Raeburn mounted the outside stairs to meet the headmaster.

CHAPTER 4

"Amazing chap, that Duke—quite extraordinary." Coulson was shaking hands with great goodwill. "Every time I meet him he seems more remarkable. Heavens, though, I wouldn't care to have to do business with him. Well, let's get these bags inside first, shall we?"

They set the baggage down beside the great empty hall fireplace. Coulson was ushering the new arrival into a panelled room which must have been the library of the mansion house. He had his desk here, leather chairs, reasonably tidy stacks of books and papers.

"Sit down—sit down." A dominie's lifetime of firm encouragement had built into his tones a flow of impulsive enthusiasm. He was tall and scraggy, tufted with grey hair above the ears, with what would soon be a dome pushing through the thinning top. It was a face familiar to Raeburn, since it appeared much in the newspapers, where he was habitually interviewed for his observations upon any new oddity in the field of education.

"Yes, sit there—anywhere you like. Drink? Whisky? . . . Well, now, let's see, I'm still completely confused by the whole thing, and as happy as a sandboy, whatever that may be. Cheers to you! Welcome to Markland . . . I suppose you are looking at the luckiest headmaster in the land."

"Nice to be here. Good health!" Raeburn let the exuberance flow around him. In time it would become measured and informative. This man's reputation was probably deserved. He had put into active practice a good crop of the ideas that few had done anything other than dabble in.

"I simply can't believe my good fortune in having Barry Raeburn on the staff here. Even if we can't look on you as a long-term fixture. We were really getting pretty light on the side of English and history—to say nothing of the other bonus items. You know, if this had happened last year you could have had the department . . ."

"Don't think about it. I'll be very happy to fit in wherever you need me. My own lot were very good about letting me get away."

"Health, the Duke said."

"Yes. Apparently I was needing a break. Shouldn't take too long."

Coulson's free arm swung round the panelled horizon: "Moors, woods, fresh air, sea air, swimming, gymnasium, rest, even—it's strange how much of that you can get here. And we have a superb matron, Mrs Gibson—expert at all the medical and food things—"

"Oh, I imagine it will all turn out to be fairly normal."

"Would you like to talk about the money arrangements? The Duke —I was wondering if he had perhaps over-simplified it."

"How did he explain?"

"It seemed straightforward. You go on to our pay roll at our rate for the job. Sorry, it's a bit short of your present level. But we'll pay you in full, indenting on a bank for the difference. The Duke wrote out an authorisation in blank which I have to fill up."

"Sounds quite easy, doesn't it? If it suits you it's quite all right with me. I'd much rather hear from you about the school."

Coulson glowed at the opportunity. "I'm afraid it's not much of a school at the moment. Just an empty building. You'll see a difference in twenty-four hours from now. Most of the staff will be here by early tomorrow afternoon, and the boys will be arriving over the next two days. Then it's hell for leather for the summer term. I'd better give you the facts and figures first."

He talked about staff and numbers, pupils and classes, houses, facilities, recreation, discipline, married quarters, the small hierarchies, the privileges, the management and administration, the special cases of food and religion and attitude . . .

"I expect you know—everybody knows!—Heavens, it's the only thing that everybody knows!—that we have one of the princes here. No problem. Likable chap—fifteen. 'Treat him like the others'—you know how irritating that sort of instruction can be, coming from the Palace. But they do mean it."

"Detective?"

"Yes, again that's very little trouble. He is around in the daytime, not far from the classroom concerned—never inside. Same at mealtimes— not far away. Sleeps in a cubicle near the appropriate dormitory. Hangs about during sport and outings. Sometimes feels an urgent need for a visual check, but on the whole the drill works reasonably. They'll both arrive tomorrow—fly to Prestwick I suppose, and car from there. I believe a modest relay of police cars will pass them discreetly from district to district."

Raeburn nodded, seeing it work: "I suppose in any case the boys themselves are the best safeguard for a case like that."

"Exactly. I think that's the point." Coulson sparkled at his perceptive new colleague. "Boys in the bunch are pretty anonymous, except to schoolmasters. I imagine we're like shepherds—we can recognise them easily. Dash it, we have parents coming here who can't tell their own lads from the others beyond five paces. Probably the clothes . . ."

"And they seem to learn to walk like each other . . ."

"They do! Well, the school now—what do we do—how do we do it . . . ?"

For half an hour Coulson talked about the school. Himself a modest scholar, he had been a deliberate rather than a passionate innovator, working his way through the tiny reputations of problem cases for a long thirty years towards Markland, which was his own creation. Here the time had come, at last, to show that the normal would respond also, and the ideas had become a system, and the system a cult, and the cult, dangerously, a fashion, so that it had to be pruned and re-dug, and thinned out. To Raeburn, there was nothing very new in it all, but a firm holding to matters that seemed worth believing in, until the time came that they seemed to work, and boys could perhaps be recognised not for their ingenuity, which cannot be taught, but because they had within them independently, something of a source of reason and truth. Thinking so, as the story unfolded from this modest man, Raeburn felt abashed that he himself at times had ignorantly taken part in easy detraction when Markland was mentioned.

"But I must be making you weary. This has gone on long enough. Let me show you to your room. We'll have dinner together later if that suits you."

"Fine. What I'd find very useful at this stage would be a staff list of some kind. Have you got such a thing?"

"Have I not!" Coulson was back to the broad schoolboy smile. "Earlier today I was playing myself with my new copying machine. You can have a set of these"—holding out columned sheets. "These are copies of the staff register pages—not only all the names, but age, home address, date of joining, next of kin, insurance numbers—you know the kind of thing; nothing confidential, so far as I know. Then here is a sheet with the non-teaching staff. Heavens! What a lot of them we need—house staff, cooks and kitchen hands, gardeners/handymen, secretarial—all that lot."

"That's really useful. I'll soon get to know them all." Raeburn scanned columns. "I see you have crosses against some of the names . . ."

"Oh, yes—you might find these helpful, too. These are people starting this term for the first time—new, like you, eh?"

The room opened off a small corridor at the foot of the main stairway. It had some good half-panelling, handsome chairs. "This was a sort of guest room, but we never seemed to need it. I live in a cottage in the grounds. A sister keeps house for me nowadays. Make yourself at home. Will this do? I'll give you a knock later." He was off, but came back to say: "I say, it *is* good to have you."

Raeburn took plenty of time to unpack his bags, moving about his new quarters, which looked into the heavy trees dropping down a slope. He guessed the sea was beyond, but could not find it through the branches. As he hung up the clothes and put away the small personal trifles, he commended the selection made by whoever had gone to his flat.

Whoever had gathered his belongings together had managed to include a good collection of his books, and he handled them with affection for a time before putting them on to shelves. He remembered how each of them had come into his possession, the often painful gathering of the money to buy them, the familiarity of the pages. He sat with some of them, reading for a time, until Coulson came to collect him.

Dinner was on trays in Coulson's room, since his sister was not at home, and the kitchen staff, almost unseen, made scratch meals for the few in Markland that night. Again Coulson talked eagerly and gently about what might be done with the facilities which had been gathered in this place; the adding brick by brick to tradition. Raeburn found himself coming back with interest to a life stream, as he remembered in the other's company what it was that made him want to be a teacher: a strange sense of sorrow for the young, the long road they had to face, their slow realisation of the solitary fate of mankind, the need for the kind of courage that could best counter their vulnerability. He remembered the clear moment of his student days when it had first occurred to him that almost everybody would go through life truly unknown. Only a handful of people would have, like him, a sustaining renown, helping to defy the emptiness of years.

"I'd better show you round the place," Coulson said, "while we have a chance." They went from room to room and hall to hall, switching on lights and leaving the darkness behind again.

In one of the outbuildings which had been added over the years he saw the classroom where he would preside—the high desk, the long blackboard, charts, maps, paste-ups of what had been done, early struggles with creativity. His lot would be in the fourteen/fifteen age group, so that some of his ideas, flushed with maturity, or mere prejudice, would take hold and be offered up later as their own.

The dormitories were plain; iron narrow beds neatly made up with grey or red wool blankets. Six or eight beds to a room, with a bedroom nearby for the young teacher who had night charge of each unit. A bundle was moving under the blankets in one bed; the light caught a dark head and eye, and both vanished into the hump as the owner ducked under.

"Hi!" said Coulson, "somebody here. Of course, I'd forgotten. All right?" he spoke out.

In a moment, a muffled voice said: "Yes, sir."

In the corridor, with the dormitory closed and in darkness, Coulson spoke softly as they walked:

"Shame, that youngster. We get a few cases like that. His people sent him back yesterday. Only child. Mother on the loose somewhere— father other interests, personal and business—no time for the kid. Won't take him. He spent all Christmas here. Well . . ."

When they reached the main hall, Coulson pointed to the heavy clock above the fireplace: "Time to turn in, I suggest. You've probably had a long day. You know your way around if there is anything you need, and there is an internal phone. My house is on it. Not much for you to do tomorrow, if you want to look at the countryside, but I'd be glad if you were around about mid-afternoon to meet some of the parents. Depends how you feel, of course—"

"Certainly. I'll be here."

In his room, Raeburn eased into the night silence of the place. For about eight hours now he had put his medical condition largely out of his mind, forcing himself to look forward since he had seemingly been preserved for some large and specific purpose. Into these reflections, however, was coming another issue, noticed earlier and almost pushed back into the perspectives of his new setting. But it would not stay there.

He left his room quietly, finding his way up the main staircase to one of the groups of dormitories. He remembered where Coulson had been standing when he was describing the boy . . .

Raeburn switched on the dormitory light, closed the door gently, and went forward to the occupied bed. The head had emerged again, and, as he thought he had seen on the earlier visit, the face was mottled with tears.

He went forward and sat on the bed. From the blankets came a hand, rubbing dry the red eyes. They still burned with fear.

Raeburn said: "Where do you keep your handkerchiefs?"

"The—the locker, sir."

"In here?" He handed one over.

"What's your name?"

"Anthony Biggs Hewitt, sir."

"I'm a new teacher. My name's Mr Raeburn. Hullo!"

He had to wait for it. "Hu—Hullo, sir."

"Listen, I've only just come here. There's hardly anybody to tell me about Markland. Is it a good place?"

"I—I think so."

"I expect you'll be glad when all your friends are back again."

"Yes, sir—they've all been home." He gushed afresh at the eyes.

"Were you home?" Face it, boy. Even now, face it.

He hid behind the handkerchief. "Not—not for long, sir."

He started to explain, in only a few broken sentences. Not many were needed. He didn't say it, but nobody wanted him. There was a family lawyer who paid the bills, and got him farmed out in the long summer holidays, on climbing expeditions, or sailing, or any costly kind of excursion where somebody else would be responsible for him.

It was a story that was ancient even before Abraham had a son to sacrifice. No one would ever be able to explain to him what made him unwanted: why no kin had concern for him. All he was ever to learn of scholarship, and discipline, and loyalty and faithfulness and joy, would come to him from strangers.

Raeburn steered him back to ordinary matters they might share: no sermons, no great revelations of truth. They settled to talk about the school, for it was all they had in common.

Eventually: "What is it you teach, sir?"

"English and history. Older classes, I think. You'll have to wait for me. How old are you?"

"Nearly ten. Eh—sir—do you do games?"

"Well, no—I don't think I'll be teaching games. This is the cricket season. Are you good at cricket?"

"Not—not very."

"Neither am I. Two duffers, eh?"

"Please, sir—what did you say your name was?"

"Raeburn. First name Barry, short for Barrington. I don't like it very much."

The eyes were fixed on him. "Excuse me, sir—can I get up—for a minute, sir, please."

"Yes, of course—if you need to."

The boy was out of bed like a young salmon, pattering across the floor to where a shelf held some ragged books. He was back with one immediately, holding it up so that Raeburn could see the title: *Every Boy's Giant Book of Sport.*

"This is really a bit young for me," he was busily leafing it over. "Yes, here!"

He held it up. It was, of course, the picture—one of the full pages in a section labelled "Immortal Moments in Sport." There was that leap again—they had coloured it, the wrong blue for the Scottish jersey— but the surge of zest in that chill, remote dormitory did Raeburn good.

"That's you, sir—isn't it?"

"Well, in fact, it is."

"I remembered it. Gosh—and it says here you got twenty-seven caps, and you were captain of Scotland. Is that right, sir?"

"Yes. Of course it was a long time ago."

"Gosh—wait till the others hear about this. What was it like, sir? Do you remember that time?"

"Yes, I remember. Of course it was a very good photograph."

Later, he was saying to the boy:

"Listen, did you have any supper tonight?"

"No, sir—not much. Matron got them to give me a supper, but I didn't feel like eating it."

"I'll bet you feel like eating something now."

The two dark eyes, above the small hands holding the open book, simply stared at him, and no words came.

"All right." Raeburn was brisk, man to man. "You stay here. I'll be back in a minute. Don't go away!"

In his room below the staircase, he pulled open a drawer. There was an item that they had packed into his baggage—a tartan-covered tin box of shortbread, and he bore it away. At the top of the staircase he made a silent call on the refrigerator in a small kitchen he had seen earlier, taking two cans of soft drinks.

"Mind the crumbs," he said, settling himself again sidesaddle on the bed. "And for goodness' sake don't spill the booze." For reply he got a mesmerised giggle. He opened both cans; gave Hewitt the tin lid of the shortbread box to hold under his mouth as he crunched.

There were eighteen pieces of shortbread in the box. Hewitt had nine of them, and Raeburn two. They finished the sugary drink, whatever it was.

"Enough?"

"Oh, yes, sir. That's enough—thanks, sir." Hewitt was red-faced with pleasure. "Super tuck, sir."

"Well, keep the rest. In the locker here—eh? I'll put it away for you. Afterwards you can have the tin box, if you like, to keep things in." Raeburn pushed it to the back of the locker drawer.

"Now, you—up you get and off to the bathroom. Do your teeth and what not. Slippers on this time. Two minutes!"

The boy was away like a wisp.

When he was tucked in, Raeburn walked to the light switch: "OK?"

Hewitt raised his head from the pillow: daring—a last request:

"Please sir. Please—sir . . ." It took many seconds.

"Yes—what?"

"Please don't tell them I was crying."

"No—I won't tell them. Down now! Good night."

CHAPTER 5

At breakfast time Raeburn found his way to the staff dining room, where Coulson shortly joined him. The buildings were becoming peopled. From the kitchen quarters came a great clashing of pots, and the high voices of below stairs.

"New staff getting run in, I suppose," said Coulson. "You won't catch me talking at that rate so early in the morning. Ridley, the cook-chef chap, is a fierce fellow. I think he was out at dawn scooping up the recruits from remote bus stations. My God, what a job! I'd better go through."

Soon after he had gone, a thirtyish woman came in.

"Hullo," she smiled widely at Raeburn. "I'm Joan Ker—one 'r.' Junior maths."

He greeted her. "Hullo, I'm Raeburn. One 'r' also. English, history and oddments."

She was staring, amused. "What do you mean, one 'r'? I could have sworn there are two in Raeburn."

"God! Of course you're right. I forgot about the second one."

Laughing, she was helping herself to tea. "We could certainly do with some junior maths around here . . . No thanks, tea is all I want. I had a breakfast of sorts before I left Edinburgh about six this morning."

She sat down at the table. "Of course, I know who you are. I was on the phone last night to the Head and he told me you had come. This will cause some excitement."

"It will die away. The reality is always a let-down."

"Can I say something?" She leaned her elbows on the table, holding the cup with both hands. "You must have heard it thousands of times and I bet it bores you stiff. I saw you score that try."

He eyed her up and down with quizzical judgment. "I'd never have guessed that. Was there a babies' gate at Murrayfield?"

"Don't bother being gallant. I know about time. I was eleven that day, and was there with a small party from the Mary Erskine School, sitting in the front seat of the enclosure behind the English goal. I may say I have shamelessly enchanted scores of young nephews and schoolboys by narrating how you were running straight for me. My moment of glory."

Unlike the others who got on to the theme, she didn't pursue the rugby topic. They talked for a time, until two men walked past the window outside.

"Here are some more of us," she said. "You'll have to pitch yourself to meet them all. These are Robin Thorburn and Ian Rankine. I don't suppose anybody has told you there are two other women teachers. The rest are all men."

She introduced the two, who gave companionable handshakes. One of them appeared to be working out who Raeburn might be, but the new teacher thought it best to leave it to them to sort it out through Joan Ker. So he went, saying:

"Thanks. I'm looking forward. Excuse me now, I'd like to find a telephone."

"A coin box in the back hall. That's the one we generally use."

He phoned a car-rental firm in Stranraer. They promised to have a car to him within an hour, and they did it with ten minutes to spare. Two cars came—a choice—the spare driver and car to take the other man back. He signed the documents and paid in cash, being careful not to let them see the wad of notes. He was finding it comfortable to keep nine hundred pounds of it dropped into his buttoned inside pocket, like a packet of ordinary letters. Ready money on this scale was a confident presence.

He chose a tough, sizable saloon of this year's model, in silver-grey. Driving the Iglietti, even for its brief life end, had quickened his appreciation for powerful cars. In any case, it was likely that the assignment for the next days would require speed.

Cars were now coming and going regularly in the school drive. But he sat in his own acquisition, and occasionally drove it yards forward and back, parking and parking again. The feel of it was coming handily to him.

A brisk woman of at least middle age came down the school steps, spoke briefly to some arriving parents, and walked straight to Raeburn where he sat at his wheel.

"Mr Raeburn?" she said, leaning to him through the driving window. "I'm Mrs Gibson, the matron. You're wanted on the telephone. It's a Mr Dale from Kintalla."

They walked together towards the main building of the school. Climbing the steps, she spoke to him, gently professional:

"If you'd like to come and talk to me any time—about diets or anything else needed. The Head has told me you've a sort of health problem on just now. Sorry about that. I hope it'll clear up soon here."

"Thanks. I don't think I really need anything—"

"You know—electric blanket on the bed—leg rest. I think there's a wee stool in your room . . ."

"It's very good of you . . ."

"You see, I have to refuse to be impressed even by famous athletes. They all need their comforts." No illusions, she was smiling at him. A big heart there, but no male of any age would be able to fool her. "But it really is nice to have you here. Wonderful for the boys."

"Raeburn," he said into the telephone.

"Raeburn?" came Dale's voice. "How are you?"

"Comfortable. No apparent problems. But I'm under new management."

"I have to go at once. The Duke and I are leaving for Brussels. Will you come to a meeting tonight at 9 p.m. in Kintalla. This is a full muster."

"I suppose I can. I'll have to ask the—"

"Transport—"

"I have my own."

"Good! That's good. Someone will give you directions. Get on to the west coast road. Watch for the main gates. If you see the lighthouse you've gone too far."

"I have the maps, you know."

"Of course. See you at nine," and Dale was away.

Coulson the Head was lingering for Raeburn in the main hall.

"The very man!" he enthused. "Some people I want you to meet."

From then until lunchtime there was no halt in the flow of arrivals. For the most part the boys disappeared at once, but the parents or neighbours or enlisted friends who had provided transport needed to be looked after. Some just to be talked to, others to be shown the school, so that they could sniff the classrooms, feel the beds, try the horizontal bars in the gym, and envy the boys loudly. To Raeburn's relief, many of them had never heard of him, but as the newest in teachers he made himself modestly available, answered the questions about modern education, with some referring back to Coulson. At short notice he made a dart to Dalbeattie, to take delivery of three boys whose holiday custodians did not find it convenient to come any further. He drove back with the trio to find Markland filling up, and lunch ready.

There were still not enough boys to require a full muster of teachers for the lunch invigilation, so he ate with a dozen others in the staff room. Ian Furness, the head of the English department, gave him a run-down of the curriculum procedures between mouthfuls. It was a useful, prolonged session, which found them after coffee strolling down the south hill road from the school, still talking.

"Anyway, we'll be closely in touch as much as you need, in the early days," Furness told him. "Perhaps too closely for your comfort. The Head also likes a look in at most things . . . Hope the health goes all right, by the way. I heard you were a bit under the weather. Still, it brings you here, and that's our luck. I'm not forgetting that you out-rank me"—he was pleasantly unperturbed by this condition—"there's not much protocol about here. By the way, you'll have the prince in the fourths class."

"When does he arrive?"

"He's here. They came about mid-morning. He just merges. Posi-tively no trouble. The only obvious element is the detective, and he does his best to merge. Trouble is he has nobody to merge with. But for the prince—"

"What do we call him?"

"David. They left us to work it out for ourselves and that's what came up. The boys all call him that too. It's one of his names, anyway —but probably not the home one. We never use it in talking to any-body outside of Markland."

"Seems a good idea."

There was a ringing of old-fashioned bicycle bells, and a straggle of boys in a long single line started to overtake them. A familiar figure pedalled some distance from the front.

Said Furness: "That's Miss Ker. You've met her? She organises bike runs in odd moments. We have a stack of ancient bikes. Would you like to join in?"

"Eh—?" Raeburn thought about it. Then: "No, thanks, bikes aren't my sport. Interesting though."

"I think I shall," he said, stepping out briskly towards the Markland buildings. "If you'd like to come back with me I'll show you where they're stacked. Take one any time. I say"—from the side of his mouth —"here's David now. Two behind Miss Ker."

Raeburn waited for the string to wobble past, greeting Miss Ker, who announced him to her nearest participants: "Boys—new teacher on left—Mr Raeburn . . ." and the hands signalled informal saluta-tions. He looked at the prince closely—probably tall for his age, hair lighter than the photographs, shoes no better than they should be, no tie. All very useful for a merger. As the line diminished he could hear Miss Ker telling the familiar story.

Raeburn hurried back to his room for his binoculars, also included in the inspired packing which had put together his belongings two nights earlier. As he came out at the top of the steps he was encountered by the matron. She stopped him.

"This is me being bossy," she said, "but I think it would be an aw-fully good idea if you had a little lie-down in your room after lunch. There isn't much doing—we seem to have a lull—and we've got to look after you."

"Well, in fact, Mrs Gibson, that's very good of you. I think I'll make it a little later, if you don't mind. I thought a short walk now, don't you think, while it's fairly warm—"

"Just as you feel. Do please look after yourself though. It's going to be a busy term. Always is."

He went off, still thanking her. Above the road, at a spot a few hundred paces beyond where he had met the cyclists, was a map feature he had already studied in his room. This was the Doon, a high green knoll, flat-topped, a place prepared for fortification by the ancient people who had once inhabited this peninsula. The name of the place, in their own or even a later language, was long since submerged in the antique Scots tongue of the district now, but it said "fort" in the oldest of the Gaelic. He made for this outlook from which twenty generations at least of the older folk had watched for their enemies from behind walls of stone and timber where nothing now remained on the summit but a saucer hollow of grass and bush.

He took his time to the top, finding himself a good ten-minute climb above the road and commanding the near-by parishes, as he had guessed. The turf-grown remains of the old ramparts gave an outside edge from which the scarped hillside sheered to a slope below. The sunken summit dipped only slightly towards its middle, the grass close-cropped by sheep and wind. To the north side there was a clump of gorse and bramble.

Focusing his glasses, he perched seated on the edge, looking to the southern roads. Soon he picked up the Markland cyclists, hardly more than a mile away as they dawdled and swerved, waiting for stragglers. Still half a mile behind them, Furness pedalled to catch up, and soon was amongst them. All got off to walk the bikes up a steep hill which Raeburn, conning their progress on his map, thought must be the outskirts of Kintalla ground. For a time the riders were screened by a heavy clump of woodland bordering the road, and then came out clearly again on the high and famous grouse moors.

From the side of the Doon hill, a voice said: "And just what are you supposed to be watching from up here?"

A man had stood up in the bushes. Heavy set, younger than Raeburn by ten years or more, he wore an oldish town suit, and a very large pair of binoculars hung from round his neck.

The man made his way over, not watching his footing, his steady eyes fixed on Raeburn.

"Who are you?" Raeburn asked.

"Oh, no," the man spoke. "—sir—" he added casually, his voice professionally cold. "*I* ask first. I'm police. Do you mind telling me your name?"

"Not at all, Raeburn. I'm a teacher at Markland."

"I see. Would you mind, sir, telling me why—"

"Same as yourself—keeping an eye on the lads." Raeburn gave him his widest, most innocent smile. "I tell you what—I happen to have my passport with me. Would you like to see it?"

"Well, as a matter of fact, if you don't mind, I would, sir."

He studied it and handed it back.

"And I think," said Raeburn, "I know who you are. But you have probably got a document also. Mm?"

The man held out a folded, stiff, black-bound card. His photograph was there, with official seals, and his name and rank: Detective-Sergeant Gordon Miller.

Raeburn waved him to a seat beside himself on the turf edge, and offered a handshake. Miller was silent, a waft of disapproval floating from him. Shortly, both resumed their viewing with the glasses. The bike cortège, in a scattered line, bent out of sight behind a knoll. Beyond it their heads appeared momentarily, until a dip took them all for a surprisingly long time. From his map Raeburn noted that the dip carried a small river with wide contours. When the heads and then the vehicles appeared, the line was climbing back in their direction on a moor route he calculated to be between two and three miles away.

"Interesting job we've both got," he said to the policeman.

Miller gave a heavy breath of assent. He was cooling, possibly reaching an inward admission that Raeburn, too, was some sort of professional vigilant.

"That's a fine map you have there." Miller lowered the glasses. To the eye, seen from the distance the cycling party was a line of black insects, moving on the road.

"Pretty good. I like these big-scale maps."

"Mind if I have a look at it?"

"Help yourself."

The policeman studied the sheet, aligning it with the countryside. "This is better than what I use—the ordinary inch-to-the-mile Ordnance Survey."

"Yes, it gives a lot of detail, doesn't it?" Raeburn knew that his map was unmarked as yet. "I thought it would be useful to study the countryside. We might start an orienteering course for the boys."

"Oh, yes—that's the thing where they run cross-country with maps? You need to be pretty fit. I don't see that as being very suitable for my chap—running alone among woods and rocks. You can guess . . ."

"Yes—I see the point." In addition to that point, he could see the discomfort for Miller of having to escort at the trot.

When the cyclists were within hailing distance of Markland, the two made their way off the Doon slopes. Miller engaged in a mild admonition:

"You don't want to be seen too much spying through glasses at some-body special. It draws attention. It brings the press around and that sort of thing."

The detective, lingering, checked the prince into the main building, becoming immediately unobtrusive. Arrivals were thinning, but there was a busy briskness in the place, with more parents and relatives about. Staff walked with authority. There were no scholastic gowns.

Raeburn snatched a cup of tea from an unattended tray in the main hall and bore it to his room. There he spent an hour or two filling in map points, making notes, reading. He spotted the name and height of the small hill near the Doon to which he might have to move if he learned that Miller was a regular watcher from the old vanished fortification. The spine of Drumdar, with its well-clothed slopes, rose a few hundred feet above the summit of the Doon, far enough inland to the west to escape any military threat at the time the Doon was built and occupied. It probably commanded more country.

The last item he had to deal with that afternoon was the staff lists. He memorised a few names, and went exploring. A few of the teachers lingered still in the staff room, Coulson with them.

"Come in," said Miss Ker. "Tea?"

"I've had some, thanks—but, yes, if there is some more going . . . How did the safari awheel make out?"

"Oh, that—we didn't go far. Breathless stuff, up all these wee hills. Wait until the end of term . . ."

Coulson waggled a finger at him: "You'll avert your eyes, I'm warn-ing you. Did you ever see such a collection of clapped-out bikes—"

"And people," somebody said.

". . . brings discredit on the school. The bikes get worse as time goes on. Chaps bring them and leave them behind."

Miss Ker said serenely: "Nothing extra on the fees for the use of our splendid fleet. Do you know everybody?"

There were more introductions. "Don't worry about names and things . . ." They were truly informal—a good team.

"I thought," Raeburn said, "I'd rove about before dinner—kitchens and everything—and try to find the people who have only just joined up, like me. Is that—"

"That would include me, then," said Karel Wehr, whose hand he was just then shaking. "German-born, as you can tell from my guttural Hamburg accent. I'm here to teach my native tongue."

Somebody started to sing a pidgin version of "Die Lorelei." Wehr was about Raeburn's age, he guessed, but possibly looked somewhat older. And even as he formulated this notion Raeburn smiled within himself at the customary human withdrawal from deterioration which his pres-ent condition made ridiculous. He and Wehr had a wry, small exchange about the ineptness of new boys and masters. Soon he escaped from this.

There were better gleanings where the servants lived and worked. Mrs Gibson, instructing a huddle of washing and cleaning women, happily introduced him to them all, with the customary thumbnail information about his sport history. He found it possible to cut out from the small herd two new girls, as marked on the Coulson staff sheets—Jessie Donald and Isobel Henderson. Jessie he was able, he thought, to eliminate at once. She was undoubtedly Girvan born, as she said, with hotel experience in some of the Lothian hostelries he well knew.

The other was down on the sheets as born in Rathmines, Dublin. She spoke like it. Was sharper than the other, in about middle-twenties, and had a good glance, steady on him as they talked. It was she who said:

"Dublin's a great place for the football. You'll have played there so."

"The best ever. I've had many a happy day at Lansdowne Road."

"Ach, well, I was never there myself. It was always Croke Park for me."

He found Ridley, the cook/chef of the establishment, who had gone in with the founder. That day a kitchen assistant called Anton Biros had started on the job. The name sounded promising. But it took a little time to be done with Ridley's reminiscences of various Raeburn exploits, including a number of oddities afield from between the wars which his enthusiasm fathered upon the more recent Raeburn. Fans fall into a number of separate and distinct categories, and Ridley, effective at feeding the mobs, was one of those who believed that every famous player remained all the rest of his life loaded with free stand tickets for the next game. At last there was a casual chance to talk to Biros, on the "new boy" jocularity level.

It was hard going, for Biros spoke little, and had an evasive eye. His particulars had him as about twenty-eight years old, Lebanese with a work permit for six months. A short man, moving easily on lithe legs. There was little to be had in the way of verbal communication. As they parted it occurred to Raeburn to put him to an unofficial athletic test of his own. He slapped him with a comradely hold on the bicep. He had often been amused in doing this to notice that the man of little fitness to whom this happens immediately stiffens up his muscle to appear formidable. Biros had no need to do this. He was fit and muscular, the bicep full and firm and relaxed. A strong man. He turned away to heave some of the great steel pans on to cleaned shelves.

Their earlier bonhomie allowed Raeburn to turn again to Ridley, the master of the kitchen, walking with him to a managerial corner.

"That sort of chap?" he asked. "I suppose they can get this kind of job occasionally. Are they good at it?"

"Oh, good enough. You have to keep them at it. This one's all right. Knows something of cooking too. They generally come for the language. Bit wee for a scrum, eh?"

The only other new man was a young Latin master with a good degree from Cambridge who had done some conscience-stricken teaching in the East End of London. He had been sorry to note the lack of interest there was in the classics. At dinner in the staff room he was being readily assured that the interest in Markland was less than ideally high. Well over six feet tall, with red hair, Martin Gray claimed only to have done some tentative college rowing.

Clearing his absence with Coulson before coffee time, Raeburn got the rest of the evening off, completed some writing in his room, and took the road with the new car to Kintalla. From the map he worked it out closely as eight and a half miles away. It was easy to find. The twilight was darkening to night, needing his dipped headlights, as he moved on to the gravel inside the big gates, swung on good springs down the wavering surface of the main drive, to come to the front steps. He backed off into the side of the forecourt.

Mounting the steps towards the door, he was picked off by a searchlight which hissed brilliantly at him from somewhere in the shrubbery. The twilight dissolved before it, while, as if signalled by the beam, fresh falls of illumination poured from above the pediment of the doorway. Isolated in the chill whiteness, he mounted the red steps steadily, looking up to see the Duke's motto carved above—"I Have My Day"—and the even higher single beam which lit the flagstaff on the front roof and showed his banner stretching there. Raeburn, expecting some effective security, had not thought of how to prepare for it other than to get out the pass with which he had been provided in the Edinburgh house. It was ready in his palm as the door opened. The broad, light-footed figure holding the door was saying, "Your pass?" in a tone of challenge, as Raeburn thrust it at eye level towards the shadowed face and shouldered past him into the hall. He wheeled round the doorman, still holding the pass close to the other's eyes. A hand came out to take his wrist and another clawed to grip his shoulder. The sway which allowed Raeburn to slip both hands hardly reached downwards to his hips. The man, catching nothing, stumbled forward almost to his knees. Raeburn plunged a right hand to the back of the collar, holding him down, while his left hand still pushed the pass towards the man's eyes.

"Read it! Can you read? Raeburn is the name."

"Higgins!" The Duke's voice spoke urgently from the back of the hall. Raeburn dropped his collar grip and stepped away from the doorway.

The man came to his feet while the Duke, stepping across the hall, said: "Close the door, Higgins. Lights out."

Raeburn put away his pass. "I'm glad of that"—as the door closed and light switches were moved. "I should say that your doorway is quite a target area. Is this how visitors to Kintalla are normally received?"

The Duke looked at him, impassively surprised, the black eyes level. "In due course, if you feel bound to investigate the arrangements, I believe you may concede that they operate satisfactorily. However, security at Kintalla will be no part of your concern." His tone did not so much change as dismiss the topic, taking another. He led the way through the hall: "I am bound to say I have considerable regard for quick reflexes—"

"Still working—sort of . . ."

"Of course, you are virtually a professional."

Raeburn laughed at him. "You're joking. There's no money in it. When I played club rugby I paid for all my own gear and most of my travelling expenses."

"Nevertheless, it brought you here." There was less ice in the voice, but it was the nearest the Duke was going to reach towards a welcome. "Like so many other things in this country, sport is a matter performed by experts under the guidance of pretentious incompetents. The British predicament, indeed."

As he was pushing open the door of a large, well-lit ground-floor room, three men who had been waiting inside came out.

"Ah yes—" the Duke said to them. "You ought to go now. Stand here in the hall for a moment." He let the door of the room drop shut. The three lined up while the Duke spoke again: "This is Mr Raeburn, who is joining us. Make sure you will know him." And to Raeburn: "These are three of my tenant farmers: Galloway of Drumragit; Boyd of Laigh Torrs; Hislop of Ben Crocket. Remember them."

Guessing that the gesture would be rarely a feature of such an introduction, Raeburn shook hands heartily with the three. Under that roof they were perhaps diffident, but they clasped him firmly and smiled, with their eyes at least. Grave men, with their own inwardness. The Duke nodded briefly, in either approval or dismissal. In a moment he was pointing them to the outside door:

"Leaving now, Higgins. Remember—lights for arrivals, none for departures."

He pointed Raeburn to the door of the room they had just left, walking ahead of him and pushing it open again:

"Come in here."

CHAPTER 6

It looked as if it might be the dining room, with about a dozen men in it. The large table was covered with maps and papers. On what was probably the sideboard, blackboards and drawing blocks, well scribbled with half designs, were reared against the wall. Most of the company sat straggling round the table as if in conference, with a few in the background working at the drawings or turning pages.

They waited for the newcomer to be introduced. The Duke was not one to linger over this.

"Raeburn," he said to the gathering. "I have told you about him. Some of you he knows already. You have met Dale, Reid and Mac-Farlane. This is Sylvester"—his hand and arm flapped vaguely in the direction of a man even younger than Dale. "He does the same sort of work for me as Dale. Next to him" (a heavy serious man like an improved version of MacFarlane) "is Laidlaw, our head gamekeeper. This other is Mr Porteous." (A dark suit, the only remotely formal-looking person in the room. He had a steady eye on Raeburn.) The Duke continued: "Mr Porteous is manager of all our estates and non-urban lands in Britain. He is called Mr Porteous by everybody." The Duke appeared to be indicating that even he called the man Mr Porteous; probably had little interest in what his other names might be, if he had any.

"You had better also meet"—the Duke said, almost as a perfunctory afterthought—"my two house guests, here for a little shooting." He indicated two men who sat relaxed and comfortably, both of them dressed with impeccable casualness. "You may perhaps know Lord Melfort."

The renowned ex-ambassador raised practised eyebrows in salutation behind an elegant blue fog of tobacco smoke. "Yes," he said, possibly in greeting. "Let us hope we have a little shooting."

"And Sheikh . . ." The Duke, with some breathing gutturals, ran through his lips the long Arabic name of his second guest, who acknowledged with a courtly nod. "You may address him as Sheikh."

"Now." The Duke turned briskly to the table. "The others here know the duties of the three farmers who have left us. You have to know. If at any time they receive an agreed signal they will each drive out from their yards a tractor with a laden trailer, as a road block. Each man will station his at an agreed spot within a few yards of his own buildings. A look at the maps here will show you that this will effectively suspend all traffic in the Kintalla peninsula. The area affected includes the school premises of Markland. With these blocks in place"— Laidlaw was pointing them out on the maps—"nothing can leave our area to join main routes, which can only be reached as you know by travelling north."

Raeburn noted each spot. Drew out his own maps and marked the places.

"Seems all right from the maps," he agreed. "I'll have a quiet look in the passing one day soon. Interesting to see how far it might be possible to—"

"How many does that make of us?" Melfort asked the Duke.

"Ten now. Not counting our three farmers, who will of course not take any active part except to put the vehicles in position."

"And of them?"

"We make it eight at maximum. Let us look at the personalities in a moment. First we should be familiar with the proposed plan of the kidnapping attack. More information has come to hand and was given to me in Brussels this afternoon. There is a credible outline available. It is clear that the intention will be to use a helicopter—"

"To get him out, you mean?" Melfort interrupted eagerly.

"That must be assumed. Or it might be to deposit such as the leaders within the target area. More likely to make the lift—"

"Then why bother with the road blocks?" Melfort had hectored his way to the head of the Diplomatic Service by means of the obvious question in a God-given tone of authority.

The Duke let him wait for it, carefully scribing a plot point on one of the maps. Then:

"Merely to ensure that we cover all the doors, and keep the action to our own back yard. Pursuing the theme of the landscape opportunities, Laidlaw will point out some further aspects—"

The head gamekeeper came to the sideboard, propped higher a stiff large-scale map which leaned there, running across it with a stubby pointer while the Duke spoke:

"The dark patches blocked in on the whole surface area represent at least an approximation at the spots where a medium-sized helicopter would not find it possible to touch down. The model is thought to be a seven-seater Skrela HC ii, which even with a full load would not be sufficient to take off the entire kidnap team. Two helicopters are highly improbable. There would probably be a planned rendezvous in Northern Ireland, only minutes away from here, either going to ground there pending the ransom negotiations, or changing to a jet aircraft for a farther destination." The Duke scrutinised them in the circle of his gaze.

"Study this carefully. Make minimum notes on your own maps, if you need reminding. You will see that in broken territory such as we have here, the low rotor clearance reduces the number of possible landing places, which now seem to be very few. Some of the road surfaces are the most likely. These are marked." He waited, breathing absently, while they transferred the markings.

"There is a scheme worked out for the defensive coverage of these points, to be discussed later. In the meantime I see that—mm—Mr Raeburn has been at work on his maps. Perhaps you will tell us about your marking code." It would be too much to say that the Duke's tone betrayed anything so cordial as an interest, but the looks of that roomful of people who presumably knew him best dangled upon what Raeburn might have to say.

He flicked open his maps, laying them on the centre of the table. "Yes—I thought this might be worth trying." He told about the bicycle excursion, the encounter with the prince's detective. "These are sight lines from the top of the Doon, covering the whole bike route. You will see that not more than about 20 per cent of it was ever out of sight from that viewpoint for more than five seconds. If you look—"

"Most interesting," the Duke broke in, exercising a casual right of centuries. "A good addition to the general body of information. While we are talking, Mr Porteous will copy the lines into the main map."

Raeburn said: "There's one thing—"

"Are we sure that is the only cycle route which they use?" said Dale.

Raeburn let the insertion hang upon the air; continued: "I wanted to say that Miller the detective—of course I'll get to know him and his style better—seems to have taken up his post on the Doon. We might be better to think of Drumdar, this other height, as our place. It's two or three hundred feet higher than the Doon, probably commands a better view of the countryside. Whoever it is could get there even if Miller was in position. The sight lines would have to be done again, but they would probably eliminate at least three of the blind spots on the Doon map—here—and . . ." He stabbed them in sequence.

"There's another thing—"

The Duke was turning to Dale. "How could anyone answer that question?" he said to him. And absently, with patience, seemed to speak to his papers as he made a note—"schoolboys—bicycles—country roads —woman leader"—his voice trailing to nothing at the thought of the incalculable possibilities.

Raeburn tightened his lips. This lot could be penetrated only in their own time. He dropped his raised papers and maps back on to the table. He was about to wonder if it was worth it, when he realised that for him, in a sense, there was supposed to be nothing worth it.

The Duke had now turned to him, the cold face with wide eyes approving, it appeared, Raeburn's further words. Said: "Something else to tell us? There was more?"

"This. The top of the Doon, a green, shallow, cup-like hollow, seems like an ideal helicopter landing pad. You haven't got it marked."

"Quite right. Insert it please, Mr Porteous. I know that place. Quite perfect. Reid, you will take over the top of Drumdar. From first light."

"Surely, Your Grace."

Laidlaw put a cross and some symbol on the main map, at Drumdar. The Duke marked his own map. Gathered up the company again:

"We shall look now at the people we have to face." He flicked a cueing hand, without looking at the man. "Sylvester."

Sylvester had the notes ready. "As far as names are concerned, we can deal only with those which the group are presently using. They have each got a number of names, but those I'm going to give you are the most likely ones for this operation. We can be certain that the leader is Casio, a European who has never worked so far westward as this. His two deputies, or next in command, or it might be that by this time they are a triumvirate, are known as Konski and O'Connor—"

"Sure enough"—Lord Melfort held his cigar in front of his downward eyes, holding the audience briefly with it. "You can always expect an Irish *nom de guerre* nowadays. Fashionable."

The Duke breathed a full measure of boredom through his nostrils, like a snake sound. He nodded Sylvester forward again.

"—These three—Casio, Konski and O'Connor—will probably be the last to arrive in the neighbourhood. They might not even come until the actual attempt—"

"Some here already then?" Melfort made the query.

"At least two are identified. Martinu and Panacz, a youngish pair released as a result of hi-jack pressure from a Yugoslav group in February, are camping as tourists in a holiday caravan near the coast road a few miles south of Stranraer. Some distance north of the Kintalla estate boundary," he added. The last information was taken in impassive silence. It was well known that holiday campers did not fare comfortably on or near Kintalla ground.

"The others, making up the eight, are known as Cove, Fung, and Lu Satu. Cove is a woman. We know all their ages or age groups, and general characteristics, and we may have identified Fung working in a restaurant round the coast to the east. All except the main three have left mainland Europe and are either here or on the way."

"The task of the next two days or so will be to identify the main body of them, as individuals," the Duke said.

The sheikh stirred, smiled gently. "And kill them."

It was difficult to detect what it was that created the Duke's disapproval, but it fell like a frost upon the gathering. The sheikh had naturally addressed the Duke, whom he presumably considered the only equal in rank present. Raeburn could not tell what it was that exploded the extra silence—some unseen tilt of the Duke's head upwards, a poising of the stiffened neck, more clamorously repudiating than a scowl or a headshake—but all present seemed even more aware of it than he, and awaited the eloquent interpretation.

He spoke, eventually:

"Not to kill them. Not at all. First, naturally, to identify them. Then the supreme requirement is to direct them towards their purpose, so that they are caught up inevitably in the commission of the crime. In the very act. At that point, and not before, they are to be killed. Executed. We have not assembled this undertaking with selected men and plans, to exercise some clandestine vengeance for crimes committed elsewhere. What this country requires is a style of dealing with its own enemies." As if by a laborious courtesy, he permitted a silence to fall.

"Of course," Lord Melfort put in. The sheikh wore still, unchanged, the soft smile which he had been wearing when first rebuked. Behind it lay a chill and arid tolerance as old as the desert itself; an innate knowledge of wisdom lying beyond the recent novel barbarism of even the oldest Western European dukedom. Within the smile and the demeanour that went with it was an instinct for continuity and survival that was old and effective even before Charlemagne.

Raeburn noticed how the Duke, without a flicker, had nevertheless recorded the sheikh's silent comment. He himself, in schoolroom and on playing field, had more experience than most of the urgent necessity to dominate. His mind lingered to learn how the Duke would deal with it.

It happened that the Duke felt it expedient to deal with the matter more in the mode of the fifth Duke than that of the twenty-first, which he was. He said briskly:

"Of course"—echoing Melfort—"we kill them. In the end. I had meant to tell you the procedure later but can do it now. We shall shoot them individually, and before disposing of the bodies each one will be photographed in close-up. The photographs will be distributed without comment to the main European and American state police departments. This will establish without doubt that these important figures have been eliminated finally. As for the bodies, we shall dispose of them in the neighbourhood. It seems to me that there is no need whatsoever to involve the local police, far less the so-called defence forces. What we are talking about is a private activity, mounted and completed by private elements of the community who feel moved to protect their interests and their future, in the absence of any official concern. I take it we are agreed upon this"—he looked up and round the gathering, waiting long—"otherwise I shall be bound to consider why we have come to-gether."

Not bad, thought Raeburn. About the only way to deal with a de-scendant of the Prophet. He gathered up his papers, speaking:

"Before we go much further, do you mind if I—"

Melfort spoke: "In dealing with crime on the large scale, I have al-ways made it a rule to assume a possible addition to the list of known enemies. It can be called the 'X' factor. The unknown. I think you will find that this innovation which I introduced is now established practice in the British FO; in fact of the major Foreign Offices else-where. It's merely the need to assume that there is an enemy within. I mean one of us."

Only the Duke could deal with it. His own men watching him, he turned pointedly to Raeburn:

"I see that Raeburn has some further notes. Please?"

"First, there is one matter that has not been considered. Two, indeed. They seem to me important."

Raeburn was folding the notes, ready to speak on the new topic. The Duke raised a chairman's finger. Perhaps two.

"The notes, if you please."

Raeburn spread them on the table. He had less than any of them to worry about.

"I managed to get hold, simply by asking the headmaster for a copy, of the complete staff lists of the school personnel, not only the teaching staff but also the people in admin, services and maintenance. They in-clude ages, home addresses, length of service, and all that. Useful for identification checks if you wanted to compare them with your list of the likely kidnappers . . ."

Dale's hand was stretched across for the list. The Duke waved him away with a sudden flick. "Go on," he said, newly brisk. "Most interest-ing. And more, I see."

"Yes, more," said Raeburn. "Five new members joined the staff for this term. I've had conversation with all of them. Here are notes and descriptions of each—age, height, physical characteristics." He reached over to hand the sheets to the Duke, who said:

"Really most valuable." For the first time, he appeared animated. He reached past Dale's ready hand to put the papers into Sylvester's. "Im-mediate check," he said.

Raeburn described the five briefly, finishing with: "I'd take only two seriously out of the lot. Biros, the kitchen man, seems to me a sure thing. A very hard man in every way; quick; accepts authority with some reluctance, although he must know he's playing a part. The school staff list shows him as aged almost thirty but you'll see from the notes that I take him as a mature twenty-five. I'd personally write out the girl Isobel Henderson, unless she slots in very accurately with someone on your black list."

"Explain why," said Melfort.

"I'm really not very sure why." Raeburn spoke direct to the Duke, whose eyes were on him. Lord Melfort was studying his cigar. "But somehow she seems quite genuine. The Dublin voice was sound. So was the idiom. There was quite a trace of Sasunnach. I'd say she had spent the last five years or so in England."

Sylvester raised his head from the papers. The Duke pointed to him, silencing other talk.

"I think we can be sure that we have Konski in Biros. Age and height seem right. Build, eyes, ears even, shape, walk—yes, this is the man without a doubt. The two new masters are out—one is too old, the other far too big. The only other candidate is the maid Isobel Henderson, who might be the woman Cove. Appearance, age, height about right."

"Thought so," from Melfort.

Sylvester said: "We have her down as Swedish-Canadian, so the language wouldn't be a trouble."

"I'd be surprised." Raeburn held to it. "There's quite a subtlety in the differentiation between Croke Park, which is for the Gaelic games, and Lansdowne Road, the rugby field."

"That's what makes it perfectly obvious to me. It isn't even an elaborate deduction on my part. Merely experience." Melfort expanded in his correctness. "A spy, or a criminal in masquerade, has only a few score essential items to learn in adopting the background of another country, but one of them is invariably the main sports venues, the points of rendezvous, the transport elements, main bridges. I have some considerable experience—"

"OK," Raeburn told the table. "I'll keep an eye on them both. Especially Biros. And anybody who knows a lot about Sweden and Canada can feed me some disarming questions to try on the girl."

"We shall pursue enquiries about Cove." The Duke turned to his own notes, while the sheikh stirred to question:

"It is easy to spend much time speaking about people. What we know is that there will be people, and there will also be surprises. However, what do we know about the occasion of the attack? When?— where?—how?"

The Duke turned readily to this part of the action. His look to the sheikh might have been one of relief; of agreement as to the priorities among peers.

"Certainly. It is time to detail what we know. It seems quite certain that the seizure of the prince's person will take place in the late evening of next Tuesday. This is Saturday, and although in the intervening days we shall not require to be constantly assembled, there are points of vigilance to which we shall be giving much attention between now and then.

"One can be reasonably certain about a Tuesday move since it will be we who will induce it. That is our bonfire and fireworks night at the castle here. Most of you will know that my son and heir was born four weeks ago, and at each of our estates we are to have a celebration for the tenants and a few neighbours. The Duchess and I with some members of the household attended the festivity at our Sutherland estate last Monday evening. Next Tuesday is the turn of Kintalla; and so we shall work our way south—to the main estates only. Five in all.

"Naturally, all those present in this room will attend. Farm tenants are also expected. Some remote relatives and friends, and a few chosen neighbours. I should expect to invite the headmaster of Markland, with perhaps the deputy head, and a representative group of the pupils, certainly not more than half a dozen, to be chosen by him. I should expect him to select the head boy, the captain of games—that sort of thing— and of course the prince. There must be someone suitable in the party."

He paused, as if trying to decide whether to tell his present company any more. "The boy's name is the Earl of Allenhope," the Duke finished.

The sheikh opened his mouth, warning any casual conversation off his verbal territory. The dutiful silence awaited him.

"A noble name," he pronounced, "is the first inheritance of the son of a noble father."

The Duke nodded almost at once, as if the point was inexplicably obvious. "Yes—quite. Well, the name is actually mine. One of mine. I only lend it to him."

Melfort had already leaned over to say to the Duke: "I remember when you were Allenhope." It was intended to have the intimacy of inside information, and not for imparting to the general company. But MacFarlane felt drawn to endorse the historic relevance.

"It was I," he said directly, "who stalked the first stag that Lord Allenhope ever shot. He was eleven years old, and I never saw a cleaner kill." He looked round awkwardly, abashed at having initiated a topic.

"That reminds me—weapons!" The Duke put out a finger at Mr Porteous. "What have you got for Mr Raeburn?"

Mr Porteous took a flat cardboard packet from the sideboard, pushing it across the table to the Duke, who kept it moving as he slid it up the table to Raeburn.

"Take that. It's Belgian. Don't open it up until you get back to Markland. You'll find full illustrated instructions inside. Language should be no trouble. Get familiar with it. Do everything but shoot—meantime. That comes later. Plenty of opportunity . . ." For the last sentences he was already back to his notes, looking at no one.

"What is it?"

"A pistol." The Duke said it with patient surprise.

"Thanks. I'll do my homework." Raeburn slid it into his big side pocket. "But first of all, at this stage, I'd be—"

"As to weapons," Melfort edged in again, dragging the Duke's attentive frown away from Raeburn, "—what else have we got?"

Nodding, the Duke looked at him, and his eyes had never been so dark. "I take it you personally will need nothing. Pistols and FN rifles for the others as required. Half a dozen sub-machine guns. Two Czech K3 mortars—these to deal with one or more helicopters. Adequate, I think. Before we disperse tonight we shall all be issued with walkie-talkies. Study these, too. They are all fixed to the same tuning. We shall have a test call round everybody at 11 a.m. tomorrow. Note the time carefully. Kintalla guests outside somewhere, please." He spoke directly to Raeburn. "The signals will usually reach to Markland—we have tried."

Raeburn stood up. He remained on his feet for a second or two, and then leaned forward, tapping gently with a pen upon the polished table top.

The stir and the asides died. The Duke ceased from his notes and looked across. After a time he said: "Yes?"

Raeburn and he held eyes for many seconds. Each had his own accustomed authority, and in his own sphere was used to being in command.

"Yes!" The Duke was half a tone higher—and louder.

Raeburn relaxed to reply. He ceased his tapping; said:

"I believe—I believe that I can shout more loudly than anyone in this room, and am prepared to take part in any competition to demonstrate this. On the other hand, this may not be considered necessary. What I intend to do is make some considered observations on the important matter which is central to our meeting here. I have no mind to abandon this proposal, and I do not intend to be interrupted again. Please inform me if this meets with your approval."

Silence dropped upon them like thunder. From Melfort, to whose chilled face the Duke had darted a look, came the breathing mumble: "Extraordinary! Extraordinary fellow!"

Raeburn, serene, digested his own crudity, and became ready.

"Pray proceed," said the Duke. "We must not miss this."

"Thank you." Raeburn put his pen in his pocket; held the Duke's eye again.

"Allow me," said Raeburn, sitting down again, "to recapitulate briefly the scheme as it now stands—the little I know of it. It has not been summarised since I came here, and I have the minimum of information. I understand you to have become aware of a plot by certain interests to kidnap Prince David, who is at school here, and to hold him to ransom.

"Your belief is that the ransom will be readily paid out of the huge personal fortune of the Royal Family. It's an unrecorded mass of wealth and needn't even be specified in the public demand. It might not even be a public demand. At any rate it would certainly be the largest single ransom ever paid. So far so good, and if the show turns out like that I shall play my full part in scuppering them, as promised."

"But that is precisely the point we reached in our agreement of almost two days ago." The Duke's pen seemed poised now, ready to tap.

"At that time, as you know, I was already busy with reservations. But I was scarcely able to express them clearly. This is the point—now. I am quite certain that your reasoning is wrong, although your facts may be quite right. I do not for a moment believe that the Royal Family would pay any such ransom."

"You *what?*"

"They would not pay! Not ever! I dare say most of your reasoning is perfectly credible, but you've come up with the wrong answer."

Raeburn still spoke directly to the Duke. "I don't know how well you know them, but don't you realise they are not in any real sense private people? Have you any idea how accustomed they are to sacrifice—to discomfort—to loss? It would hardly occur to them to try to buy themselves out."

He spoke on, and now the Duke's head, the face utterly without expression, was shaking to and fro in a negative finality. It still swung for a time after Raeburn had finished speaking, and shook still while the lips moved:

"You are, of course, wrong, if I may be allowed to say so. Perhaps an understandable lack of knowledge about that level of life. Not a single nuance of your ponderous reasoning has failed to come into the present calculations. I trust you will spare me the need to proceed through the whole sequence of the logic; and as to your second point, if it is of equal weight, perhaps you will be good enough to put it aside."

As he spoke he was glancing at the watch on his wrist, and he made a faint gesture to Dale. The younger man turned and switched on a transistor radio at the very moment the late-night news headlines were being announced.

The first item skipped through some reference to the economic conference, where nothing much had happened. The second item was suddenly mentioning the Duke's name ". . . whose multinational business interests have made him the head of one of the most powerful commercial empires in the Western world. In Brussels this afternoon he signed a deal with a group of assorted European brewing concerns which will place him at the head of the biggest beer syndicate in existence. The Duke, who is believed to be in residence tonight at one of his country estates, was not available for detailed comment, but earlier today our reporter at Brussels airport, Bill Martin, asked him:

Reporter's voice: "Your Grace, what's going to happen to the beer?"
The Duke's voice (muffled, on the move): "More—and cheaper."

The item went statistical in money and gallons, and the Duke waved Dale to switch off.

"Quite enough for now," said the Duke, standing up. It was the unmistakable rise of dismissal. "Stand by everybody for the bleeps at 11 a.m. tomorrow."

His staff people melted out of the room, long used to exits. The Duke left Lord Melfort and the sheikh behind, taking Raeburn lightly by an arm to lead him to the door of another room off the hall.

"Please come in here," he told him. "I want to speak to you."

"I want to speak to *you*," said Raeburn. "Urgently."

CHAPTER 7

"Brandy?"

The Duke had poured himself a steady splash and, with his nose in the goblet, was already deliberating, rocking cupped hands in a slow motion.

"No, thank you."

He allowed himself to sink into the largest chair. Shortly he took a first pull at the brandy, surprising Raeburn by the volume which the lean jaws imbibed. No doubt many generations of practice had gone into developing that capacity. The glass globe came away from the mouth, and the rocking resumed. Then the Duke spoke:

"Urgently?" It was a cue—a permission, almost an instruction, to speak.

Raeburn sat in the chair on the other side of the fireplace, schooling the anger out of his face as he brought in a smile that he hoped might carry a show of indifference.

"Is it always difficult to get a hearing in your presence?" he asked.

"A hearing?" The glass raised again, and at the same time the eyebrows went up a fraction. "I'm not aware of any impediment to further conversation at this time. Please feel under no constraint."

Raeburn laughed, for the first time since entering that house. "You know fine what I mean." He walked to the sideboard and poured himself a dram of one of the celebrated whiskies which ranged there, and sat back with it. "How do you expect to get the best consensus of points of view if people can't get a word in? Or is the whole scheme so cut and dried that there isn't room for another idea?"

"In fact, it is."

"I'm not saying for a moment it will alter my decision to come in with you. I'm in."

"Good." For a moment the Duke looked almost genial.

"But I haven't the slightest doubt you are wrong in your belief in how the Royal Family would behave."

The Duke was nodding in a seeming effort to comprehend. "One has opportunities—close opportunities at times—to see, judge, certain behaviour, habits . . . There are others also who have, long since indeed, during the planning—who have made their contribution . . ."

"And what if the kidnap people have come to another conclusion—say something like mine?"

"Ah then, we shall be somewhat wiser. Let us say in the meantime that you have made your point. You know enough of the counter-plan to realise that your theory has very little chance of being put to the test."

"But," said Raeburn finally, "I think you're right about the kidnapping but wrong about the target. These chaps may change direction. For example—and this is my second point, in spite of you—you ought to look out for your own safety. No, don't interrupt me, for God's sake!"

The brandy glass was waving him imperiously to silence and Raeburn stopped as the Duke said: "But I must. The reason I asked you to remain with me was to talk about *your* safety."

Raeburn stared—stumbled: "What? *My* safety! What about my safety?"

The Duke laid his glass aside. "If you have no objection, I should like to discuss your disability. Briefly."

"My what? My disability!" Of course the man was ruthless, but it seemed an offhand way to describe a death sentence. "Of course, if you want. Carry on. You know as much as I do."

"I think I do. When I was in Brussels today I had a meeting with a doctor who has been of considerable service to me. His name—Dr Sanger—may be known to you. The Nobel Committee awarded him their medical prize earlier this year for work in a quite new field—the development of drugs which permit the alteration of the hormonic values in the bloodstream. Sanger at present works in Zürich. In fact, I ought to say that he works for me in Zürich. In all of my business interests, the only significant charitable undertaking which we pursue is the support of the Zürich Specialist Clinic, an interest which I undertook a number of years ago for reasons of a deeply personal character.

"In various fields of medical innovation, some work of an important nature goes on at the Clinic. Well, shortly after our meeting in Edinburgh, I spoke on the telephone to Sanger and gave him what I knew of your medical history. I took the liberty of telling him that I was concerned to secure for you a return to full health, if that might be at all possible. May I take it that you have no objections to raise, so far as the matter goes at this stage?"

"But—but—" Raeburn had lost coherence. "—But it's impossible. Thanks, of course—but I've been written off. Nobody's fault. You shouldn't bother. Why should you bother . . . ?"

"Naturally Dr Sanger made some direct and expert enquiries. He is accustomed to taking nothing for granted. By the time he came to report to me in Brussels earlier today Sanger was extremely well documented. As one would expect, in a case like this nothing whatsoever can be guaranteed. But I must tell you at once that Sanger is of the firm opinion that your condition would yield to almost immediate surgery."

It was Raeburn's hand pounding on the table. "Impossible! I'm not sure that I want this all stirred up again—my specialist is thought to be about the best in his field. He knows! I talked to him at great length about surgery—I would have had a go at anything, however risky—and he said it wasn't on. This Sanger, away in Zürich—Brussels . . ."

The Duke was going patiently on with his omnipotent nodding:

"Yes. Mr Torrie. A most eminent name. Although I had naturally never heard of him myself, I was impressed by his high standing in the appropriate department in Zürich. He and Sanger have had a number of consultations, in the first place by telephone. In the end Sanger was flown by one of our company aircraft to Edinburgh early this morning, where they went over all the clinical evidence, examined the X-ray plates and other articles. It was possible at that time for Sanger to give Mr Torrie certain information about two new items of apparatus we have recently had constructed for the Clinic. They are reasonably portable. I shall mention the importance of this in a moment."

"But why—why—why should you do all this?"

"It appears that the element of surgery in the case is scarcely so important as the possibility that the Sanger hormonic principles would be the main factor in the post-operational phase. It remains to say that your Mr Torrie has become most enthusiastic about the whole project and desires to be associated with it. Here is what has been arranged, if you agree to it. I may say that I felt so inclined to guess that you would agree that I have instructed the finalising of all the details.

"Next Thursday—of course we shall have finished with our kidnap plot project by that time—next Thursday the special apparatus and some operation equipment will be flown by us into Prestwick airport, bringing also Dr Sanger and some of his colleagues who are eager to share in this experiment. I hope the word does not sound too irresponsible." The Duke drooped his mouth in a momentary hinted smile. "Plans have been completed by which use will be had of the operating theatre in the excellent Ayr County Hospital. I am afraid you will have quite an audience. Doctors are incurable voyeurs. Mr Torrie will of course take part. You will be conveyed from Markland, presumably by road. Your own Dr Grant will be on the scene, and he will be in touch with you beforehand. Probably travel with you. The operation will be overnight Thursday/Friday. You know how doctors love to dramatise their affairs!"

"I—I simply don't know what to say."

"In such a case the best tactic is often to say nothing."

"I mean—you have me all disposed of."

"Rather, we are trying to ensure that you will not be disposed of."

"If I seem astonished—even dubious—it's only because I thought it was all over."

"Nothing is all over . . . there is a good deal of human ingenuity going on here and there."

"I didn't think I even had a chance."

"Well, enough of this speculation. Let us leave the rest to the people who claim to be experts. The situation appears to be that they are prepared to risk their reputations. What about you? Are you prepared to risk their skills?"

"Yes. Yes, of course."

"I had no doubt about it. Now, there is a great deal to be done, even between now and tomorrow morning." The Duke flourished and flicked the slim black notebook in which he had been writing throughout the planning session, as if it held a hundred riddles. "And you have no doubt much to think about. You will remember to stand by the walkie-talkie for tomorrow's bleep session at eleven. You have your own transport for tonight?"

"Yes—I got a car. By the way, thank you—for all that . . ." Raeburn had never felt less articulate, more inadequate. "I still wish you'd give me a chance to say . . ." His voice trailed off.

The Duke walked through the hall with him to the door. There were no more words, no handshakes. Higgins stood back, taking the opening door with him. It came to a firm close even before Raeburn came off the last step on to the gravel of the drive.

Conning the car gently back to Markland in the wake of its headlamps, he had much to think about. The Duke and his power saturated his thinking. Here was a man apparently with the powers of a deity. Already he had pulled Raeburn like a puppet from the certainty of extinction, not on an impulse but with a devious purpose into which the man fitted, for all his fame, like a small toothed wheel. Now there was another purpose afoot, with their creature inert upon an operating table, and the knives plying, the new inventions crackling and sparking.

It was something new for Raeburn to meet, and to come to know, anyone who could set aside the terminal purposes of life, after the farewell rituals, the sentence, the winding-up. He felt a surge of gratitude and curiosity about whatever short chapters might lie ahead. And there were new people in his life, suddenly, in these last two or three days. He had been needing that.

On the long bend of the road at Cessford Wood, a mile or two short of Markland, there was a sudden small tremor in the steering wheel, and he had to wrestle to keep the car straight against the speed he had built up, dropping mileage and easing her into the level stretch of road running towards the base of the Doon.

Like all mishaps, he had no chance then to know what happened, nor to remember later. He was in the midst of a lurching, bumping slew, fighting to steer the car, which was insisting on tracking into the roadside ditch. He had the impression that the vehicle had leaned suddenly away from the crown of the road. Carefully, steadily, he increased the pressure on the brakes, the steering still answering. At some time in these seconds he must have switched off the engine, so that by the time he had got her to a halt and stepped out, the night was profound with blackness and silence. Only his beams cut the dark ahead. To the rear the lamps turned the road to blood. Far off in the windless night there was the voice of a hill burn running endlessly to Solway.

As he stood there, holding the driving door opened, both feet planted on the cool tarred road, and not a sound near him, he suddenly became aware of an immense whisper upon the road behind—an unidentifiable force, rushing and crushing upon him. He strained, in that second or two, to detect what menaced, and at once it was at him, a black and whirring shape, destroying.

It leapt at him out of the night. None of the fabled athletes he had evaded and outpaced had ever made him move at this speed, with no one to see. He slammed the driving door shut and with the leverage gained he swerved from the waist down in a single movement that put his feet a full yard from the car. The thing whirled past him, just below his leaning face, tapped grindingly at the front end of the car, and spun to the hillside, dying out of the lamplight among the scrub bushes and heath on the far side of the ditch.

He had identified it as it went past. It was the near-side rear wheel of the car, which had come off its axle to leave the car three-legged and slithering as he controlled it to a standstill. He was on a long downhill incline, and the wheel had pursued him, rolling to overtake the car, taking a free run on the crown of the road. It had been coming fast and heavily for him at knee height, and it would have broken both his legs if he had not made that jump.

By the reflected light Raeburn could not see enough to tell what had taken the wheel adrift from its hub, but he could feel from the bolt ends that their nuts were undone. Somebody had loosened them enough to ensure that the motion of the car's own riding would shed the wheel. The bolts were not stripped, and there seemed no other hub damage. Nor elsewhere on the car, except that in its passage by the front of the car the wheel, still in full flight, had tipped the end of the bumper and bent it fully outwards like a straw.

Raeburn felt for the ridiculous merchandising package in his wide jacket pocket where the new pistol was stored, and smiled to think he had no idea how to work the thing. It was time to be away from here. He doused the lights, locked the car, and skipped fifty yards along the road to take his bearings.

The night was not too dark, and like all nights it became lighter as he grew used to the gloom. There was a half-moon. A cottage skylight window half a mile across the moor showed where, perhaps, a fretting baby was being comforted; although as he looked it went out to signal that those inside were reaching towards the morning. A great ghost of light moved regularly to touch the tree tops of the Doon and the lower points of the eastern end of the Cessford Wood. This was the lighthouse of the Mull of Galloway, with its long beam twice as lengthy as its darkness. There was no traffic. Nothing moved on the road. He could see from his watch in the scanty illumination that it was after one in the morning.

As the minutes passed there was enough light to walk and to see. He made good progress along the road, finding the bends ahead, realising that they were already familiar. After a time he could pick out the grass verge from the metalled surface, and went on it, to silence his betraying footsteps. He was level now with the low summit of the Doon.

The trouble came not from that side but from his right, where a dry stone dyke ran to fence the grazing fields. He was walking the turf border of the road, where gorse bushes sprouted between road and dyke, when he saw—was it?—yes, certainly, a figure twenty paces ahead come over the wall, seeming to scuttle out of sight into its shadow towards him.

He might have stopped, but his instinct was to keep walking, with eye fixed at the point which the moving wraith would be reaching if it kept up its crouching run at the same speed.

But suddenly the figure was at him—immediately in front of him, risen from the bushes, having covered the distance like a dart. No time to think this one out. Raeburn stopped at once, hands ready, and gathered. The man had a weapon—it might be a club—no, he was aiming it—

Raeburn's eye had kept track somehow of the route the man might be expected to cover, and of his speed, since he had first crossed the wall. And as he waited for the thrust, or the swing, or the bullet, there rose another figure from the expected direction. This shadow stood suddenly over the assailant from behind. An elbow went round the throat, so that you could hear the neck muscles crack; another arm seemed to plunge, taking a grunt from the near figure, which was left to drop quietly on the turf. Raeburn was aware that he himself was still left in the heroic pose of combat which he had struck a few seconds before.

"Reid," said the upright figure immediately. "Reid. You mind me, Mr Raeburn—I'm one of the Duke's men. We were at that meeting tonight. Reid, they call me. Just you wait there a minute and don't be worried. We'll get this sorted out, quiet like."

Reid was on his knees, rummaging in the grass. He spoke again: "I wasn't able to give you a word of warning. I'm sorry—sir. You shouldn't be having to put up with this kind of trouble, and you not very well . . . See, we'll have a bit of light." He seemed to take a pocket torch and prop it lit on the grass. Beside the crumpled figure of a man, he was wiping a knife clean on the turf.

"God Almighty! What happened?"

"First, are you all right, Mr Raeburn? You shouldn't be walking, eh?"

"Don't worry about me. My car broke down. It's a mile up the road. What in God's name is all this? Who is this? Is he dead?"

"Aye, right enough, he's fair snuffed it. Ach, the whole thing is straightforward enough. You heard the Duke tell me to watch out from Drumdar. Well, MacFarlane ran me round here an hour ago, and I was having a wee recce when I spotted this character. It occurred to me he was maybe waiting to do you in. There would be no other reason for him to be here at this hour. They must have crippled your car, sir. So when I heard your footsteps I knew he was an ambush."

Reid, familiar with death, had rolled the man over like an animal, shining the torch around the indeterminate face.

"Who is he?" asked Raeburn.

"Well—I don't rightly know, but he's one of the caravan pair. He's either Panacz or Martinu—one or the other. I don't suppose it matters. I've seen them at the caravan."

"What if the other is hereabouts?"

"Aye." Reid pondered. "If he is, there's trouble still. But I don't think it, or they would both have gone for you." He had taken a pistol from the dead man's hand, looking along the extended barrel. "He was doing it right too. A silencer. Mr Raeburn, would you hold the torch for me, please."

Reid stood up. "On the face, sir." Raeburn shone the torch on the young face. Reid, at full height, untensed, pointed the gun and fired it, with a gasp as its only sound. There leaped into the middle of the forehead a round hole from which a little blood immediately oozed.

"Why the hell did you do that?" There was no getting used to death.

"Just while he's—while he's—kind of new. The bullet hole will show he can't be anything but dead. That's the way the Duke wants it. Mr Raeburn, sir—where's your own gun? You had a gun."

Raeburn took out the package. "Still wrapped up. I don't know how to use it."

"Dear me!" Reid scooped the box from him, tearing into the wrapping and clipping, clicking. He slipped the blue-black weapon into

Raeburn's pocket. "There, man. It's loaded now, anyway. There's the instructions and some clips in your other pocket. I wouldn't touch the gun until you've read them, unless maybe you have an emergency.

"I'll need to be getting away." Reid had moved to the base of the dyke and was gathering things. He came back with a slung rifle, binoculars, a haversack dangling, bearing them as one well accustomed to such gear. The torch went into his pocket.

"If I was you, Mr Raeburn, I would get back fast to that school tonight. Will you be seeing the Duke early tomorrow?"

"Probably. What about . . . ?"

Reid bent, heaving the dead man in a single grip at the back of his collar. With a swing he took him over his shoulder like a kitbag.

"Tell the Duke I've put him into Locker 3. He'll want to send maybe Mr Dale to take the photograph."

"You're not going up Drumdar tonight, are you?"

Reid was stepping across the road, the dangling man, Panacz or Martinu, at his back:

"Ach, I'm used to being out at night."

Raeburn saw them out of sight two steps beyond the far edge of the road. He heard them cross the fence, and for a moment was aware of Reid's laden footsteps among the low trees. Soon the silence came. He turned and ran for Markland.

CHAPTER 8

For an hour after his arrival back in the small hours of the morning Raeburn had sat in his room, familiarising himself with the pistol. It had been a cautious beginning, but soon he could load and unload the clips, grasp the weapon suddenly, slip off the safety catch and lock it again, grasp, aim and trigger it. Soon he could do it without looking at his hands. The instructions were clear—not even technical, except for a dozen or so new words for some of the parts, and these were clear in the illustrations. He was astonished at the comfort of it, the natural shape and feel of the thing, matching his hand and arm like a companion. With some safety pins he shallowed somewhat his left hip pocket, and there the pistol waited its task.

In the morning he went through the motions again, feeling a satisfying mastery over the silent blue steel. The morning bell at Markland was at eight o'clock on Sundays, an hour later than on the other days, but long before it spoke he was roaming the building. At the coin-box telephone he put in a call to the emergency overnight number of the car-rental firm in Stranraer, and was relieved to get an alert if muffled response at once.

"Oh, aye, Mr Raeburn. You're early. Is the car doing you all right? . . . No! God!—A wheel off. How did that happen? Wait a minute . . ." There was a fumbling second or two, and the voice came back, dentured. "Sorry—I'm still in bed. Are you hurt? Well, that's something, to have you all right. Where was it? Have you told the police? Will I?"

"Rather you didn't. I have my suspicions. I'd be glad if you'd leave that bit to me. I just want the car back."

Raeburn had told the story in terms of a mere mishap. Nothing about the apparition of Reid nor of the stranger now installed in Locker 3, wherever that might be . . . "Trouble is that I really need the car all the time. I just don't want to be without it."

"And how did you get back to the school at that hour of the night?"

"On my two feet."

"Man, though, it's very unusual. Wheels just don't come off your modern car."

"I think you can forget about blaming any of your people. I'm pretty sure somebody interfered with that wheel. If I can prove it I'll let you know."

"Aye, and the police too. We can't have—"

"I'd rather you said nothing in the meantime. Maybe I'll catch them the next time—if they try it again."

"Well, we'd better get it back to you. I doubt if it will have come to much harm. I know the spot. From here it shouldn't take half an hour —say another half-hour to get her on her feet, and then it's only minutes to Markland. We'll no' be long."

"You mean you'll come right away?"

"Ach, there's plenty of time before the kirk. I'll take my own lad with the truck. We have the garage here too."

A clashing of pots drew Raeburn to the kitchens, from which came all the nutty, hot waft of porridge smells and a great momentous frying. There seemed to be a full muster here, with Ridley the chef more lurking than presiding. Girls carried trays of cups, plates and cutlery to the dining room beyond. Young men with white close caps, and hair styles not limited by the school rules, moved among the smoking pans and kettles. Raeburn's eye at once—he hoped unobtrusively—picked up the man Biros, who was slicing bread with an old-fashioned long plunger machine and racking it into a series of toasters. With an occasional free hand he agitated by the handle a frying pan crowned with eggs and bacon.

Ridley came over at once: "You're up early, Mr Raeburn. Did they not tell you there's a long lie on Sundays?"

"Yes, they did. But I've been up most of the night anyway." Not softening his voice, he gave a rueful description of the mishap with the car wheel, making the location a mile or so away from the actual spot, and the walk to Markland that much longer. The impassive Biros was within easy earshot, flicking at the toast; slicing; sizzling.

"Here, that could have been serious! Were you hurt?" In the mood for drama, was Ridley, finding himself exclusively in the company of this star turn of his obscurer days. "No? Lucky you! We don't want you out of action. That happened to me once. I lost a wheel off a car in Glencoe. A good while ago now. If I hadn't been pretty fit in those days . . ." He described his agile escape. Then:

"Here! I'm talking too much! Tell you what—that sort of thing makes you hungry. What about joining me here for breakfast? I always stoke up before the customers. Chef's privilege!" He motioned a finger at Biros. "You! My breakfast. And the same again for Mr Raeburn, with porridge first for Mr Raeburn. Not for me."

Raeburn was pushed towards a desk in a corner, which had suddenly become a table set for two. He took the porridge for the internal comfort of it, while Biros delivered the large-sized plates of bacon and eggs.

"Toast! Milk! Spoon!"

Ridley had a voice attuned to cutting through kitchen clamour, so that he almost never merely spoke. It was a yelp. Biros served precisely, and not slowly. While he still moved at the table, Ridley intimated to Raeburn:

"Got to keep them at it—these chaps. Make them hop—eh?—captain?"

To Biros he said, pointing: "This gentleman—Mr Raeburn—great football player—rugby—you know!" He sketched an oval with his hands. ". . . Caps—you know?"—shaping a cap on his own head.

"Yes, chef," Biros said slowly.

Soon Ridley was talking again, genially, half a fried egg hovering near his mouth: "Well, it's great! Fancy me sitting here in my own department having a meal with Barry Raeburn. Tell me—here's a thing I've always wanted to know—what sort of breakfast were you supposed to take in the old days? I mean before a game . . ."

Raeburn was finishing, and satisfied, and now wondering how he might escape this pressing fan, when Mrs Gibson the housekeeper came through the kitchen, saying: "Excuse me, chef." And at once: "There you are, Mr Raeburn. I was told you were here. The garage people are outside with your car."

Among his grateful words on the way out, Raeburn stopped to say a thank you to Biros, if only for the appreciation of seeing again that quick and wary light in the eye, the unobtrusive placing of the feet in the stance of a man used to defending himself. Biros gave him a single nod.

In the forecourt below the steps waited his car, back on four wheels, and a truck with a youth standing. The father was dangling the keys:

"Not a word from us. If you have your suspicions I'll leave it to you. We got three of the five nuts in the last half-mile of the road before we reached the car. The wheel had taken a dive into the heather. None the worse, though. No damage. We straightened the bumper."

"Glad if you leave it to me, then. Some crazy youngster, maybe . . ."

"Maybe no! There's more than just mischief here, I would say."

They went off with no fuss.

With so many of the men teachers supervising the morning meal, the staff dining room was almost empty for breakfast. He got a smiling welcome, however, from Joan Ker.

"Just for once," she told him, "we won't call you late. But don't let it happen again! Help yourself to the goodies. Breakfasts are the best thing here—eating-wise."

"I cheated." Raeburn could only grin back at her apple-cheeked face of smiles. "I've been about for a while. Got breakfast in the kitchen from the boss himself."

"There you are, see! The favourite lodger. What was all this in aid of? Did he give you tea or coffee?"

"Tea."

"Coffee now, then." She handed him a cup, and Raeburn told the few of them a version of the story about the car wheel. He felt he was growing evasively smooth. Before they could get in with their supplementary questions, he asked: "Anybody seen the headmaster? I'd better report to him."

Joan Ker said: "You'll find him in his study, swotting up for the church service. Full turnout expected."

Coulson was there, a breakfast tray hardly touched at his elbow while he riffled among Bible and hymn book, taking notes.

"Come in, Barry, come in. I'm mugging up the good book. We have a sort of church parade in the hall at eleven-thirty, and some of the parents are still around for this first one of term, so we like to make a show. Good if you can come."

"Sure. Eleven-thirty? Sunday suit?"

"Well, collar and tie anyway. I heard about the car bump from somebody. None the worse?"

"Man and car still in one piece. Can I slip over to Kintalla . . . a quick word with the Duke. Guaranteed back by eleven-thirty."

"Certainly. Tell the Duke I think we are getting on fine. I hope you have a good singing voice—we're rather light in the basses."

"I lost it long ago, shouting to flank forwards. But I can turn the pages."

Coulson turned back gratefully to his rummaging among the texts. "Watch it, though. Seems to me you're being a bit strenuous. Maybe a check-up . . ."

The quiet morning countryside, still early, had a Sabbath calm, mild air, a high, faint, blue sky wisped overall with a white underfelt of cloud. No one walked the roads. The cars were few, since there was hardly a place to go except Kintalla, where visitors came only to plan.

Raeburn parked the car discreetly on the far side of the Kintalla forecourt gravel, and started a crunching track towards the steps. A woman came forward from the scattered trees to encounter him. He was aware of massed chestnut hair, the utterly apt brogues, and some stylish informality about the tweed skirt and the short-sleeved jumper. She would be about the same age as Joan Ker, and what he noticed in particular was that she wore the same kind of smile, in welcome. It was the first he had seen in this place.

"Mr Raeburn!" And the handshake was firm. "I knew you weren't far away. You've come to teach at Markland. I hope it goes well."

He stopped. "To tell the truth, I haven't started yet. But there seem to be other things to do in this countryside. I'm here to have a word with the Duke. Do you happen to know if he's about?"

"He's inside. I'll take you in." They walked together. She smiled again at Raeburn's look of what might be enquiry, and said: "I'm the Duke's wife. I was Edith Haddo. Hullo again! I recognised you."

He struggled to recall whether he had given her the wrong kind of speculative look; dismissed it. "Sorry—I should have thought . . . Your —" Well, if not that, what did you call a Duchess?

"Oh," she laughed, "there's more to it than that. I'm Bandy Haddo's sister," and laughing still, she took his two hands in a brief clasp.

"You're not!" It couldn't be. Bandy Haddo! Bandy had been a playing contemporary, in another Edinburgh club. A good forward, he had never quite made it to the international scene, but had a few years of district representative games. They had often met on the field, and after it. The Haddos had been some kind of Lothian lairds, not well off, trying to keep going with farming. He never knew there was a sister.

"Bandy! Where is he? Is he . . . ?"

"He went to New Zealand. Farming. Doing all right. He came home for my wedding. You should see how fat he is!"

"Aye—he had a tendency . . ."

"A bit older than me, I'm bound to say. A man when I was hardly into double figures. I always miss him. Decent to me. We had seats in the Murrayfield stand for that game when you jumped—I suppose everybody talks about that one."

"Well, well, Bandy! Give him my regards . . ."

"I'll give him your address—I know he'd like to be in touch." They walked on, unspeaking. Who was he to think of starting a correspondence with anyone.

"The baby?" he asked. "How is the baby?"

She appraised him, the smile still hovering. "That wasn't bad for a bachelor. Come and see." She led him towards a nursemaid and pram emerging from the trees. "I feel that since we are almost old family friends I can give you some schoolgirl cheek."

The nurse, in some sort of uniform, fussed and tucked at the pram's contents as they approached.

Raeburn looked gravely at the sleeping scrap, with its blue eyelids and pulsing head. "I've never seen such a tiny Earl," he told the Duchess.

"Neither have I. But then he doesn't know he is one." She pondered some problem, seriously; stated: "You know he might not be allowed to play for Scotland, even if he's good enough. Born in England, and I'm afraid more English than Scottish in him."

"In spite of you?"

"In spite of me."

"Pity—we could have done with some blue blood in that team."

They went laughing towards the door. It opened and the Duke came to the top of the steps. His sallow look of absent concentration showed no change to see them. At once he turned back into the hall, with a summoning flick of the hand to Raeburn.

"That means me," said Raeburn. "Goodbye for the time being, Duchess."

"Edith," she said, and turned back to the pram.

He and the Duke sat again in the smaller study room, like an office, which they had occupied alone in the small hours of that same day. Raeburn had started to backtrack on the medical undertaking the Duke had embarked on for him. ". . . felt I hadn't expressed as fully as I meant . . ." but the Duke cut him off at once:

"Have you come to withdraw from the arrangements?"

"Not at all. I just wanted to say, in case there was any doubt—"

"There are no doubts in my arrangements, and presumably none in your response. I have told you that I dislike inefficiency. It would seem to me inefficient at this point to allow you to die, and inefficient also to engage in too much discussion on the topic. You have not come here at this hour of the day, have you, to rehearse matters already settled?"

"Not at all. I came here to endorse some of my early inadequate courtesies, but they can easily be put in abeyance. The main purpose of my visit, however, was to tell you that the war has started."

The quick edge was into the Duke's voice: "Started? Explain."

"And that there have been casualties. There is a dead one already."

"Dead! How do you mean? Has someone contradicted my orders?"

Raeburn laughed at him. "That's the worst of the enemy. They don't seem willing to follow your plans." He told the previous night's story— the cast wheel, the man at the dyke, the emergence of Reid, Locker 3—"whatever that may be."

The chill eye of the Duke warmed with a guarded passion as the tale unrolled. "Good!" he said. "That was good! Reid did well."

"Speaking for myself," said Raeburn, "I'd rather he was on my side than against. As for Locker 3 . . . ?"

"A sort of shed—a building in the wood. It's a game larder serving the north side of the estate, with electricity and water. Useful for storage when the bags are big—hanging game—cold day lunches—just part of the equipment. You'd better see it."

The Duke pressed a telephone switch and at least two voices from separate responding microphones answered him. "Sylvester," said the Duke briefly, and put up the switch.

In a moment Sylvester had tapped the door and entered.

"Tell him," said the Duke to Raeburn, and the whole story was told again. When it was finished, the Duke said:

"Both of you, go to the Locker. You do the photographs, Sylvester, and bring back here everything useful. I want you to be clear of all that in time for the eleven-o'clock bleep round-up. You"—to Sylvester— "I want you on the shore of Loch Talla." To Raeburn, he said casually, "Anywhere in the neighbourhood of Markland will do."

"Sir," said Sylvester, leading the way from the room.

Sylvester took time to collect a pair of haversacks, already packed, which he slung into the rear of a car collected from the back courtyard of the castle. He led their cortège on the same route that Raeburn had taken the night before, skirting at last the main road below the Doon, and drawing to the recesses of a lay-by some distance beyond.

"No point in getting the detective worried, if he's on the prowl today." Leading the way, Sylvester strode over the fence and through the thick young trees on the north base of the Doon.

Locker 3 was an oblong hut, high-pitched in the roof, and perhaps bigger than a suburban villa garage. It was immensely strong, built of locked logs, with no windows, but one skylight of opaque glass in each of the two roof pitches. It stood in a small clearing out of sight of the road, with its solid door pointing uphill.

Sylvester put a small, flat steel key into the lock and swung the door easily open, stepping in. "Come in," he said to Raeburn.

Inside it was more than half dark. Sylvester's hand ran over a section of the inside panelling like a Braille reader, and in a moment touched a switch to light two bulbs high to the roof. It was brilliant for a moment after the gloom, and they could see the other inhabitant.

From the roof beams along one side there hung a short row of butchers' hooks, an arm's length from the wall, and he hung from one of them. You could imagine how Reid had simply heaved him up there, spiking the bunched nape of the jacket on the polished point. He was younger than Raeburn had expected, peaceful and swaying slightly, perhaps with the compression of the opening door, the toes pointed in their light shoes, the arms straight. His eyes were still open. Making a triangle with them, in mid-forehead, was the black drill mark of the bullet, and it made death indubitable.

As Sylvester appraised the scene, Raeburn asked, breaking the silence:

"Panacz or Martinu?"

"Martinu, without a doubt—but I'll check." He was opening one of the haversacks, lifting out cameras and articles. "These are the two who were sprung a while ago as a result of a Yugoslav hi-jacking. The other one, Panacz, is presumably still in the caravan up the road, looking like a tourist and starting to wonder about Wandering Willie here."

Sylvester made his first checks from a notebook, folded back at an opened page. "Mm—that's right, fairly dark brown eyes—skin sallow Mediterranean—hair dark brown nondescript, curling a bit around the back of the neck—ears that shape—it's Martinu all right. One more thing"—he had an inch tape out—"we'll just run the tape over him." He went about it briskly, in two sections. As he was working on the lower half, from the waist down, he remarked: "We'll just take the measure to the heels. The toes being pointed will throw us out."

There was water in the building. Ranged against the opposite wall was not only a stove and oven but a sink with taps. Raeburn turned towards it and drank a glass of water. He perched up then on the edge of the sink to watch Sylvester at work. The young man by this time had some inking and paper apparatus out of the haversack and was taking fingerprints.

"Do you do much of this?" Raeburn asked.

Sylvester shook his head. "No. But with the Duke, you learn to expect anything." He paused with a trace of concern. "If it worries you, why not wait outside?"

"Carry on," said Raeburn. "After all, I saw him go."

The cameras came out last. Sylvester took several negatives with a close-up flash gun. Finally a polaroid, the hanging man absently looking with dull eyes. In moments the colour picture pushed itself out of the camera.

"Quite good," said Sylvester, content. "One will do." He showed the picture casually, before folding it away in the notebook. Then he emptied all the pockets—a sparse collection, not much more than a thin wallet, some kind of passport and a few other papers, coins, a thin-bladed folding knife.

Sylvester had to struggle to get his hand out of the second hip pocket, for it was fisted on to some contents, and the slumped stiffness of the dead buttock was sealing the tight opening. He almost giggled, wrenching the hand out at last, and at once held out the open palm for Raeburn to see. Resting there, beaded blackly with oil drops and already smearing the skin, were two wheel nuts.

"Mine!" said Raeburn.

"Undoubtedly. Busy times last night in the castle courtyard. He loosened three, and took away two. They would reckon that gave you a few miles before the wheel came apart." The Duke's man pondered them briefly. "I'd have thought a real professional would have got rid of these."

Sylvester folded away all the items in envelopes, and tapped the swaying figure to stillness, groping at the same time for hidden pockets. It was when he took off the shoes to search them that Raeburn went and leaned at the threshold of the open door, looking out.

Shortly he heard Sylvester washing hands at the sink, and turned to find him packed. "Better get a move on," the younger man said. "It's after half-past ten, and I've to be up at Loch Talla by eleven for the bleep exercise." He hung the second filled haversack on another of the vacant hooks.

"Fresh supplies for Reid," he said. "He'll collect them after dark. And by the way"—he opened a wall flap and turned an electric knob to its first position; a thin whine started somewhere—"that builds up some cold air. This place will be none the worse for a touch of the chills in a day or two."

They left the locked door behind them, forging through the fingering larches until they came to the road. Sylvester was into his car at once and had the engine started.

Suddenly he was leaning out of his window, with his notebook at a page:

"I nearly forgot. Take a note of this registration number, will you? It's the car that Martinu and Panacz have—had—well, you know what I mean, there's only one of them left. You might see it roving about the roads."

Raeburn noted it. "Useful. I'll remember it now that I've written it down."

Snapping the book away, Sylvester was moving. "You're all right? I have to go."

"Fine. See you soon. I'll hear you on the air." Sylvester's car darted out of the lay-by. He was round the first bend before Raeburn touched the tarmac.

Markland grounds were peopled with stragglers roving out for vague purposes in the morning air. Parking his car behind the buildings, he saw a wisp of runners on the far side of the games pitches, and waited to see them home, although his time was running fast to eleven o'clock. They were herded, he recognised, by the energetic French teacher whose name was Patrick Kavanagh, to whom he called as they eventually pounded past:

"How far?"

"Three miles—or maybe a bit less." Kavanagh stopped gratefully. "But they're soft—the blighters. Me too." He shouted to the scatter of finishers: "Dressed and in places for church by 11.25. Don't hang about in the showers." To Raeburn, "Did somebody tell you about the church parade?"

"They did. I was on my way to change."

"Well, don't let us stop ye. I could have done with a sweater less." He ran for the changing rooms.

Raeburn waited to see them all arrive. He never failed to marvel at the variety of boys, and here they all were again. There were the endless competitors, who would never, until they became senile, stop trying to win; the others who would never try to win if it had to be done strenuously; the many who could never win anything, however hard they tried, but would be in the pack and who might one day, and once only, have a Pentecostal inspiration; those who would look as if they were trying so long as authority watched; the others who would dodge authority, take the easy way, cut the corners, drop out for a lap and come back strongly for the ending; and beyond all these, those to whom the miracle of puberty and the start of manhood had already brought the vision of achievement and who would never thereafter know again the easy-going inconsequence of boyhood, nor be spared the weight of the unattainable. Most of them made a brave finish, knowing his eyes were on them, all of them by this time knowing who he was. As they strove, even the dodgers, not to breathe too heavily, nor let their legs tremble, he realised that it was this that had made him want to have dealings for his own lifetime with the young, in the hope that he might remind them of what they carried within them, or perhaps even let them learn to seek it. He himself would fade from memory, and soon, but was it not possible that one of these, for some good reason, would still be remembered two hundred years from now—three, four hundred years?

"Better them than us." Raeburn turned to the voice, to find at his elbow the width of Detective-Sergeant Miller, who nodded to him in a kind of morning friendliness.

The detective's face moved easily to the official look. "I wanted to say to you that was a bad thing that happened to the car—the wheel coming off. Have you found out any more about it?"

Raeburn shook his head offhandedly. "No. It could have been serious but I got away with it. It's all fixed now. It just means I check up in future."

"You'll have told the local police?"

"As a matter of fact—no. They must have plenty to worry about. I may have been careless myself . . ."

Miller was immobile with disapproval. "You see, sir, in the police you get a feeling for what might be important. In fact, earlier this morning I took the occasion to phone the county chief inspector to ask if he had been apprised of the incident."

Raeburn made his eyes wide. "You told the police? Without even checking up with me? Is that how you work?"

The detective's face had congealed suddenly into a wary stolidity. He replied: "I took that liberty—sir." They faced each other for a while, until Miller added: "I have a duty—you understand, Mr Raeburn? They may call on you for some information."

"It can be got for the asking." Raeburn turned and left him. The chap had no doubt his solitary worries in this governess job, but whoever had selected Miller had perhaps not made enough allowance for the temperamental flexibility the role required. There wasn't time enough at this moment, or Raeburn would have thought it worth while spending five minutes getting on terms again.

He got to his room in time to throw the switch of his small transistor radio and hear the pips for eleven o'clock. Before they had finished he had the walkie-talkie out from the bottom drawer of the wardrobe, extended the aerial, and had flung up the window to lean with it upon the sill, so as to help the frail carry. The second after the long-drawn sixth pip of the time-check sounded, the Duke's thin, purposeful voice crackled from the tiny speaker, hard held against Raeburn's ear.

"Eleven o'clock. I shall address you each according to your identification number as listed on the instrument." Raeburn was having to lean out of the window to clear the crackling and invite a faintly louder signal. Pasted to the small gadget was a paper with his number—6—and another strip which listed all of them, starting from Dale as 1 and finishing with Melfort as number 13, with 14 listed as a spare. The Duke himself was down as number 12. His voice went on, unidentified, as if it was an unheard-of matter in that circuit to have to guess who he might be.

The dialogue began, running on without a pause or stumble from any of them:

"One. Come in. Can you hear me?"

Dale's voice answered from somewhere. It occurred to Raeburn that it would be useful to know the call points. "Yes, sir."

"Are you in the proper place?"

"Yes, sir."

"Very good. Out. It occurs to me that some may think it would be useful to know the map locations from which the numbers are responding. Not necessary. It would diminish security and add nothing to effectiveness. This is no more than a signal and efficiency test to cover the area. Respond quickly please and no superfluous words. Two. Come in."

Damn him, Raeburn thought. How did a cold fellow like this read thoughts so truly!

"Yes, sir." Sylvester answered remotely from Loch Talla. "Nothing to report. In place as instructed."

"Out. Three." This number was Laidlaw, the head gamekeeper, and four was MacFarlane. Both replied from some vantage point of the estate, and were dismissed.

"Five. Come in."

"Here, sir." Reid came over clearly from the top of Drumdar.

"Was it a good night?"

"Fine—comfortable—grand day now; quite clear."

"I heard about your visitor . . . Out. Six—come in." This was Raeburn, and a small affability might have lurked in the tone of the call-in.

"Here. In place. Leaning out of a window to help the sound, and able to guarantee I can't be seen."

"Very clear. Enough now—"

"A quick point"—and Raeburn made it. "The local watch-dog—know who I mean?—has reported last night's mishap to the police. Promises me a follow-up. Understand? What do I do?"

The pause lasted hardly a second. "Nothing. We'll get rid of that. Keep him happy if you can. Five."

It was the call for Reid again, who came in at once. "Aye."

"Change of plan," went the voice that carried all the decisions. "You will be relieved at soonest by Four. Come back here when he is in place." He seemed to turn aside, to Raeburn, saying: "Six. Explanations later."

"Of course." Raeburn had realised that because there were so few things to keep account of in his new life, it was possible to concentrate on every item he encountered, and he was already busy in his mind with an earlier fragment heard from Reid. "Nothing like keeping it in the family." Something about Reid's brother—cousin?—being deputy chief constable.

"Quite." Again, maybe the faintest hint of approval. "Out. Seven."

Mr Porteous made a ponderous entry and exit. Then Eight, Nine, and Ten followed. They were the farmers Raeburn had encountered as they left Kintalla the night before; the men who would set the tractor road blocks if these were needed. The Duke ripped them in and out.

No nuance of voice signalled a change of style for the two house guests. The sheikh answered to Eleven with courteous precision, anxious to be in action. Lord Melfort was the last, at Thirteen, to which he answered without disguising his aloof amusement:

"Lucky number!" He added, deliberately—"Out!"

"Quite so." The Duke cleared his throat gently across the county. "All come in listening for fifteen minutes twice a day, at 11 a.m. and 5 p.m., the latter time only by special arrangement. This number—Twelve—will be constantly open. Report anything of significance. All out!"

There was still plenty of time for Raeburn to get ready for the church service. He dutifully dressed in his best dark suit, with a white shirt and the Lions tie he hadn't worn for years. Better give Coulson a show, he thought, tying it, for the headmaster had looked embattled among the gospels and the hymn books earlier. For that reason also Raeburn got to the hall ten minutes to the good, expecting to join the other teachers and welcome some parents. It was already crowded, boys in place, teachers at ends of rows, and even the piano manned by Joan Ker, who twinkled a distant eye of recognition at him as he came to the door. At the back of the hall were some flushed rows of tweedy parents, hoping to be thought mere visitors who chanced to be in the neighbourhood, although they kept up a constant surreptitious craning to find some unidentifiable adolescent face in the crowd.

A tall youth, in the school blazer and dark slacks, and a good three inches taller than he, met Raeburn at the door:

"Mr Raeburn? Sir?" It was murmured with some grave respect for the impending rites, mingled with as much awed deference as was proper man to man. He would be about eighteen.

"Yes. What's your name?"

"Fenton, sir. Walter Fenton. School captain. Last term, though." He eyed Raeburn's neckline. "Lions?" nodding at the tie.

"Yes. Hope it's all right. I never know when to wear it. Thought it would please a dad or two."

"You were right. They'll go mad about it—mine too. He's here. I wish they wouldn't come. It's always better when they go away at last and we get down to it . . . I was to find you a seat. What about this?"

He installed Raeburn at the end of a row of parents, and the hall now waited in silence for the headmaster, who was, indeed, at that late hour, changing his shirt. Miss Ker, with plentiful use of the soft pedal, touched off gently some familiar four-finger psalm tunes, so that the gathering was held together, perhaps more effectively than with some classic introit. There was a pause between each fragment, and a restart before the shuffling renewed; the clock crept onward to 11.30.

Then the lanky Coulson came in from the end door, and the school thumped to its feet, some of the shoes having been lifted high off the floor to await this ritual, while prefects watched and noted.

It was a brief ceremony. The head said nothing memorable in the opening welcome back and prayer, although some of his simplicity lifted the words with part of the purpose Raeburn had held from their first meeting. They sang a hymn and a psalm, begging forgiveness for grievous sins, although most of them were still some distance away from the start of their true sinning. A boy rose from among them to read a lesson from the Old Testament. Inevitably, it was the prince who had been selected. (Quite right, of course, Raeburn thought across the room to Coulson. All these outsiders expect a show.) His voice was breaking, and in the schooled family tones, so familiar, he husked and squeaked his way through a remote divine promise that was given to a wandering tribe hardly embarked yet upon its destiny. Soon they were free, and spilled into the corridors and the steps above the ranked cars.

There Raeburn, with Coulson or Furness or Kavanagh and others, played his part in ushering the parents away. A few of them mentioned some vague or real connection, but he didn't have to dredge too hard for replies, while many of the observations were uncommonly sage or apposite. With the last families separating among the remaining cars, Coulson took him by the elbow and steered him up the steps.

"Thanks indeed. You've worked hard. Now we've just ourselves left. Much better." He waggled a jointy long finger. "After lunch, a lie-down for you. A sleep."

"What? Not even a wee cycle run?" Joan Ker was at their side.

"Oh, you!" Coulson glowered at her in mock exasperation. "Give the chap a break—"

"No," said Raeburn. "In fact, I think I'd like to go—"

"Three-fifteen leaving," she told them. "Time for a little lie-down before that. Old clothes, of course."

"Don't let her wear you out." Coulson stalked off leaving them laughing.

"I liked your playing."

She made a mouth. "Simple stuff, you'd notice. Anything worse than two flats sinks me. For the advanced performances Mr Rankine the music master takes over—like when we do *The Yeomen of the Guard.* Tell me—how is the health, really? Will you be all right on a bike? We don't go far."

Raeburn said, after looking at her, "Well, I just do what the doctors tell me. I'm pretty sure there's nothing against bikes. Say, do we change before or after lunch?"

"Before. I'm off to get my jeans on now"—and she went.

On the way to his room he saw one of the masters at the entrance-hall telephone, holding the receiver and signalling: "For you."

It was Sylvester. "Mr Raeburn?"

"Yes."

"Just to tell you we have got rid of the possibility that the—the authorities might talk to you about the car mishap."

"Ah—yes. The relative?"

"None other: the Duke appreciated your deduction as to how it would be done. Our colleague—shall we mention him as Five—spoke usefully to his kinsman. We'll hear no more. His Grace would have spoken to you himself but he always attends morning church service when in residence at Kintalla."

"Good for him. I've had some myself, here."

"He wanted you thanked, and told."

"For what it's worth, you might note that there's a cycle run starting at three-fifteen today. I hope to go and try to keep it to the previous route. Don't know yet if the chief inhabitant will be awheel."

"That's useful. I'll make it known. OK for now, then. Expect to see you here soon."

"I expect so. Goodbye."

CHAPTER 9

He seemed to be awakened by a gentle tap on the door, and as he came up from the easing sleep he was almost smiling at the thought that it must be one of his boyhood memories. Raeburn had lain in his most knock-about outdoor clothes on the top of the modest bedcover, not expecting to fall asleep. With his opening eyes seeing directly into the face of his travelling clock, he made himself aware that the time was ten minutes to three—five minutes before the hour being the time the clock told, plus the five minutes with which he always cheated himself by putting his clocks forward.

Only his mother had ever been able to tap a door like that. She had been still for twenty years. He remembered her tap now with a surge of fondness. It had never been sudden or peremptory, but a soft stroking arousal, with tones of expectancy for what the waking would bring, the brightness, the promise, the sense of adventure she seemed all his remembered life to have been able to carry to him. Calling up the sounds now from his memory, he could recall how that tapping, on the dim bedroom door of his youth, had seemed to raise notes from the timber panels. He had never heard them so clearly in his mind as now. Funny that he should be so taken with this memory in the strangeness of this place, with the elation of what lay immediately ahead, and the dark beyond it. It was doubtless true, as they said, that a man like him coming to that last stage found it easy to recall younger and fitter times. Although as he lay he realised that he felt, for the first time for—how long? He couldn't remember—a remote hint of a strength that once was normal. A positive absence of ailment.

With his mind rambling to wakefulness, he was suddenly conscious that it was about to remind him of something. Something? Yes, the bicycle run. But immediately the tapping sounded again, with all the modulations, the patterns of his mind, filling it . . . He sat up. It was real this time.

A voice followed it; scarcely a whisper. "Sorry! Are you awake? It's Joan Ker—I thought I'd remind you about the bike run, if you still—"

"Yes! Fine! Good!"

"Over twenty minutes yet. But just if you're sure—"

"Count on me to be early, in time for the talk on team tactics."

"Oh, thanks."

In the corridor he met Miller the detective, and stopped to pass an affable and helpful moment:

"Have you heard, by the way, that there is a bike run this afternoon, starting about three-fifteen? Thought I'd mention it, in case your chap may be taking part . . ."

"Really, they ought to tell me earlier. What's the time—my God! I'll see them assemble, and if he's there I'll get up that Doon."

"If there's anything I can do—I'm going myself."

"Not much in fact. Tell me when you come back if you see anything unusual. Not much happening in this neck of the woods. Thanks for telling me, by the way. I'll go and get my gear."

Behind the sheds about nine boys were assembled, with Joan Ker mildly sorting out the dilapidated collection of vehicles. The rules seemed to be simple: those who had got a decent bike the last time out got a decrepit one this time.

"Test brakes and chains. Tyres." She was having no trouble with them. "No, Tom, that one isn't for you. It's for Mr Raeburn. You know the rule—the best we've got for the newcomers, otherwise they'll never come again."

Raeburn wobbled a trial circuit or two of the cobbled yard. It had been about twenty-five years since he had ridden a bicycle.

"What do you think?" Miss Ker asked.

He made himself dubious. "I think I agree that it is the best bike in the herd. Not saying much, is it?"

"Miss Ker," said a middle-teenager, adopting an adult frown. "Do you think this new teacher is going to be hard to please?"

She considered it gravely, and decided: "Benefit of the doubt for a few days. After that, it's every man for himself."

They bantered their way aboard, round the front drive and into the roadway. Not far from the gates they passed the trudging Miller, his binoculars slung, and a haversack, bound for the Doon and another of his unquestioning vigils. As they passed him he lifted his hat, perfunctorily vague, it might be in the direction jointly of Miss Ker and the prince, who was riding in the pack.

"Always on the job," said a voice from among the schoolboys, when they were out of hearing.

"By Royal Appointment," murmured another.

"No personal remarks!" Miss Ker braked herself nimbly into the middle of the pack. "You'll need your breath for the enormous hills ahead, you out-of-condition lot. Spread out! Not more than two abreast. You're hogging all the road."

Raeburn started to drop back so that he could join her. On the way he was overtaken by young Hewitt, rocking his small rump on a too-high saddle.

"Hullo, you!" said Raeburn to him. "How are you doing?"

"Very well, sir, thanks."

"Enjoying this? I can tell you I'm very rusty. Can you hear me squeaking?"

Hewitt listened briefly, and shook his head, grinning.

"Everything all right?"

"It's great, sir."

"Listen, Anthony Biggs Hewitt"—the face glowed to be so remembered—"what do they call you in the school?"

"Biggs, sir. It's my middle name. I don't know how it started."

"Do you mind if I call you Biggs?"

"No, sir—that would be great."

"Listen, then, Biggs . . . It's always great. Remember that. It's up to you. OK, then, pedal on."

Hewitt thrust on forward, and as he went, from the rear, his ears were pink with happiness.

Another pair outflanked Raeburn as he dawdled, coasting slower alongside him to pay their wheeling courtesies. They were Fenton, the school captain, and the prince.

"How long since you did this?" Fenton asked.

"I was just calculating," said Raeburn. "Shall we say a quarter of a century?"

"Speaking for myself," said Fenton, "I couldn't say a quarter of a century with any personal conviction. How do you like Markland, may one ask, Mr Raeburn?"

Giving him a nod of equality and appreciation, Raeburn told him: "You could serve time in many a worse place. The company's good. Bit stern in the discipline, though."

Fenton agreed, with some formality. "I think you'll find that the excessive discipline only applies in selected quarters, sir. Such places as junior maths." Miss Ker was overtaking them, and Fenton spoke up so that she could hear.

"I heard that," she said sternly. "Cheeky!"

"Goodbye." Fenton spurted ahead out of earshot.

"Time to go, too," said the prince. "This is no place for a younger son!" The two swept through the straggling field.

She came alongside him, and smiled. They went along in silence for a while, and there seemed no need to talk. After a time, he said:

"A good lot, this. I like it here."

She let some time go by. And, even then, spoke in detached sentences: "Yes . . . Good—that's the word—the place is good . . . good boys, good teachers. But then, nearly everybody's good, don't you think? Or maybe you don't."

He waited, trying to choose his words. "I don't, you know. I'd like to. But in fact there is a lot of positive wickedness about. I wish it weren't so. Does that sound—"

"Cynical? No—you may be right. I wish you weren't. I wish it just arose out of thoughtlessness, ignorance. For example, as you've found out, there is a case here . . ."

He nodded, and said after a time: "Wee Hewitt?"

"Yes. Wee Hewitt."

He let it stay at that. By this time he was able to wag a head towards the Doon, now behind them and emerging visually from the surf of leafage and shrubs at its foot. "See that? The Doon. Since it's clear you are the courier and trail-blazer for these expeditions, would you like to make the task easier for a toiling public servant?"

"You?"

"No! God, do I look like a toiling public servant?"

"Well, no riddles then. Who's the sufferer?"

"I was referring," he said, "to Detective-Sergeant Gordon Miller, almost one of us, who at this moment should be emerging on the summit plateau, out of breath, not having been told of plan or route, and who will be training his binocs on the lot of us, and wishing he were driving a car around to book traffic offenders somewhere."

She rocked her head back and forth in thought, before saying: "You know, it's a recreational option. David gets the chance along with the others, and has taken to coming lately. I suppose the policeman could come too, if he wanted. He looks a sad sort to me, though. Do you think we should take him along? Is that what you meant?"

Raeburn risked one hand off the handlebars to flap a signal of appreciation and pause to her. They swept, in the rear of the string, down a slope into a hollow, across a low parapet bridge, heaved up around another corner, his treacherous stomach muscles wearying, until they came out to the flat, straight road again, and could see all the pupil riders strung ahead of them.

He took some grateful breaths before he answered: "No, that wasn't it. I thought . . ." (how the devil did you put this! It was going to sound interfering anyway) ". . . I met Miller and told him there was a run on. I just—it seemed to me it might be a good idea if the bike runs could take the same route for a few times running. He must have his worries, following the show. You know?"

She was thoughtful for a moment or two, then said: "I suppose so. You ought to know that this is the fifth time we've gone exactly this way. Three times before the holidays and now this is the second time this term." She looked at him levelly. "I was beginning to think it's time we had a change. I can see difficulties in sticking to the same routine."

"I suppose you could be right." He stumbled on with his confusion. "Still, I'd give it a few more times yet. It might be an idea if you were to ask Miller."

"Not I," she said crisply. "It's up to him. I don't see him thanking me for cueing him up." She pedalled ahead suddenly.

His mind laboured to think how he might disarm the offence of his clumsiness, or if that did not matter, how he might diminish any suspicion he must have left. She was now straight ahead of him, and she turned back to him, twinkling, with a nod towards the hedge.

"Car," she said.

He steered into the verge and coursed along it, while her bell sent the warning ahead. He heard the car now, which drew up slowly to pass them—a nondescript black and battered object, with a large engine. It cruised alongside their line, seeming not much faster than they might go if they needed to speed up. As the driver came alongside, he turned to look at each cyclist he passed. Raeburn held his eye first. He had a face round as a globe, with a short overall bristle of hair. Raeburn found himself taking in the car's rear appearance, the clutter in the rear window-ledge, the boot bumps, the trembling, rusty exhaust pipe, the tow-bar . . .

His hand dived into his jacket side pocket, after the card he always kept there on the right side for noting urgencies he would otherwise not remember unless he had written them down. That number on the car. The registration number that Sylvester had given him. There it was, for sure, on the black car that was in among them! He could hardly bear the effort required to take the card out slowly, unobtrusively, his eyes intent on the number plate ahead until the car drew off into the straight distance of the road. But he hardly needed to look at the numbers he had written on the card.

Of course, they were the same. This was Panacz—forlornly cruising in the search for Martinu, who had not returned the night before. Panacz, who for all his violent successes, was not likely to guess that Martinu swayed on a hook a short way back, and would not come down by himself.

Raeburn guessed that Panacz would drive by Kirkmaiden to circle the Kintalla estate, for at least he must have known what Martinu had planned. He had probably driven him there last night, failing to pick him up again at some midnight rendezvous. The black car was now out of sight, the road before them clear.

He and Joan Ker were overtaking the line of boys, who had bunched, starting to wheel off the road to the left upon a level of close

turf and low heather which ran flat for an acre. They dropped their
bikes and ran for the grass levels beyond the fallen stones of the dyke
which had once fenced the moor for grazing, and which now could
keep nothing out. One of them had brought a football in a saddle bag,
and they were already kicking it in the frenzy of release and joy that
comes with even minimum skill when there is a ball to take to the air.
In a moment they were all into it, some half-formed teams and rules
prevailing.

Miss Ker leaned her cycle steeply on the heather bank and sat upon
a turf mound. She said to Raeburn: "You know a lot more about this
than I do, but it won't take a minute less than half an hour. Kind of ritual. They need to let off steam."

"Then what?" he asked.

"Then we just go back to Markland. Same way." So he sat beside
her, and they watched the play for a time.

She asked: "Are they good at it?"

"No," he said. "But it doesn't matter. Hardly one of them will ever
make a first team anywhere. It's very easy to tell. But that's not the
point. It's not going to be their life, and I do believe they're lucky in
that."

She nodded in the direction of the tiny Hewitt, playing goalkeeper,
throwing himself like a fish after a soaring shot. "What about him, for
instance?"

"Yes—he's got problems. But every outing I'll bet he gets more
confidence. The big fellows are doing well by him. They bring him
into the game . . . Can I ask you a question?"

She raised eyebrows at him. "I was going to ask you one. But you
first."

"OK. How did you know I had found out about him? And what?"

"I don't know what." Her answer was ready enough. "I only know
that something enormously important happened to him because of you
the first night you arrived at Markland. I've no idea what. That lad
will worship you until he is an old man."

Raeburn's look was on the playing space. "I can't think of him as an
old man. But no doubt he'll make it. Some don't. You know, I don't
know about residential schools. I dare say someone like you gets a lot of
confidences and hard-luck stories. Mm?"

"Oh, well, you know about spinster school teachers. We're not supposed to get too involved. I think we're not expected to understand the
problem, whatever it is. The closed book of life. Coke and sympathy—
nothing more.

"That's about it." She went on. "Now for my turn. Here's my question. Ready? Simply this." She looked at him steadily. "Would you like
to tell me what exactly you are doing at this school?"

He stared at her in silence, shaking his head in puzzlement. And she laughed gently.

"No, no!" she said. "Please, no innocence. I'd rather you told me it was none of my business. But you are not here as an ordinary teacher . . ."

"That's just what I am. Had a bit of health trouble and my last school were good enough to call this a sabbatical—"

"Nonsense! You know too much about some things—too interested in this and that. You are here keeping a special eye on something—somebody. What I don't understand is, why you? You're too well known."

Raeburn laughed for her: "Yes, I've dragged that too long, thanks to some enduring fans, but I could do without it. They won't let me go, and grow up. Tell me, what other suspicions have you?"

She had coloured by now. "Maybe I've said too much. But you—all this coming and going. And the health thing. What about that, now. What is the trouble? You look fine to me, I'm glad to say."

The treble tumult of the boys behind him went on as, laughing, he rolled backwards on to the nape of his neck and kicked his legs in the air. Then, it was as if a bullet had entered him, tearing through his inside.

He yelped, with his legs collapsing, and clutched his stomach. There had of course been pain, in the early days, although they seemed to have drugged it away while he was in the clinic. But it had been only a remote hint of this devilish smite. It was mortal, draining him. Suddenly he knew what it was going to be like to die. He tried to sit up, managing to prop half-upright, his head lolling, sight fading in the drenching sweat of pain that would shortly overwhelm his heart.

He was aware of her staring at him. It had started as a smile, now wiped and pallid with an agony of apprehension as profound as the physical change that rent him.

"What is it?" he heard her say. "Oh goodness, what is it! What's happened?" There was a rising sob there. "What can I do?" He had fallen back, bunching such belly as he had in the two hands, as if he might still the demon inside. He felt her hand touch his forehead, the other trying for his pulse. The thing lashed on at him.

"Come here!" She was calling over her shoulder. "Boys—here!" And the steps were thumping on the heather. He could not open his eyes. She shouted again, sharply. "Just the older boys. Two of you—Walter and Philip—that's all. The others stay well away."

The two were kneeling by him, with her.

"What's the trouble?" It was Walter Fenton, the school captain.

"Mr Raeburn's taken ill . . . Mr Raeburn! Can you hear me? Can you speak? If you could tell us . . ."

Somehow, there was some easement; only enough to point back feebly to the possibility of life. He tried to open his eyes—failed—at last made his voice go: "Sorry! Sorry! . . . happens sometimes. Goes away —usually . . ."

"Try to sit him up—that might help," she was telling the boys. "Slowly. Gently." They held him there.

"Better," he said after a while. "Thanks . . . Sorry." Long gaps between his words.

"Here's a car coming. Stop it, Walter." He could feel her take over from Fenton, her arm round his back, Raeburn's left arm over her shoulder. Then: "Can you hold him there, Philip?" and she was away, talking to the driver of the stopped car.

She was back soon. "Gently, then. How is it now? I think your colour is coming back."

"Better," he said, after a time, but he couldn't see her.

"Do you think you can stand up? We'll lift. If not, not to worry. We've enough here to get you aboard." The lads were big. He felt briefly their braced arms, and he seemed to be on his feet.

"Good! That's good! Now, it's only a yard or two." She was in full charge. "I'm going to lift each leg inside," and she did, with a grab on the tweed cuffs of his trousers. "Fenton will go with you to Markland." Now they had him on the seat, Fenton's arm still holding.

"Walter," she was saying. "When you get there, Dr Coulson and Mrs Gibson right away."

"Sorry," said Raeburn. "Tell other boys—sorry—the young . . ."

"Yes—yes—I know what you mean. Don't talk." She might be saying to the driver: "Thank you very much—the young man will show you where to go."

The driver eased into motion and they were travelling.

"Won't be long, sir," Fenton said at his side.

Easing his hands away from his front, Raeburn grew surprised that the thing did not pounce again. Suddenly it cleared like an indigestion kink. He felt the sweat start to dry on his face; opened his eyes.

"Thank you," he said to the driver. "Feeling better." They were already half-way back to Markland. The driver nodded. Then he turned to look closely at his emergency passengers. He had a face the shape of a football, with an inch-long scrub of brown hair from brow to nape.

As Panacz turned back towards the road ahead, he picked up Raeburn's eyes in the driving mirror, flicking stolidly from him to the road in an endless series of steady flashes like a traffic lamp on a roadside excavation. Raeburn stretched round to his hip pocket, taking the pistol by the butt, easing it out slowly and into his side pocket. The squirming of this manoeuvre made Fenton drop his sustaining arm and relax into his seat.

"Really better, Mr Raeburn?" the school captain asked.

"Yes—really. Silly, that. Sorry again."

"We heard you had a health problem, sir, but that was a bad bout. An old rugby injury?"

"No—I don't think they're quite sure what it is." He was holding the gaze of Panacz in the slit of the driving mirror, guessing that the easing of the pain, which lifted more and more, must owe something to the flow of responsive nerve juices that was going on within him. He was being driven along by an international criminal, a man known to the police of a dozen countries, and whose eyes were dead and half-lidded and as still as those of the mate in the Locker whom he could not find. Raeburn guessed at whether he should try to give the ready Fenton some warning, and at once thought not. They would soon know if this was to be Panacz's day.

Here was Markland coming, and a figure, by now familiar and easy to recognise, was seated casually on the low wall at the gateway. The car bent in towards the entrance, stopping, while Biros rose from his position and came towards their driver.

He had, it was clear, recognised the car, and was ready to find the expected driver. Panacz thumbed a gesture towards his back seat and got out. Biros stared in at Raeburn and the schoolboy. A few seconds passed. There was no plan ready to burst into action.

"Ill," said Panacz to Biros, his flat pudding face offering nothing of recognition or conspiracy. "You help, please?" Fenton was opening the rear door, while the two on the gravel of the entrance muttered in swift sentences of which Raeburn grasped nothing, and which might not even have been a language. All the time Panacz was miming, to show how they would both shoulder Raeburn into the school building.

A swift walking step shod in heavy shoes came across the road, round the car, and on to the gravel. Reid, his rifle slung, put a hand on the chest of each man and firmly moved them back from the car. Raeburn came out by himself, standing there while Reid took a grip of his bicep and faced the two strangers.

"Thank you, sirs, and that'll do now," he told them. "I know this gentleman, and I'll take him up to the school. I know the way."

"Thanks," said Raeburn to both.

"Yes, indeed, thanks," said Reid. "We'll not need you any more. You looked after Mr. Raeburn well, mister"—to Panacz. And half-lifting Raeburn, Reid had them both moving to the gates and through them.

Fenton said: "I'll see the headmaster." He was running ahead of them towards the stone stairs.

"Can you manage it? I could carry you. What went wrong?" Reid, the hard man, showed distant concern, as if more for the problem than the invalid. "I had the glass on you from Drumdar top and saw it all. And I knew it was that foreign bastard's car. Can you manage?"

"Yes. Getting better. Slowly, though."

Reid had one of Raeburn's arms across his shoulder, held there, and with his other arm pulled the man to him. They limped on through the gate, out of hearing.

"Happens sometimes," said Raeburn. "I'll be all right after a lie-down."

Their hip bones were pressed together. Reid grunted in his throat with something that could be a chuckle. "I tell you, sir, it's as well those two weren't helping you. I can feel the pistol clear in your pocket. You would be better with her in the back pocket."

"I was getting ready . . . You know who they are?"

"Fine that! I've been watching Panacz for the best part of a week. He's been on the trot since early this morning, looking for the one that's hooked you know where. As for Konski, or Biros, he sits on that wall like a puddock, and he and the other fellow have had two conversations today already. I doubt there's not much doing in that kitchen. By God, it's as well the sheikh wasn't hereabouts. He would have shot the pair of them, just to keep his hand in."

As they progressed, Reid stole a look over his shoulder, and was speaking again at once: "They're both jabbering still. This is the first day they've been so open at it—they'll be dead worried about the other fellow not showing up, and him not all that far away either. They'll wait a while before they see him. It looks though as if things'll be about to start. You're managing better already, Mr Raeburn . . . Here's the headmaster."

They were half-way now to the steps of the school, and from the door Coulson had come running, taking the steps two at a time towards them. Even at that distance they could see blackly the ready furrows on his wizened face. He was down on the level now, the spindly legs still lifting and jogging concernedly towards them.

Reid moved on evenly, still supporting Raeburn, and saying: "I'll be off, sir, as soon as he comes here. Leave me to tell the Duke. You can be sure His Grace will be talking to the headmaster. I hope you'll be all right. There will be big things doing, anyway, in the next day or two. I hope you will be in trim to enjoy yourself—"

"So do I. It seems likely. Thanks for everything."

"Man, I hope it's me that gets plugging one of them at least. The ones on two legs are more sport than stags or hares any day . . ." He raised his voice to the panting Coulson, now in earshot. "He's fine, sir. A wee turn. He'll be telling you himself. Right as rain now . . ."

"Barry—my God!" Coulson had him by the jacket lapels. "You've been trying too much. What went wrong? My fault—"

"Nothing of the kind." Shaking him off, Raeburn saw over the head-master's shoulder the figures of Fenton and Mrs Gibson; the matron, at the top of the steps, and she was skipping down in their direction, with the school captain in attendance.

"Ach well," Reid was smoothly playing it down, "you won't need me any more the day. I'll be away." He had turned lightly and was gone, speaking musingly as he went: "I'll maybe have a wee word at the gate with the kind gentleman who gave him the lift in the car. He seems to know his way about these parts . . ."

In no time the headmaster and the matron had Raeburn in his bed-room, and they were stripping off his tie and jacket. He caught the jacket as it fell from a sleeve, hooking it over a chair back so that they could not feel the gun weight. Coulson was at his feet, untying the shoe laces.

"Doctor—" he was saying. "Have to get the doctor."

"Absolutely not," said Raeburn. "I'd just like to lie down, I think." He gave a brief account of the onset. ". . . must have got a twinge from the bike. Unusual exercise. Anyway, my own doctor is coming in to see me in a few days . . . No need to worry. Honest!"

Mrs Gibson had gone away, to return immediately with some tea on a tray. She was telling the headmaster: "We should leave him now. If he feels like sleeping, that's the best thing. Take some tea if you can." Off she went.

Coulson fussed still, holding the pyjama jacket for him. "I certainly feel I must tell the Duke. This is the kind of thing he would want to know—judging by what he said about you the first day . . ."

Raeburn got rid of him at last, and was gratefully working his way among the blankets when Coulson was back, with an apologetic knock at the door:

"Sorry. Coulson again. You can't get shot of me . . . Joan Ker has just come in, worrying about you."

Coulson opened the door a few inches. Sensing she was there, Raeburn spoke up to her:

"Hullo! I'm quite OK. How did the run finish?"

"Rotten. All worried. We just pedalled back like mad. Some more worried than others."

"No need."

"What happened?"

"Bikes, I think. Cycling's not my game."

"Pain?"

"Not now. Fat of the land. Tea in bed."

"It was awful while it lasted. We have to get a doctor."

"That's all settled—"

"I'll tell her." Coulson was pulling the door shut. "Give a shout if you need anything." He heard their footsteps to the end of the short corridor.

When he woke, it was dark. He had slept for a long time, and yet needed more. After a tentative stretch, which brought a hint only of the clawing within, still subsiding, he reached to switch on his bedside lamp. It was near to midnight.

He pondered briefly the wisdom of phoning Grant, the doctor; then guessed at a better idea. From the wardrobe drawer he took the walkie-talkie radio, its aerial still extended, switched off the bed lamp, and gently eased up the window so that he could lean out. Drowsily warm from the bed, the cold air struck him like a shower of water, so that he reached back to lift the eiderdown and wrap it over his shoulders.

"Yes?" The voice, becoming familiar, responded the moment he pressed the button.

"Six." Raeburn spoke gently. The moon had not risen enough to light the lawn, and the trees were a whispering mass of darkness.

"I know," the Duke said. "I can identify your instrument on my panel here. How are you?"

"Better. Some sort of spasm only—so far. You knew?"

"Coulson telephoned me. In turn I have spoken to Dr Grant. He will come if you want."

"I think I can wait until Thursday."

"Wise. So does Mr Torrie. And, indeed, so does Sanger in Zürich."

"You mean—you've spoken to them all!"

"Naturally—no need for prolixity. Three quite separate theories; none of them of special significance."

"Well, I'll be damned. How am I . . . ?"

"It is not the intention to use this method for small chat. Please be available for the eleven-o'clock call tomorrow. Otherwise, out." Raeburn could not think of any riposte to the click which severed him from Kintalla. He replaced the radio, wondering if it might be an increasing involvement that was making him care whether the Duke spoke or not. He lowered the window silently and sat on his bed, the light on again.

The tap on the door panels had more weight, perhaps more authority, than the last one which had fallen there.

"Who is it?"

"Headmaster. Coulson. Can I come in?"

"Of course." Raeburn swung his legs under the blankets, sitting up.

Coulson was carrying a tray, with two cut-glass tumblers on it, golden and steaming.

"Good man!" he said. "How is it now?" Raeburn told him. Coulson was happy: "I knew you would shake it off. You've had a good sleep. I looked in once or twice, prompted by Miss Ker, whom you seem to be stirring to unexpected heights of anxiety. No comment necessary, thank you." He laid the tray upon a bedside table, pulling up a chair along-side.

"Good! This is very cosy. You like toddy, I suppose?"

"Of course. How did you—"

"I was keeping a lookout, and when I saw the light below your door I simply carried the fixings—they were all ready—into the kitchen to get the water, which requires to be just off the boil. I take it that you know how to make toddy?"

"Yes—I suppose I do. Whisky, hot water, sugar—"

Coulson sighed. "I dare say a crude version can be made in that way, by just splashing the ingredients you mention together. Well, it's too long a story for now, but if you look closely at the glasses you will see that the whisky is floating discreetly on top of the water. In fact, the whisky is cooking in that position. I am about to stir the contents of the glasses. They are ready for the operation. Silver spoons, by the way." One in each hand, the spoons tinkled their way round the glass rims, and the smell of the brew within was pungent and needful. "Remind me"—as he stirred on—"to instruct you fully, one day, in the proper making of toddy. At present"—he handed one glass, not too hot to hold, taking the other himself—"all you have to do is drink it."

Raeburn sipped. It was liquid paradise. "Are you sure you should be prescribing?"

"This will ensure you get to sleep again—the real sleep of the night. No questions." They drank, rapt; murmuring with pleasure.

Coulson collected the glasses briskly, getting his tray ready to go. "I put off Ian Furness, head of English. He wanted to come in and spruce you up about your first class tomorrow—the Civil War. I said you had probably heard of it; and had taught class before. Well-meaning. Sleep well." At the door with his tray, he turned a knowing eye on Raeburn. "I expect my only duty will be to give the latest bulletin to Junior Maths, who will be hovering."

As the door closed, Raeburn was slipping down to the pillow. A heavy tidal run of sleep took him away.

CHAPTER 10

"One has some difficulty in understanding," the boy was saying, "why the leading people on both sides—and there seem to have been some pretty clever ones—failed so badly to see what was coming, and to start getting ready for it."

"I think you've mentioned something that should always be kept in mind," Raeburn said. "It is a fact that, just then, in the early part of the seventeenth century, there were indeed some very talented men around, in Court and Parliament, and as you say, looking from here, they seemed to have missed the point, and they went on missing the point for another hundred years or so. Why, do you think?"

"It escapes me. Perhaps they were not so bright as we think. Or civil war may just have been inevitable."

"No. Nothing on that scale is inevitable. What we are examining are the origins and causes of the Civil War." Raeburn was enjoying it. The readiness of the teenagers before him to join in debate, to speculate, was a bath of freshness after the stuffing of pupils which was mostly all he had known. Moreover, the dialogue had a piquant edge if only because the boy standing here at his desk in the midst of the classroom, searching into the changing motives of an old and powerful story, was the prince.

"Well now, our textbook is not much more than a summary, so we'd better find out one of these days what the school library can do in this field. There's been some truly great writing about the period—still guessing, a bit partisan—you take your choice—but reaching close to the real human core." Raeburn searched for one or two of the thoughts which had, once, first impressed him. "Look at the French. They had most of the intellectual and philosophic talent that was going in Europe at the time. Very bright lot of kings. Not so dull as they're painted, that Louis lot. But it took France the best part of another two centuries to get to the stage we're talking about. And like us, they had to do it the hard way."

As he had expected, they laughed mildly at the French reference; and settled almost immediately.

David was smiling. "Who," he queried, "took the Versailles crowd seriously?"

"Themselves, for a start. Oh, yes, I know about the fun and games. But they did a day's work as well. Without a Parliament."

"Yes," David said. "Of course, our Parliament got shut down. One of them, anyway."

"Good idea?" asked Raeburn.

"Bad idea," was the pupil's answer.

Raeburn nodded him back to his seat. "Thank you, David." He spoke to the class: "I assume it is generally known that *we* had a Parliament hereabouts at this time. Later in the same unpleasantness we had it shut down, too. Any comments?"

Philip van Moubray raised a hand, and then stood:

"Perhaps I may declare an interest." He had an uncle in the House of Commons. "I am mostly from the Netherlands on my father's side. It should be remembered that the Dutch people suffered severely as a result of the civil war in this country. There were many naval battles and landings—"

"Yes, Philip"—Raeburn settled encouragingly. "Tell us about that, the effects upon your country, the Dutch side of the story."

Van Moubray was ready with his tale of the two fierce and improbable enemies. It had been a trade war, and a navigation war for the control of the crowded seas at their shores, and an empire war with eyes on the lands in the globe's curve. The Dutch had had victories, modestly referred to in the British tale, and the thing, started by Protector Cromwell, had gone on in spasms for a long time. But in the end the Dutch had come to ruin, and needed to begin again.

In this way the lesson passed: a discussion, a debate, a steering.

His spirit had lifted to the stimulus of it, not only because the boys had grown to a habit of discourse that forced him to bring to the front of his mind the questions he had once made himself answer, but also because this was true teaching, and learning, the double bargain with the future. Looking back down the years, he was already grudging the promotional progress that had brought him one of the best junior headmasterships in the profession, and the administrative tangle of trivia it carried, rather than the two-generation comradeship of the ranks. He had, of course, always had some advantage from his sporting record, but it seemed to mean something less at Markland than it had elsewhere, for here there was a questioning of everything. And yet it would all be over for him before the week was out. Even if the unheard-of Dr Sanger were to perform the miracle, for how long must he lie, cut and reduced, while other lives went on, but scarcely his own? This Duke had surely taken something on himself . . .

A bell rang for the end of the lesson, and Raeburn drew it to a close. The class stood for him as he gathered his books and gave them a brief farewell, making for the door. The boy nearest to it got there first to open it for him, to say with mature and casual measure:

"That was really pretty interesting, sir. Thanks. A lot of new stuff about Cromwell . . ."

Raeburn said, backing off down the corridor: "Good. There's always new stuff about Cromwell. Lots of writing, apart from textbooks. We must have a look at what's in that library of ours."

He found his next class in a room on the second floor. They were five senior boys with low grades in history, people who would always be afflicted with a blank on the side facing the endless, gripping human narrative, and who would have to memorise rather than feel. Furness had set them to read some chapters on the economics of trading, from the early days of the empire more or less up to date, and as they got to their feet for his entrance they were flicking through the pages, actively hoping to light on some fact about which there might be a teacher's question.

"OK," he said. "I think we might put the books away for the moment and assume you have done your holiday reading. I shouldn't be surprised if there isn't another style of attacking this subject. However, names first. Mine's Raeburn. Yours?"

They spoke their names. In the middle of it the door opened quietly, but Raeburn held to his small audience until the last lad had spoken his name. Immediately, a voice from the doorway said:

"Coulson."

The headmaster had his face round the door, grinning.

"Hullo, headmaster."

"Mind if I come in—?"

"I don't suppose," said Raeburn, "that anybody in Markland has more right to come in here than you have. However, in the interests of democracy perhaps we'd better put it to the vote." He turned solemnly to the class. "In or out?" And they laughed their headmaster in.

"That's a relief," said Coulson, settling into a back seat. "This is about my worst subject. I thought I'd take the chance to catch up. Please go on, Mr Raeburn"—catching his eye, twinkling in accord—"if you don't mind."

By good luck, Raeburn had remembered the old true story of the group of early Glasgow merchants who built and equipped a ship, filled her with goods, and sent her merchandising to far parts. After a year or two she came home to the Clyde, and they boarded her at the quayside, calling upon her master to produce the account books. He confessed he had no training in the production of account books, but "Here are my accounts," he told them, heaving upon the cabin table a bag of gold. The merchants knew a good thing when they saw it, so on the next voyage they sent a fully fledged accountant to keep the tally. Alas, when they came home the second time, there was the clerkly man with a neatly engrossed set of account books, but no bag of gold.

It was easy to move on, within the practical frame of the human adventure of buying and selling, to how those who did it best believed least in the checks and probes of authority—and whether they were right or wrong; and above all, to the need for entrepreneurs, ready to take risks not in the heat of battle or piracy, but with the cold firmness to spend and venture and wait alone and unsupported for results—and whether such men were more valuable or less valuable to the community than those who watched from the sidelines of less hazardous duties.

He told them how some in their own generation would have much to do with such problems, and would actively participate in shaping the events of their time. Certainly the merchant of today traded in a world where the dangers were hardly less than they had been when men took to the sea in ships loaded with the labours of their craftsmen and kin, and vanished with high hearts over the edge of the world. The class spoke and argued deeply about these affairs, feeling their way to conclusions that in some cases they would not lose as the years went over them.

When the bell went, Dr Coulson was first on his feet. "Boys, I'll bet you enjoyed that as much as I did. No doubt Mr Raeburn will be glad to let you cut away for your break. I'd like to have a word with him."

When they were alone, Coulson took Raeburn by the elbow:

"Barry, two things. The first is that it was absolutely unforgivable of me to crash in on your lesson. Forgive me. I really was concerned about your bad turn yesterday and couldn't bear not to have a look at you on the job . . ."

"Well, thanks. We were all glad to have you. As you can see, I'm fit. Yesterday was . . ." He left it there.

"And that brings me to the second point. That was a masterly lesson. You did to them what I want Markland to do to such fellows. They've all got something good—important. Not great exam-passers, but what in God's name does that matter! I say! What's the time? Nearly eleven. I have to rush. Sorry. An A-level tutorial—doing it myself . . ." He turned at the door. "I won't be at coffee. But you take your time. You have a free period now, eh?"

"Yes."

"Well, take your time. Lie down . . . Got to go. More anon—"

It spared Raeburn the need for an excuse to break off for the Duke's radio call. Yet he was late in reaching his room, where he switched on the walkie-talkie before he stretched for the window, meaning to throw it up and lean out. But something changed his plan, and instead he turned up the volume to its highest and crammed behind the window curtains, forcing the small instrument against his ear to muffle the sound and make it private to himself. The Duke's far voice, already at Reid, number Five, on Drumdar, was so diminished that it was almost possible, momentarily, to think that his authority had somehow been reduced.

". . . just been in Locker 3," Reid seemed to be saying. "I would think it's about time we got him out of there, and no mistake. There's signs—"

"Do that!" The Duke was unbelievably tinny. "The photographs are quite adequate . . . Possib—use electri . . . draw—'tention . . . 'port —telephone."

"Aye."

It was Raeburn's turn, and with it came what seemed to be a fortunate surge of energy in the frail small handfuls of communication. It started even before the Duke's voice came sharp-edged:

"Six?"

"Here—" Raeburn was beginning.

". . . not likely to be anything from you today—"

"Hold on!" Raeburn forced his tones into the instrument, pitching at the urgent, hissed whisper that means the noise of emergency without shouting. "Something to report!"

Hardly a second of pause, before: "Go on!"

Raeburn leaned on the wall, lifting the heavy curtain a fraction away from the far edge of the window. "I'm right inside my room— hence the poor signal. I was just in time to avoid opening the window fully and looking out. Biros is watching the window from the shrubbery opposite. Almost certain it's him—white shoes and pants showing, rest concealed by branches. This means—"

"Confirm!" The voice was unguardedly urgent. "How soon can you confirm? Quickly!"

"Immediately," said Raeburn. "I'll lay down this receiver and get binoculars. Hold on—starting now."

In a moment he was kneeling on the floor, back from the window, the glasses trained through the two-inch gap low down to which the window was permanently open.

Biros it was. His face was dappled by some intervening leaves, but unmistakable; while, below, the pale faded blue pants and the soiled white shoes were hardly covered. He had binoculars, too, glassily intent upon the window.

Raeburn lay flat on the floor, feeling his way to the walkie-talkie, lifting a cushion over his head and the instrument. This time he vocalised a harsh whisper.

"Back again! Can you hear?"

"Go on!"

"Biros—no doubt. I'll identify him missing from the kitchen in a moment. I'm keeping well back from the window—sure he can't hear. He's spying for me with glasses—"

"Proves there's a leak within . . ." The voice of Melfort slipped in smoothly.

"This looks like a wee job for me, sir." It was MacFarlane's voice from his calling place somewhere in the moor. "I could be off the hill here and into the wood in just a few minutes—less maybe—and just put him away. That would be another we could do without. Right, sir?"

"On no account." The Duke's voice, climbing the intervening contours of the land and the ultimate walls, was making Raeburn's set crackle with anger. "Attention, everybody! Do not come in on this medium with casual speculations. No one is to be killed or disposed of except in self-defence or emergency . . . 'derstood? . . . 'plete oppor— 'morrow . . ."

The wave of reception had died, and even the tones of the master had dwindled to a bleat with no meaning, and finally an impotent silence.

Raeburn backed stooping to the door, let himself out and made at once for Ridley's kitchens. When Biros came in through the rear door, carrying an empty garbage can, Raeburn was already leaning against a cupboard, drinking a cup of coffee poured by Ridley's own hands, and listening. Biros dumped the can, lifted another which was teeming with leavings and humped it easily away, padding on his soiled white sneakers. His pants were faded blue and, if he noticed Raeburn's presence, he made no sign. The back door swung after him.

"Solid bone for a head, that fellow. Goes about like a zombie. He's taken about ten minutes to empty that first bucket," Ridley said. "I keep him for the heavy jobs. Never mind, he's got some big crates to unpack in the cellar next. Another cup?"

Raeburn was free until the last period before lunch. He took his binoculars and rounded Markland to the woody band of cover opposite the side of the house where his room window was on the ground floor. Among the trees there he found the ground where Biros must have stood, although there were no footprints on the brown leaf-bed of many winters.

Through the glasses, he was surprised at how little was visible of the room's interior. Anyone standing inside more than a yard from the window might be faintly visible, perhaps no more than a grey illumined face and hands. A speaking instrument would not show. Lower down, where the window was raised, the gap was merely a crack. He could make out the outline of the armchair's edge, but only, he felt, because he was familiar with the upholstery pattern. Further to the right, there were the backs of books, in stripes—his own. The window opening at this distance would show perhaps less than half the diameter of a binoculars' large lens—too small a section to be identified, he had no doubt.

By mid-afternoon, his last class over, he felt a need to take to the moors. Almost the only change he needed to make was into his hill shoes. In ten minutes he had the car out and was away. At the front gate of Markland he came upon Joan Ker, striding out, well shod for rough ground. She turned brightly to him as he stopped the car.

"Going my way?" He opened the passenger door and she got in beside him.

"What's your way? And should you be going alone anyway?"

"Two questions to which I don't have the answers."

"You know, you could have another attack—"

"Unlikely. Anyway, I'm due some special treatment soon . . . You didn't say where *you* were going."

"Just out. Like you, I'm finished for the day, except for dinner duty. I think I ought to come along and keep an eye on you. Where to?"

"I thought Kintalla, or thereabouts."

"Oh, you're visiting! Sorry. Let me out."

"Not visiting. I'd simply like to have a look at Kintalla from the high moors behind. It seems interesting from the map. Let's go." He had the car pointing southwards, and opening out.

"Yes," she said, "you would know about what's in the map. It's all a mystery—and it gets more obvious all the time. I may say I'd be more concerned to see a map of your inside—if it's any of my business."

He reflected, and answered: "That's been done pretty thoroughly too."

It was a mistake, for she was on to it with a pounce of concern: "Why that? What for? They don't do that for nothing."

He drove on, silent for a minute or two. Eventually he had an answer formed, but she cut in again:

"You've got to tell me."

He said: "I'll probably tell you one of these days."

"I'm sure you know you can trust me."

He nodded merely, looking ahead, and she seemed more content.

They swept aside on to one of the moor roads, topping out above Talla Head where the north channel of the Irish Sea ran and beat, and a mariner could set an uninterrupted course almost due south to Santander. He parked the car and they began a plod and scramble to the higher ground. The car shrank beneath them. They could look into the courtyards of the farms on the low ground. Coming to the crest, they moved some distance down the farther slope.

"That's Ireland yonder, in the haze." He let her use the binoculars. "You're looking almost directly into Belfast Lough."

"Great!" She swept the horizon. "I looked it all up recently. Durham and Donegal are actually north of us at this point. I suppose you know?"

"I do. I looked it up, too."

"Where's Rathlin?" she asked. "I have a soft spot for it, because of Robert the Bruce."

"And the spider. It's far north."

"Oh, I say, there's a castle down there. Among the trees. I suppose that's Kintalla."

"It is—Duke and all. They live there from time to time. He's also the Viscount Kintalla."

"What's he like? Powerful? Feudal? Aristocratic?"

"All these things—he's big. He's big business."

"Yes. He owns everything. What about the Duchess? Is she here?"

"If you give me the glasses, I'll tell you." He took them from her and swept a brake of gorse and heather lower down. "Yes, I thought so. A bit strenuous, I'd have imagined, so soon after . . ."

An auburn head moved on the slope, bobbing upwards until the whole woman came into view. Raeburn could not remember if she wore the same skirt and cashmeres, but they set her off as trimly as he remembered from the first day.

"Who . . . ?"

"That's her. The Duchess. This will teach you to talk loosely of the proprietors."

"God," she whispered.

"Not quite. Near enough."

"What do we do? Should we be here?"

"I'll introduce you. I suppose I could call her a fan from 'way back."

"Like me. What do I call her?"

"Duchess, or something. Or nothing. The name's Edith, eventually. She's friendly."

It was a friendly enough face which came up to them, blowing with the effort:

"Hi! Do you mind if I sit down? The legs have given out. This is the most strenuous trial-run since the late performance." She blew a few times, and directly to Joan said: "Hullo!"

"Duchess," Raeburn said, "this is Miss Ker. She teaches at Markland."

"Welcome to Kintalla." She raised a friendly hand, nodding warmly, and turned severely to the man: "Barry! I've told you the name's Edith. If you don't use it I'll start calling you Uncle Barry or some suitable schoolgirlish name. Does he call you Miss Ker? I thought Markland was the devil of a place for informality. Did you ever see him play?"

"Often."

"Me too. Who's looking after him down there? He's not been well, you know."

"She knows," said Raeburn. "Everybody's on the job down there, especially the headmaster, and the brisk Mrs Gibson, the matron, egged on by Joan Ker, here. By the way, it's Ker with one 'r.'"

"That's good," said the Duchess. "Keep them guessing. I used to be Edith Haddo, and one and all thought there should be a 'w' at the end. I always had to spell it." She was wry: "I'm never very sure what my name is now."

"There's a thing"—from Raeburn. "—I've often wondered—all these titles the Duke has—do you have them all too?"

"I've never been very sure." She grinned, gleefully uncaring. "I never seem to meet anyone outside the family I can ask. I know that the Garter King and the Lord Lyon disagree about the whole thing. But then they disagree about every procedure . . . Does that sound disloyal to something?"

She pointed out to them the far shadows of hills and bays; named the near braes and howes of the estate land; showed the marches, the roofs of one or two of the hill farms.

"That white speck away over there is a shepherd cottage called Binnanee. It's on the very edge of Kintalla ground, and nobody seems to know why it was built almost on the crest of the hill. You should be able to pick it up with your glasses." Raeburn was now focused on it— a plain white façade with an outhouse or two, typical of the district. He could imagine the inside, the kitchen and parlour looking out to the front, and the steep, straight inside stair leading to the two attic bedrooms above. From the chimney, in the quiet day, a pencil of faint blue peat smoke reached up and quickly dissolved in the updraught. "The shepherd lives alone." As he watched, a tall spare man with a pale blob of face fringed by a tangle of black hair and beard came out, gathered an armful of peats from a stack at the gable, and ducked back inside with them.

In a short time she asked them: "Are you coming to the party tomorrow night? Perhaps you've heard about it. Really a celebration for the son and heir. I know there is a group from the school . . . I do hope you'll both be coming." She said to Raeburn: "I'm sure you'll be there anyway." To Joan Ker: "Please come too—special invitation. That would be nice—otherwise the Markland party is sure to be all-male."

"No doubt," said Joan. "Well, if you think—"

"Yes—do come. It should be fun, mainly for the Kintalla children, but drams and things for parents and friends. I hope no speeches. Something for everybody except the baby . . ."

"What's his name?" asked Joan.

"Ah—we're still arguing about that." The Duchess was musing. "By the time we work our way through the obligatory list there won't be much left for a mother to offer. I hope he'll come through with a pet name of his own. We had them in our family."

"Yes," said Raeburn. "Her brother was called 'Bandy.' "

She said, a little absently: "Yes, dear Bandy . . . I miss him . . . Let's all go down and have some tea."

But the Markland pair were sorry. "One of us," said Joan, "is on duty at the evening meal. He gets away with it, but I have to do the schoolma'am turn."

"And the car's on the other side of the hill."

"Another time, then, and we'll see you tomorrow night. I suppose I'm on duty at the evening meal myself, now, come to that." The Duchess was up and ready to go. "I must say I'm glad it's downhill now."

She said to Joan: "I'm so pleased you'll come to the party. Not so many of my own friends come here to Kintalla." To Raeburn, half-severely: "Keep well." And she swung off down the hill.

They watched her through the fence gate and into the castle trees, where she turned to wave, and bent out of sight along a path. They turned to their own slope behind them.

"Nice," said Joan. "Old friend?"

"Not a bit. But I've just discovered lately that I knew her brother. She was a lot younger . . . It can be no picnic married to that particular Duke."

"You shouldn't be talking and climbing too—after yesterday. Give yourself a chance. We're not in such a great hurry, anyway."

Yet they were soon at the roadside, where he unlocked the car and let them in. As he reached to the starting lock she rested her fingers briefly, forbidding, on the back of his hand.

"Tell me now," she said.

CHAPTER 11

"Now," she said firmly.

He was silent, not looking at her, although he knew her eyes were on him, trying to meet his. The key was in the starter, and he left it there, curling his hands on the wheel and dropping his gaze to the backs of them. This was his own affair, and beyond the doctor it had never occurred to him to seek a confidante or a comforter. The Duke might turn out to be a freakish exception, but there was no likely solution to his common enough condition. It was a thing to be kept to oneself, even into the blank beyond silence and speculation. There still lingered in him, in spite of the certainty of the scene to come at the hospital operating theatre some time soon—when was it? how many days?—a kind of regret that life seemed now to be reaching back to the muddle of its longer-term normality. That Duke was probably up to some experiment of his own; something perhaps to do with the products in one of his businesses. You could do that kind of thing if you were on a big enough scale. Anyway, it didn't matter. Raeburn realised he had doubted from the beginning of the story whether he would see Friday morning. A pity a decent doctor like John Grant had been conned into it. Torrie too. Where would they stand when the patient didn't recover and it was revealed that they had changed their minds about the medical facts? It was only some sort of stunt at the best. Even if it added some wretched days or months. His own answer had been right. There surged in him a wish to be back at the parapet of the Dean Bridge, unobserved, the end so cool and decided. Now here was this likable Joan Ker seeking to get into the confusion, as if there was something to be solved by a bright word of friendly concern. Who was he to burden the like of her with his hopeless tale? In the deeper things of his life he had never been able to open his mind much to confession or relief, and it was no time to start now. To a stranger! If it were to be nothing more than the weak humiliation of having even one more person know all this, and one not involved, like the Duke and his hangers-on, in some grand design of her own. This was something you wouldn't do even to somebody who was infinitely closer to you than any single person in your whole life—and there had never been anybody like that.

He knew the truth of this, and, like an unsuspected enemy, the truth, as it will, betrayed him. He would not be able to explain why, then or ever, but he started to tell her. Staring fixedly at the backs of his hands, he went back to the beginning, which was already dim even in his own mind. To the first taps and pangs, the signs of wrong, the medical visits, the routines turning swiftly to menace, the dialogues with Torrie . . . and on to the last visit and the tryst with death on that recent night above the Water of Leith. There came then, measured from him in a narrative that might have been shaped for the hearing by some irresistible authority, the net and the man in the net, the recovery in the Duke's house, and the arrangement of the appointment to the staff at Markland. He made no mention of any part of the kidnap countermoves, nor the further meetings at Kintalla. Not a word about the death of Martinu, the burning car on the moor—all that he left out. Instead he brought the Duke to prominence by describing the planned surgical operation, and his own frank disbelief in its outcome, although it had the apparent agreement of the doctors he had come to trust. Joan Ker made no interruption, asked no questions, and the story came at last to its end, which he marked by raising his hands from the wheel and dropping them in his lap.

He turned at last to look at her, and was amazed. The tears were streaming from her eyes, so abundantly that instead of channelling their way the moisture had spread all across her cheeks, so that her face was covered in wetness, like a child crying. She was not staunching them, but with one hand was trying to hold her trembling lips. Still, a cry burst from her, and she sobbed at last:

"Oh, no! Not you! Oh, please, not you—not Barry Raeburn!"

He reached vaguely to her. In refusal of his story, her head was shaking: "You—you might be dead by now. Not to die, Barry—please— not . . ."

It was a revelation to him of some depth of emotion and reality that he had never encountered. In late years nobody had cared this much about him, and even friends seemed to be fewer. This was an astounding outburst of concern. Renowned as he was, it was something he had never known before. He had read about such things and occasionally, among his married friends, mainly at their funerals, he was aware of deeps of experience that might match this. But she sat beside him now, uncaring about the figure she cut, and the merry dignity that had seemed to define her was turned into a splashy agony that alarmed and suddenly moved him.

He reached a hand to take her free one, and she seized it, bending her face over it so that the tears dribbled hopelessly among his fingers. When at last she looked at him he noticed what he had not seen before, the brilliant brown of her pupils through the thick clarity of the water. She tried to speak, and could not. Motioned then to him, like a child, for his handkerchief. He gave it to her from his front pocket, remembering as he handed it over that it was one he had washed and ironed himself. He could never get the fold-over corners to match. And at once she was using it, not to wipe her own eyes, but the back of his hands where she had drenched them.

He realised she was murmuring still: "Oh, no! Not you—not you— it's not—mustn't . . ."

He stared as this went on, and gave up trying to tell her what he had started to say. Some actions more disciplined than these started to come out of her conduct. She was now mopping her face, dabbing like a boxing second rather than like a woman whose tears were the frequent tools of her trade. He interrupted this brisk performance in the only instinctive way he could think of. His left arm went round her and drew her on to his shoulder and chest. Other than that he did not touch her. She leaned there, busy still with the handkerchief. Looking down, he could see that her face had turned white, changing from the juvenile red of the crying to something that in a way was more purposeful, less lost. He remembered how his mother's face had changed in that way when great issues were afoot. It was foolish of him to have set all this in motion.

"I'm sorry," he said. "It was foolish of me. I shouldn't have told—"

"Stop talking like that." She was still relaxed on his arm. "Let me think. God! If I was only clever. Tell me about that doctor. Sanger—is that the name? Who the devil is he? I think I remember reading about when he got the Nobel—"

"Pretty famous, I think. New inventions about our mortal frames. Might be an honour to be cut up by someone so—"

"Stop it, Barry! We haven't time to be talking like that. Heavens, he's taking on something if he's taking on the Edinburgh College of Surgeons. I know that much. My people are medical. Torrie is president. That's pretty big, you know."

"Not too big to change his mind."

"Don't be clever! You've agreed to all this?"

"Yes."

"Good! Quite right." Suddenly she was crying again, and he let her. After a time: "I don't believe you've told me half of it. It doesn't explain nearly everything. But, oh Christ! I hope it works."

"That's why we're trying it."

"But you—had you given up or what—?"

"I suppose so. On the best advice available . . ."

"All the times I've thought about you—it's been so often—it was never about somebody who would give up . . ."

"Well, you know, some games you can't win."

"Would you do it again? Give up?"

"No. I think not now. Might as well see it through this time."

"Your friends, though. What about your friends?"

"I'll tell you about my friends if you tell me about yours." In a little time he started to speak to her about the friends, and the lasting quality of friends, that a solitary person can gather and hold, with no household round him, no habitual enlarged routines, no sharing, no blessed conceding. It just didn't happen, and one was left like that. As he talked he felt it must be maudlin, for he had never shared, except in occasional banter, this searching grasp for a life mode that even those who followed it could rarely express. So that when he came to an end, she was silent, and was enough in touch with his mood to wait before replying:

"Yes. I know all about that. You needn't tell me."

"It's just that I've been at it considerably longer than you."

It was she who stirred first, beginning to sit back in her place as he let her go. "I can't believe it," she was saying as his arm came away. "All you've told me—none of my business—hard to believe. Including this."

"Well, it's all true. Including this."

"—have to get back. Sorry if I've mucked things up—said the wrong things."

All he replied, looking at her, was: "Joan." And he quickly turned away from the glad tears. He drove her back to Markland.

There was no time for him to lie down for an hour before the school dinner time. Only Coulson, the headmaster, and he foregathered in the staff dining room, all the other teachers making a large muster along with the boys in the school dining hall, to mark the start of the actual term.

"Good!" said Coulson. "Just the two of us. That lets us talk."

But he stayed among the generalities until the meal was nearly ended, saying at last:

"By the way, I've had the Duke on the telephone. Some of us are on parade for the bonfire and fireworks in aid of the son and heir. He agrees with my list—you and I, captain of school, captain of junior school, the prince, of course—we took the detective for granted—Van Moubray—you know him?"

"Yes."

"And I thought of the youngster Hewitt—remember?"

"Yes. Good idea. It's a youngsters' show anyway."

"That makes eight of us. Plenty. Good of him asking . . ."

"You've an extra." Raeburn told of the invitation to Joan Ker.

"No problem." Coulson was happy. "That was a good intervention by you. I ought to have thought of it myself. Gives us a good balance to the unit. The Duchess, is she friendly—formidable? I don't know her."

"Think of the Duke—then the opposite. I don't know her either, really. But some of her people—long time ago . . ."

"We should leave here in a party about seven tomorrow night. The younger ones should have some sleep before we go. Yourself too. How are you feeling, by the way? No—recurrence?"

"Nothing at all. There is something, though, I should tell you—"

"That's interesting, because there is something I wanted to put to you. Anyway, you first." Coulson leaned his head, smiling, on thin elbows, waiting.

Raeburn said: "It's about my health. Something has come up which perhaps I . . ."

Coulson raised pedagogic hands in understanding. "Let me tell *you*. It's about the operation. Thursday night? I want you to know—"

Abashed, Raeburn was in quickly with: "Head, I'm terribly sorry. I should have been the one to tell you first. I suppose it was the Duke—"

"None other! But Barry, don't look so guilty! It's the best thing that could happen. You're very wise to get on with it. We can easily make do for a few weeks. The Duke assures me that is all the time it will take, and you'll be back as good as new. It's great news. Well done!"

All Raeburn could do was to shake his head. What was this bloody Duke doing, to dispose of him this way! A few weeks! A likely tale, and it suited that shifty aristocrat for some complicated and large-scale purpose of his own to get him on to a hospital table, when the other way out would have been certain, apt. Heavens, by this time he would have been buried in the family place at Haddington, and the short process of forgetting the daily detail of him would have started. Who had the right to dispose of another life in this way? Now that Raeburn thought of it, in the light of that day—had he the right himself?

"Can I be allowed to make my case now?" It was Coulson, still smiling.

"Yes, of course, head. Sorry to keep you waiting. I was daydreaming. Strange things happening—they need adjusting to."

Coulson was leaning back in his chair, thin hands now clasped round a thin lifted knee. And the smile. "Some of the things are perfectly natural, it seems to me. That's not the point at the moment, though. Well, listen."

He leaned along the table to put a hand on the other man's shoulder, and turned him so that they looked at each other. The smile, still there, glowed with friendly seriousness.

"Barry," he said. "I've been thinking about this for a long time, but more intently since you came here the other day. I have to think of leaving the school. No—don't interrupt. I'm already well into my sixties, and I must be showing signs of losing touch with the young. It's a heartbreak, but such things must be—"

"I never saw anybody, of any age, more in touch than you are—"

"Fine—that's your view, and thank you for it. But as you know, there are all these pulses to be checked, the endless management acts of judgment, the—the—kind of renewal constantly needed. I don't have to tell you, and what I have been doing for five years is looking for the man, in the hope that I could find him and train him. I haven't—"

"Some very good chaps on the staff here, all believing in you—"

"Agreed. But in the few days you have been here I have become convinced that you are the man. I'd like you to take over from me, gradually, if you like, during the next twelve months or so. No, please don't say a thing just now. You have the touch, the style, I don't know what you call it—but at Markland there is the chance to put into practice the things they've been telling you for twenty years are impossible. Me for forty-five years. It's marvellous! The world is full of people who will never know what a privilege it is to be at the schoolmastering. What is it that makes a good schoolmaster? I can't say. All I know is that you have it, and it is a gift of God. You're shaking your head. What worries you? Are you frightened of it?"

Raeburn worried at it. "Not in the least. You don't know how grateful I feel that you should even think of it. It would be magical if I were even normal. You don't know the hopelessness of it. I tell you, to run this place you must at the least have somebody with a future."

Coulson had taken his arm away, and was back hunched in his chair. That strange authority, that understanding, went on. He said:

"Of course, I don't know what they've told you, and I could tell from the first you had no expectations. But you and I have certain limited knowledge of this Duke. He was very offhand about your condition. You know what he said? He said: 'Raeburn does not believe me. But you may. Certainly it will require a miracle. But I expect miracles to be done when I ask for them.'"

"But even if he is right, is he the kind of man you would buy a secondhand headmaster from?"

Coulson laughed, not hiding his relief, as if it were over and his argument had prevailed: "Barry, keep your wittier stuff for the hard fellows in the seventh. They take a lot of amusing. When you come back, hale and hearty, we'll talk about the financial set-up and the snags, and Heaven knows there are plenty. I dare say I could be around for the odd tutorial, but in fact it's not a good idea for the old man to be in there looking over people's shoulders. I know you've never made a thing of it, but that rugby career goes a long way when some of the temperamental chips are down . . . Eh? At least say you'll think about it."

"I will. I'll think about it. It's the most amazing thing that's ever happened to me. Well, professionally. No, in fact, ever."

"Grand! That's enough for tonight. What about a walk in the grounds? There might be a touch of daylight still."

But it was dark as they followed the thinly gravelled paths, talking of general things which turned back invariably to the school, or to schooling as a whole. Raeburn, embarrassed by his burden of today's intrigue and of his own death tomorrow, and by another one which had emerged that very day, was aware that Coulson, for all his lightness and informality, was less chatting than instructing. All his creed was coming out now.

In a way, Raeburn was distantly interested at how many things, in the long list which Coulson was rehearsing, were old and ordinary wisdom—thoughts about education and the young that he had already reached long ago in his own mind and had almost assumed could never be put to the test, if only because of the oldest of all human predicaments—that the chance and the responsibility so seldom ever came together. Although the other preoccupations lurked powerfully in his mind, he tried to pay intent regard, for he might never, for the one reason or the other, never hear this gathered harvest of purpose again. So some unflagging zeal for what Coulson, too, looked on as a cause kept him listening and responding.

They walked discoursing among the gravel paths and across turf ways, hardly noticing how the night had deepened, the time passed. An aircraft, flying low inwards from the western sea, pushed its noise among their talk, and they had to speak louder as the thing flew overhead. It wheeled above them, seeming to show no winking navigation lights, and at one stage seemed to brush their trees, the outline showing how it finally wheeled slowly away again to the west.

"I say!" Coulson had stopped walking, and looked upwards with his hand on the other's arm. "That fellow's low, isn't he. I'd say he was lost —taking risks, eh . . . ?"

"It's a helicopter. An expert might tell from the engine noise, but I got the shape of him as he turned."

"Well, good luck to him. I hope he comes to no harm. Amazing, isn't it? I suppose at least one boy in every three in the school here would be able to tell us the make and equipment. Dangerous things, helicopters —except for—"

"Headmaster, here's the front door. We've passed it a dozen times already and if you don't mind I'd be glad to slip inside and put my feet up. Forgive me, I've really enjoyed our talk; what you tell me has been so stimulating—unexpected—so much to think about . . ."

"Barry," the older man held him for a moment by the sleeve, "excuse me for all the long-windedness. Thanks for the patience. Off to bed with you. To be continued."

They were inside the hall. The headmaster pushed Raeburn gently towards his end of the passage. Out of sight, he darted to the handle, was inside in the darkness of the room, and had the window up and the walkie-talkie in his hands as he hung from the window, already speaking.

There was conversation in the instrument, but he interrupted without pause in his hiss of alert: "Six here! Helicopter overhead—"

"Go on!" The Duke bit the words out as the other voices cut off. "When? Where? Describe—"

"I am in my agreed place. Helicopter was low overhead—came from the west, made one or two turns, headed back roughly westwards half a minute ago or less. You may hear engine noise picked up by my microphone . . ." He held the instrument full out towards the diminishing reverberations.

"Impossible to tell. Transmission noise due to distance. We have been tracking for at least half an hour. Had lost his engine for some time . . . Essential to keep his whereabouts. Most of the numbers have already dispersed to their normal call points. I have dispatched Thirteen to the high cliffs on the coast and Eleven to the farthest south point of the estate . . . They will come in when they reach position . . ." Raeburn smiled in the darkness to the image of Lord Melfort and the sheikh rushing off on their lone sorties.

"Thirteen," Melfort said to the microphones.

"Eleven," the sheikh whispered, far distant.

"In place?"

"Naturally." Melfort was in with it at once, hardly giving himself time to shade the response into the offended tone which would come from his disapproval of this disciplinary line-up in the hearing of the others. There might have been a sigh of assent from the sheikh.

"Six! Was there a landing?"

"None at all. Certainly none within a mile or more of here."

"Look for it everybody. Listen—keep tracing."

Raeburn put in again. "Six here." He was thinking of Reid on the Doon. "What about Five? He should have picked up my sounding."

"He was in with the location report from your area some seconds ahead of you." It was the Duke's normal voice, laden with chill awareness of error. "We had finished with him when you arrived on the air."

"And the odd three?—What about them?" Raeburn pursued it. "I mean Eight, Nine and Ten. I know they have a minor part, but for a check like this it would be useful if—"

"You will be pleased to hear," the Duke said, "as I was, that it occurred to them to make contact also. Their reports are limited but useful—"

"Ten," said a voice of the district. It was the farmer Hislop of Ben Crocket, which Raeburn remembered was the farm whose hill loomed near Talla Head. "Helicopter coming. He's low down, making for the sea. No sign of landing—"

"I shall take over from here," cut in Melfort, assured that he would be recognisable without identification. "I can see him. I am on the cliff with no lights showing, and he is moving I should say at full speed—enough light to show him the coastline—going down—still down." Raeburn's radio lost power suddenly, as some mysterious ether wave failed and the searching sounds fell through the tiny machine. He kept listening for many minutes, hearing sometimes stray words and thick phrases, none of which made sense. After a long time there was another surge of power, but the transmission seemed to be over, and nothing came through. He made no more effort to stir it up. No sound of an engine hinted in the night. About midnight he slid the heavy window down, drew the curtains, lit the lamps, and read until the small hours, flicking the switch of the walkie-talkie at every chapter end. It remained silent.

By the time morning classes started it seemed that all those in the Kintalla party knew of their role. It seemed to have been intimated with some casualness before the dormitories had emptied, but Mrs Gibson, the matron, came to the staff coffee session to make her plans known and lodge a moderate protest about the short notice. She explained about the need to make sure that the boys changed their underwear, socks and shirts, and had no buttons missing. There would also need to be special cleaning of shoes.

"Sorry, matron." Coulson was apologetic. "Really, though, don't you think the chaps will want to make an effort themselves. I'm not much of a believer in kit inspections. I think if the form masters make sure they have a good scrub after lessons, they might be able to look after the rest themselves."

"All very well, headmaster." She knew better. "But you know what boys are. If they think, some of them, that it's a dressing-up affair they'll go to great lengths to dodge the column. Just to see if they can get away with it."

"Ah, now—it must be terrible to be disillusioned. Well, chase them up, and we'll reinforce any orders in that line you have to give."

It gave Raeburn a chance to move to the side of Joan Ker: "How are you?" he said, low. "Do the rest of us need to change our underwear?"

She laughed, in the manner of the normal staff room encounters; then said: "But I'm terribly worried."

"What about?" They held to undertones, speaking closely.

"You don't need to ask. That was terrible—all you told me yesterday. I still can't believe it, but I'll maybe know more after we've been at Kintalla. I feel I have to speak to that Duke."

"Well—suppose we keep it to ourselves for just a little longer. I'd be grateful. He's not the kind of Duke who gives out much information."

"Will you ever forgive me"—and yet she remained more concerned than abashed—"for that awful outburst. I've only one thing to say about my performance. I meant it."

He looked into her face, schooling the look to an external casualness. But, eye to eye, he was astounded by the kindling he saw.

Inadequately, he said: "Sorry—and thanks. I think I'm bad at worrying people. Kind of habit—"

"You're good—to let me share it." He let her go.

The eleven-o'clock radio call was brief. Nothing could be added to the information of the night before, but, said the Duke, "I'd like a meeting here tonight at say 6.45 p.m.—that is, before the entertainment starts. The information we have will be collated. We shall also make final the plans to counter the move which is due to be made tonight. Any observations? Out!"

CHAPTER 12

"I wonder when we should actually set off? I mean, so as to arrive at what might be thought to be the right time, by Kintalla standards." Coulson, standing on the front steps of Markland, was putting the query to himself.

Walter Fenton, the school captain, and Raeburn were with him. Fenton allowed the other some time to make a reply, and then offered:

"Mrs Gibson is putting the rest through their paces, sir. Shall I try to speed things up? It's getting on to half-past six."

"Yes—do it tactfully, though. Some of the fun and games for the younger children are starting before seven, and we mustn't go tramping in late. Ah, here they come."

Mrs Gibson led the way through the front door, followed by Joan Ker and the boys: the prince, Peter Murdoch, captain of the junior school, Philip van Moubray, and Anthony Biggs Hewitt, looking tiny but glistening. Miller the detective was already beside the school van in the courtyard, unobtrusively obvious.

"Well, have a good time all," said Mrs Gibson. "Who's got the bag?"

"I have, matron." Murdoch held up a suitcase.

"The bag?" Coulson asked. "What bag?"

Mrs Gibson dealt with it, putting on her sensible voice: "Not much, headmaster. Just a few overnight things for them—just in case."

"Overnight at Kintalla! Most improbable. Let's go. All aboard!"

They climbed in, Coulson announcing with joy: "I'm driving. Fasten seat belts, if you can find any. A good cross-section this, I should say. Ready?"

Van Moubray waved an imperious hand to where faces watched from high windows. "I suppose," he said, "you could say I represent the international or non-native element."

"—And I'm the wee one," Hewitt said boldly, and reddened like a sunset when he heard how he had added to the laughter.

"What am I?" asked Joan. "The feminine requirement?"

"By special invitation," said Raeburn. "Special."

They went merrily to Kintalla, Coulson presiding at the wheel, rather than driving. The van had trundled many a long mile on these roads, and beyond, to distant sports fixtures, railway stations, ski-ing sorties, and was losing its zest. They sang a song or two, led by Coulson, who had not added to his repertoire for at least the lifetime of most of them.

When it was over, Coulson, slowing up, said: "First prize in voice production goes to Signor Hewitt, for best soloist."

"Viva," cried Raeburn. "Viva Biggs! Viva everybody!" and led a burst of clapping which had the youngest almost swooning.

It was Dale who stopped them at the gate. He pushed open the door of the van, leaning his head casually inside.

"Welcome to Kintalla, headmaster and chaps—and lady. All correct. Don't get out yet. There's a line-up, with the Duke and Duchess and their two chief guests shaking hands. Why don't you stay in here, let the van creep down the drive, and when you see the reception line, park where you are in the drive and get in line. Eh?"

"We know our place." Coulson flourished a small salute. "Best behaviour, everybody." He started the van.

Dale took Raeburn's eye. He beckoned towards the outside with an upward tilt of the head. Said with diffident assurance: "—Mm—Do you mind . . . ?"

Raeburn left his seat, saying: "If you'll allow me, headmaster . . . I'll join you all at the great get-together." He pulled the van door shut after him as it started to drift down the sloping gravel drive, while he and Dale stepped ahead.

"Quite a crowd," said Dale, moving through the wandering family groups; and when they were more alone, quietly, "No—it's nothing very much really, but the Duke thought you should probably have a look at this, if only to memorise a few new faces." He was leading the way into the trees, to where sounds grew of occasional explosive crackles. "It's the fireworks chaps. Five of them—you'll see the framework of the set piece in a minute. Most of the stuff will be set off from a clearing in here. It seems they like to bring a few samples to try first. That's the row you can hear . . ."

"Yes, of course—the firework people. That must add a lot of worry to your security problems. What do we know about them? Five—"

"No worry. At least in my view. Security clearance—100 per cent. But he wanted you to have a look at them." He pointed the way round the thicker brakes of trees. Then was saying: "Do you mind carrying straight on—that direction. There's something else I have to do for the Duke. Keep walking towards the bangs. Maybe a word with the chaps, then about-turn to come out. You'll be back in time for the hand-shaking."

"Quite all right." Raeburn walked on into the darkening wood, leaving the crunching steps of Dale diminishing behind him. He strained his sight below the branches ahead, with the sample firework noises coming louder, and even the visual whisper of the flashes now streaming round the trunks. Here in the deepest thicket of the wood, robbed of the little sunlight that ever penetrated, the tree trunks enlarged themselves and became only outlines—ambush points—stage flats to hide some part of the long threat of dusk and doom; and Raeburn, who ever since the night of the Dean Bridge had imagined he would never again be stressed by the trivia of mortality, felt a sudden small grue of menace.

He had quickened forward to meet the men, when one of them stepped out from behind a tree, only a few yards off. His arms were raised ahead of him, as if he might be showing one of the display rockets. Raeburn signalled him in a casual gesture, and was about to tell his story when he was suddenly aware who the man was now standing stolid before him, braced on parted legs, double pointing with the instrument in his lifted hands.

There was no doubt about the round dough-face of Panacz, the scrub of hair, the utter absence of expression. Even his passive pallor lightened the twilight, and clearly in front of him, pointed, aiming, steady, was the pistol with the silencer, the neighbour of the one carried and so held by Martinu.

Raeburn waited for it, and knew there was no swerve or doubling that could serve him. He wondered, looking to the muzzle, if it would flame, or merely cough up gently a wisp of smoke and sound.

Panacz was now tensing to pull the trigger, and when the shot went off the pistol did not even jump, or show a muzzle sign. The sound roared in Raeburn's ear, above his right shoulder and, still looking into Panacz's face, he saw there the black gash spring to the middle of the forehead. The moon-head hammered back, like a struck boxer's, and Panacz fell backwards and prone, the arms still vaguely holding up the weapon. At the level of Raeburn's knees, on the right side, something smote him like a Welsh forward's tackle, and he was bundled sideways to the ground. Sprawling, he turned to grapple.

A man, his tackler, was lying half on top of him, the felling spring relaxed, and voice noises that might have been meant to be reassuring like "Aye—Aye—Aye" coming from him. Raeburn found himself beating and clutching at a hard head of thick hair. It rose to look at him, overwhelmed with decorous concern.

"By God, sir—have I hurt you?" It was MacFarlane, rising, and in turn, with a hand like a clamp, heaving the other to his feet.

"No. But—"

"You're all right, Mr Raeburn. Sure?"

"Sure. If there's one thing I'm good at it's falling. But what the devil! You've shot him . . ."

"Aye. But—well—I had to get you out of his line of fire. When they go, they often pull a cocked trigger. I've seen it many's a time. A bloody near thing, if you ask me." MacFarlane, back to his gamekeeper role, was brushing twigs and leaves from both of them.

He stooped then quickly to lift his stalking rifle where he had dropped it on launching into the tackle, cherishing its butt and barrel, drawing the bolt, loading up another single as if he might be a man who needed this assurance.

Raeburn walked over to the fallen Panacz. Apart from the hole in the forehead, it was the same face. He still had little power of comparison, but Raeburn knew it would take him a long time to get used to the open eyes, dimming but still looking. He recognised also that the hole was at least twice the size of the one Reid had given Martinu. Otherwise the face was undamaged.

Putting a boot under the shoulder, MacFarlane turned the body over with a single heave from the hip. The back of Panacz's head seemed to have come off, untidily, and MacFarlane bent to push it back.

"Keyholed," he said, briefly. And directly to Raeburn: "I was worried you were going to move. As it was I nearly took your ear off, but a fit man like you might have tried a jump for it. It's as well you didn't, for my bullet would have gone through the two of you." As he spoke, he hauled the dead man by the belt towards a near-by hollow, the body bending almost double as it trundled. Emptying the pockets, he pushed the thing into the dip, tore off some branches to put on top, all the time scraping old leaves to the grave with his boots. In a matter of seconds Panacz was out of sight, and would take a lot of finding.

Raeburn had been following up and down: "But tell me—what happened? How did you know—I mean, what made you come here? I thought we were to let them assemble—"

"He'll be all right in there—well, until I can come back for him. And of course there's the photographs." MacFarlane scraped once or twice to hide the trails. "Well, you know, sir—it was easy. I've had my eye on him for an hour. He came over the east wall, and he's been in here since, and when you and Mr Dale started off for the heart of the wood I thought I'd better not be too far away. We can do without him, if you ask me. Maybe you'll tell the Duke. He'll know what's best."

"I'm seeing him shortly. Has anything else happened?"

"Nothing like this. I don't know what you were meaning to do in here, Mr Raeburn, but you would be wise to be making tracks for your own party."

"I think so. It was Mr Dale who suggested—"

"It's not for me to say anything, sir. This way. I'll see you to the edge of the trees. I hope I didn't hurt you there. It was a right tumble you took."

"None the worse. Though if it had been my left knee you would have had to carry me out."

"Ach well—like enough I could do that too."

Where the trees thinned he stopped. "I'd be wise to stay in here for a while. You'll see the Duke knows. Give him that"—handing over the few things from the pockets. He swung back to the darkness of the wood's heart.

The Markland van had dropped almost to the end of the drive, and the party had descended to join the last of the line. Raeburn joined them as they walked, and, sure enough, in front of a great marquee, there was the line-up. Coulson shook hands along the line, stopping to listen gravely to some proverbial statement from the sheikh. Then he introduced the others, the boys first. Beside the Duke, who nodded as if in tentative agreement rather than recognition to every newcomer, the Duchess shook hands with warmth, and made conversation with them all. Raeburn and Joan Ker came back to her, and they stood together, recalling the meeting of yesterday. The grounds were thick with people, most of them moving with diffidence about the domain. Over towards the shrubbery a conjuror was setting up his tricks, and a ring of audience thickened quickly about him. The Duke came across again to Raeburn, with no preliminary words, his lips thin:

"An item of business inside—due now, I think." He led the way.

Raeburn said a word of excuse and followed. The Duchess spoke after them. "Supper at seven-thirty sharp. Don't be late, either of you. We have to think of the children."

The Duke walked, heedless, to the steps. Higgins was at the door, this time on the outside, and he pushed it inwards for them both. Soon they sat in the dining room where the first conference had taken place. The only others there were Lord Melfort, the sheikh, Mr Porteous and Sylvester.

The Duke laid down the notebook he had been looking through. Keeping his eyes on it, and resting his hand, stiff-fingered, upon his forehead, showing the jet ring, and with his elbow supporting this weight of authority and decision, he said:

"To business!"

With a deep breath, enough to hold the silence, Raeburn said: "Before you begin, Duke, I have something rather important to mention."

It was impossible to tell by what unnoticed alteration of his features or posture the Duke indicated a far-off irritated disapproval. While he spelt out his silence, Melfort, handling his cigar and looking closely at the glow, spoke quietly: "No doubt."

Without looking at Raeburn, the Duke sent in his direction a tiny movement of the head which, if it had been larger, might have been a slight nod. It seemed to be his invitation for Raeburn to speak.

"If it makes any difference to your plans, Duke, you ought to know that the total of your enemies has been reduced by another one. Panacz, one of your suspects, was killed here in your own grounds ten minutes ago."

It was the first time Raeburn had seen the man's power of impassive anger. The head came up, the fingers withdrawn, the lank hair falling over the draining face, and some blast furnace of fury within made his eyes fierce with flame. They waited.

"Who has done this? Who has disobeyed my orders? It was made unmistakably clear that disposals were to await the start of the action."

Raeburn was able to be quite calm. "Before I give you the details I am bound to give you my opinion that the man responsible acted in an outstandingly able manner. You are most reliably served in that direction."

"I shall judge that."

The story was briefly told. At the end he slipped across the table to the Duke the thin handful of items that had been in Panacz's pockets, and these were handed on to Sylvester without looking.

The Duke seemed to be pondering. While he was silent, Lord Melfort came into the conversation.

"Some misunderstanding here," he judged. "Probably a mis-hearing. As some of us know, these men were security cleared long ago. They have your own passes, haven't they? Are these not the same individuals who arranged the display at your place in Sutherland? And I imagine they will be moving south as the festivities go through the rest of your places. So?"

It was a direct question. After a time the Duke said: "Yes." And later: "Quite . . . perhaps."

He heard some new rhythm of attentiveness from the sheikh, and gave him a listening gaze, the first time he had looked up.

"I have to say—if I may be permitted—that this incident seems to lessen the importance of the whole affair." The sheikh was explaining. "Here we have another killed. We shall soon have none left to deal with. A pity. I personally had hoped there would be a hue and cry." He smiled, ruefully baffled, and stretched himself unobtrusively.

"Ah yes—action, of course." The Duke had finished his preoccupation with the Panacz affair, and looked round the table almost agreeably. "You will want to have my view about the plans I have for the final phase of the situation. We have a few minutes only. I should mention first why we are so few in number. An hour ago"—this was addressed mainly to Raeburn—"I thought it suitable to gather in all those of our party already available, including my two house guests, and outline the plans so that they could join the people outside and be available, if required, for defence or any other service. They have had their briefing. Now I should tell *you*.

"I have not departed—there has been no need to—from my conviction that the kidnapping of the prince will be attempted on the road between here and Markland when the school vehicle is on its way back at the termination of these festivities. The grounds and events will of course be policed most vigilantly in the course of the evening, but the information leads inevitably to a plan located at some distance from Markland ground. The school party will be discreetly escorted at some distance, by our own cars, which will be ready to close in when the attempt is made, and of course there will be other cars and parties placed at strategic points and ready to close in, not only to provide extra defensive power but to headlight the scene with car lamps. In the end the whole action will not take long. The enemy will have little time to be surprised that we know anything, and especially that we know so much. When the assault starts, Mr Raeburn here, as the only one of our party actually travelling in the vehicle who is armed and in the picture, will perhaps be inclined to join in and take part on the ground. His knowledge of some of the suspects will in any case be valuable. Before leaving the van he will ensure that all the occupants are already lying on the floor, protected from the firing, which will in any case be unexpected by Casio and his people. No doubt the detective will also play some part, but it is likely that all will be over before he has grasped what is happening.

"We all know that there was helicopter activity over the area in the course of last night. There is good evidence to indicate that a momentary landing, or at least a near-ground hovering, was made, and that the remaining members of the kidnap and ransom party are now on the ground in the territory. Mr Porteous will point out the deduced landing spot"—that official was doing so—"which we believe to be on or near the roadway a short distance to the south of Ben Crocket Farm. Hislop the farmer was out with his dogs immediately, appeared to pick up their scent, but lost them at the Crocket burn. Reid has been well over the area with the spaniels for some hours today, but with no results. However, we may be sure that the full team has arrived. Or perhaps one short. They are probably flying the helicopter themselves, which would leave one less in the immediate quota.

"It should be said that the approach to Markland territory was made by the helicopter with great skill and an intimate knowledge of the ground. It may be assumed that the flight was made from the north of Ireland, involving a sea crossing of a minimum thirty miles, but probably more. We have, naturally, a private contact with the official radar system, and nothing was registered on the screen. I need not mention where the screen is. The deduction must be that the machine flew all the way practically at water level. Our own observers report that it came overland up the cliff gully at Talla Head, where a cleft in the rock conceals anything from a lateral vision. Thereafter it was overland, but low, and only an occasional trace, disappearing at once, showed where it had been. These traces, scrupulously reported, allowed us to check our own observations as we networked by walkie-talkie last night, but showed that we cannot expect a radar warning of the approach again. The helicopter went back by the same route, obviously bound for some home-base in Ireland. That much is clear."

The Duke allowed a silence to fall, and none stirred to break it, until Raeburn said: "Another thing is clear; an ambush in the gully at Talla Head."

The Duke turned a hard black gaze on him, before speaking. It was Lord Melfort who said: "If there's one thing a schoolmaster can be, it's obvious." He fussed at his cigar with studied patience.

"Thank you, Raeburn," said the Duke. "That has been thought of, in your absence. Starting three hours from now, the gully will be manned by the sheikh, armed with a portable rocket-launcher, as well as his other weapons."

"Fine," said Raeburn. "Long may the obvious prevail."

The Duke's hand, raised in acceptance, and assisting his shrug, perhaps held a silence on Melfort, who had started to respond.

"A point to add." Raeburn had had the thought before dressing for tonight's excursion. "The man Anton Biros—you know, Biros the kitchen helper at Markland. Today was his afternoon off, and he isn't normally due to report until tomorrow. I confirmed that before I came—"

"That's Konski," said the Duke. "So he is in place already. Excellent!"

"The girl then"—from Melfort. "That girl who has a job in the school and who we decided is one of the mob. What was the name . . . ?"

"You're thinking of Isobel Henderson." Raeburn was heavily restrained. "I'm satisfied she's not one. Anyway, she's on duty at this moment for the school dinner."

"Best kind of alibi," Melfort declared. "It fits. She'll be over here by nightfall, on one of those handy bicycles."

"To do what—?" Raeburn was voicing stridently, in spite of himself, but the Duke waved him to silence, saying: "Cove. That's the name of the woman in the case. We shall not know until she's dead. Soon enough."

The sheikh leaned forward. "So far as concerns those who might have taken employment, or otherwise identified with the community, it might have been the intention to leave them at their duties, so as to create a base for, say, ransom negotiations."

"Not likely." Melfort had to speak so fast he had no time to remove the cigar. "You see—"

"That has been taken into account, although it did not seem an item to be laboured. Since there will be no negotiations. I take it there are no more items to be discussed. Very well—we are expected on the lawn." The Duke rose and left by the door, leaving them to follow.

When Raeburn, with the others, came to the front door at the end of the hall, the Duke had already passed through it and was outside on the steps. The Duchess passed him as she came into the house.

"This is me rounding up the stragglers," she told Raeburn. "Here is the point in the proceedings where we show off the junior. He's already been seen and goo'ed at by all present, but this is the official bit."

She ushered them outside, coming with them to take a stand beside the Duke, while the rest of them descended and stood near the forefront of the gathered audience. Higgins still shadowed the door recess inside, with the doorway itself standing wide like an antique symbol of hospitality. A thought made Raeburn slightly smirk—the thought of the castle's Duke of ice, damned with a cold mood of aloofness that would for ever seem to make him a monument to inhospitality.

Joan Ker, standing at his side, nudged him, whispering sideways: "Be serious. It isn't supposed to be funny."

He nodded directly at her, holding her eye. "It's the contrast. You have no idea what a hard fellow he is."

"He is doing all right for you, by all accounts." A hinted smile or a grimace lifted the corner of her mouth as she turned away.

The ceremony could hardly have been shorter. The nursemaid, in her severe russet uniform, brought the baby up the steps and handed him to the Duke. The father spread his two hands and suddenly lifted the scrap aloft, a miniature mummy, held like a sporting trophy by a winning football captain, not polished but swaddled. He said not a word, nor did his people in that silence; until it was clear that there was to be no speech nor greeting, and they spilled out a measure of hand-clapping, which went on and swelled.

Like a cue to the rest of them, a white-bearded ancient, tremulous, shaking even at his great spread of shoulders that told still of once stalwart days, lifted a voice: "A guid yin," he said. "A guid yin. A bonny bairn. Bless the hoose." He set them going, and phrases came from here and there. "Aye, bonny!" "Oh, the wee Earl!" "Fortune to him." And women let tears drop, as they do at the pitifulness of humankind, from weakness to weakness in so short a span.

The Duke ended it by turning to the Duchess, handing her the baby like a baton of authority. Then he swept his hand in a gesture towards the dining marquee, stepping down and through them, leading the way. Almost absently, he slowed at the old man, and still without words took him at the elbow, steering through the others, who came in family groups and followed.

There was a top table spread, and the Duke went there, pausing only to hand the elder to a spinster daughter or niece. Melfort and the sheikh joined him, and stood, like all the congregation, until the Duchess came in, when there was a rich outburst of clapping and cheers. After a time the Duke held up his hand, and they were quiet, with great extra hushings for the children and the garrulous.

"Mr Murdoch." It was the name of the parish minister, who came forward importantly, lifting a hand and bowing the head.

He set forth in prayer, while the spread tables waited for them. It was a long discourse, for he did not often get the opportunity to demonstrate in the presence of important strangers how much he was at ease in the company of the Almighty. He chatted through some routines, finding no fresh phrases for the mysterious truths of which he was a custodian, but inserting shrewd and thankful references to the setting and the source of the bounty. Then he dealt with the child at length, assuring him of much success as well as responsibility in the years ahead, adding also some personal footnotes of the family: generosity and excellence which had gone into legend, or were perhaps still to be hoped for. The entertainment was touched upon with appreciation, and an undertaking given that all present would try very hard, now and in the future, to be worthy of these attentions. Raeburn's wary look was soon roving the tent, finding many another sinner so occupied. He gave a perfunctory frown to one or two of the Markland boys, catching Joan's look, at which he winked. Other and smaller children, wearied of waiting, were caught open-eyed by vigilant mothers, and mildly punched, or gathered by a hand sliding over the head to press it to the strong hips to whose height they reached. As the minutes passed, here and there at the tables elderly folk sagged and sat down, the hired catering chairs grinding and squeaking with impatience themselves.

It finished at last, and there was a great sitting down and serving of plates, opening of bottles, hissing and whispering of instructions, growing thunder of conversation relaxed, waving across the table spaces, lifting of glasses, wandering of children on visits. Dr Coulson, the headmaster, along with one or two other notables, had been waved up to the top tables, but the Markland boys had been shown to a table which had perhaps too many spaces for them; but they sat there, plainly aching with apprehension in case the teachers should join them.

A table for two, one of many pressed against the canvas walls, looked inwards to the main company, and it was there that Raeburn had steered Joan, so that they could sit side by side.

"Fall to, peasants," he said, when the sounds of the feast were loud enough to suppress his words.

"You had your eyes open during the prayer," she said. "Bad example."

"I refrain from giving the old and obvious retort."

"Yes: *'How did you know?'* I was watching."

"There, you see . . ."

"You can count on me to be watching from now on."

"I think I'd like that."

"But, God forgive me, I don't think I can wait until Thursday. Why so long? It's two days from now. What on earth are they waiting for?"

"Big things are doing. My problems are not the only ones on the agenda."

"Whose agenda? Anyway, I knew it! How do you come to be involved? Don't tell me it's none of my business. It will always be my business. Never an end to it."

"Joan, an end to everything. Sooner for some than for others."

"Don't say that! You're just an entry in some big shot's diary. *A few social matters to be attended to first. Let me see. I am afraid Thursday is the earliest I can manage.* Life and death for you, at somebody's convenience."

"Sorry if it looks like that. Hardly true, though. You see, the 'life' alternative was only added a matter of hours ago. And may I say I don't want to start wishing I hadn't told you."

"Please don't feel like that! For all it terrifies me, and I can't bear it, I'm twice the person I was before I knew."

"Good! But why?"

"Just because you wanted to tell me."

All this was strung out, like long-threaded beads, among the general uproar, the meetings, the servings, the silences drowned by adjacent noise. And they kept to their own public normalities, the smiles and nods to each other, the waving hands down the tent, the joint acknowledgment to the far-off headmaster at the top table, who had been looking round for them.

A band had come in. There were eight of them, two fiddlers, two accordionists, and the rest, and every tune they played was native to the land, a dancing tune, speaking some special message of word and note to practically every soul under that frail roof. Most of them looked from time to time, in vain, to see if the Duke might be stirred or even happy. But for them all, as they drank and ate and remembered, old and young, the music brought finished days of remembered joys, or of nights immortal still to come.

She said: "I've never danced with you."

"Pity! And you should say 'not yet.' You know that at the best it will be quite a time before—"

"Don't say it! If there is nothing else, I don't want to look back on cynicism. What I was trying to say was: 'I've never danced with you. But I feel as if I had.'"

"That's good. Thank you. I like that. I'll keep that one especially."

"I suppose you've danced a good deal."

"Like mad. Well, that music—it does that to you too. Bone of our bone. I can see it does."

"Who with?"

"Watch the grammar! Everybody. Some more than others. Same as you have done."

"Not quite. Well, nearly—"

"And everywhere. Village halls, Edinburgh ballrooms, big match receptions, Perthshire kitchens—there was a simply beautiful red-haired girl in Auckland, at a party after a Lions game, and we danced the whole night. Duke of Perth, my favourite, Dashing White Sergeant—"

"That one needs two partners."

"Yes, I suppose there was another one . . . Petronella, Strip the Willow, Waltz Country Dance, Foursome Reel . . . she knew the lot."

"I hate her, for a start."

"Positively no need. Untouched by human hand. You well know that even in Scottish dancing the permitted tactile areas are strictly limited. You will now recount briefly your own experiences on the dance floor!"

"Experiences—hardly a one."

"What then did you mean by 'not quite'?"

"Oh, you know—when you are really young it's hopeless. One's so shy. Others can carry it off. Then when that passes, the time has gone a bit, friends are away married; there are no occasions . . . Do I sound abandoned?"

"Only linguistically."

A short gesture from Raeburn had brought the young Hewitt quickly to their table. The man said to him: "Biggs! Here! We have a plateful left of cream cakes and another of mince pies. How about carting them back to that hungry mob of yours?"

"Oh, I say—can I, sir? Oh, super!" Off he went towards the hands already grabbing.

"That will make him popular," said Joan, as the other table stuffed and saluted, with happy grins.

"Yes. You like them all."

"I really do. Until now, I've taken it all as my life, and thought myself lucky. There's something—I don't know—something about boys.

They need—they need so much care. Oh, damn it, I think I'm going to cry again! I haven't cried since Sunday—almost."

"Well, don't now. Pretend to make up or something."

"How do you know about that?"

"Listen. The time has perhaps come to tell you something important—"

"About you? Only if it's about you. I can't stand too much else."

"Yes: sort of. I'm not really very sure that I have the right . . ." He told her about what Coulson had told him about the future at Markland. It took astonishingly few words. But they were enough, and her face lit so much he had to start a warning.

"Careful now," he said. "No excitement. No signs. It's a long way off."

"But it's marvellous. It's perfect. It's right—everything's right about it."

"I have no right to count on anything. The whole idea of being able to go on is new to me . . ."

"Count on it! You must! Think of it, though. We could do anything. All the chances—the boys. Wee Hewitt. He wouldn't even need to try to go home. We could keep him, holidays and all. It's absolutely the thing for you to do."

"*We?*"

She was silent, even downcast for a moment. "—Well—of course I mean the school."

"You said *we*."

CHAPTER 13

"We had better," said Raeburn to Joan, "compose ourselves for more general courtesies. Look at the Duke. He is on his rounds."

It might seem that the Duke had scarcely joined in the dinner. He was touring the tables, where he knew almost everybody; speaking to the farmers about the stock and the prospects of crops, the prices, the costs—and like him they tended to be expert in farming lore. He knew the teachers of the one-teacher schools, and spoke to them—and to the hotel-keepers, the few fishermen, joiners, dykers, sawmillers, mechanics, most of them, but not all, in his own employment. Mr Porteous went with him, occasionally taking notes as something of interest to the estate emerged in the conversation.

When he came to the Markland boys he waved them back to their chairs as he had done for the others who had stood for him. He spoke to some of them, listening with a veiled attention. To the prince, while all in the marquee craned guardedly to watch this mighty meeting, he drifted past only a single look of absent affability.

"Clever that," murmured Joan. "That was a truly regal trick. Must be fearfully difficult."

"Just to show he could do it," Raeburn said.

Then the Duke was at their table, leaning over so that they could not rise in any case. "It won't be long now," he said, apparently to them both.

Raeburn stared wide at him. What was he doing, saying this in front of—

"Thursday night. If I don't have a proper chance to speak to you again before that, good wishes." Directly to Joan, he added: "You know about that, I hope?"

"Yes, I do," she answered.

"Good. I've also mentioned the matter in the briefest outline to Dr Coulson, who ought to know what is planned. He approves."

They might have talked further, but while Raeburn was starting with a mumbled "Thank you," Mr Murdoch the minister was ingratiatingly at the Duke's side, speaking:

"Not to interrupt, Your Grace, but I was hoping you would have a special word with old John Noble of Binnanee Farm. I don't think he is well—wasn't at church on Sunday. I'm told, the first time he has missed for thirty years or more."

"Certainly. Where is he sitting?"

"I haven't found him yet." The minister drifted off again, but the Duke moved to another table, sallow, remote, dutiful. The Duchess gathered a little coterie of women here and there in the tent, and laughter came from these groups.

Raeburn and Joan spoke together again: "What if you hadn't told me?"

"What if—? How on earth did he know I told you? I didn't tell him I did. You're the only one I've told."

"I'd say it's because he knows nearly everything."

"Well, he thinks he does."

"What else does he know? About you . . . ? About here . . . ?"

But the headmaster was on them, laying a hand on each of them at the shoulder, and beaming below the halo of his thin, tufted hair.

"Great, Barry! Just great! Just get this out of the way and let's get on with the real things."

"I'm not sure that you're supposed to know."

"Never mind, I know now. He takes an interest in you, in a big way, it seems. He also told me that very few of his business colleagues seem to have much idea of junior maths." To Joan: "We were talking about you too, I'm afraid."

"Bandied about, that's me."

"You could have a worse fate. Anyway, I'm off to the fireworks. Things are looking up for Markland." Off he breezed, sweeping up the schoolboys on the way. The tent was emptying towards the lawn.

"Everybody seems to be working for you," she said to Raeburn.

"Yes. I can't get a word in."

It was dark outside, and they separated for a moment, trying to catch up with the Markland group ahead. Dale came alongside, taking a short grip of Raeburn's upper arm, his mouth close.

"All set?"

"Reasonably."

"This is it—tonight. That was good work, by the way, in the wood."

"Not my work. My contribution was modest. You probably know the details."

"Who was it then? Not you?"

"I'm the teacher, not the historian . . . I'm looking for Miss Ker. Ah, there she is. Joan, you know Mr Dale."

"Sorry, I don't think so. I can't even see him. Are you with the Duke? I'm at Markland."

"Yes, I'm on the run, mostly with the Duke. He takes a lot of keeping up with. We do this show almost word for word again on Friday night at Allenhope. The fireworks men go immediately after their show. Same with the house staff, except for a cook or two and a bed-maker. Caterers back to base in Dumfries. House party off on Thursday."

"Busy day, Thursday," Raeburn said.

"Busy day every day." Dale led them to seats where bushes screened them from the evening wind.

"His boss doesn't seem to tell him everything," Joan was saying as they settled. "That Thursday reference . . .".

The opening maroon tore aside all sounds, except for the squeals of pleasure as it reddened its own echoes in the woods and the middle-distance cliffs. Then rockets went up, leaping, rising, undying until they faltered suddenly at the peak, bursting their lives away in coloured glowing baubles that dropped and dripped, quenching themselves in the void like seeds that renewed the growth of other flaming stalks leaping aloft. Bright wriggling shapes swam in a black sea—"Fish!" said a hundred voices as the shoals darted over them. More than the cracks and the bangs were the giant seashell hissings as new lit toys rushed up, drawing the eyes, the voices, the unrestrained words of sheer happy thankfulness. There was no age at which a human heart could fail to lift at the sight, or find it tedious. It was perhaps the only form of entertainment in the whole world that nobody could be found to complain at.

It finished with the set piece, which turned out to be a fiery simplified version of the Duke's own crest, with his eagle supporters identifiable in the exploding blaze, and for a moment even his ancient motto could be read, here modernised to: "I Have My Day." Some of them spoke it, for they had seen it often, at the gate pillars, above the castle entrance, even on his ring—those who had been near enough. Now the blazon was dying.

A bonfire spread beyond the trees, drawing the crowd across to revel in the heat and light. It was enough to see them all to the gate, and soon the place was emptying. Coulson, with his attendant schoolboys, came up to say: "No hurry for our Markland lot. The Duke said we should probably wait until most have gone. Wants to give us an escort, I think. Something else doing."

It was Sylvester who joined them with a tray of sausages and long forks. "Extras, extras! Pity to waste a cooking chance." The boys were soon reaching to the spread embers as the bonfire in turn faded to wood ash. Coulson was joyfully in amongst them, and then the other adults took part, cooking and eating, with Miller the detective last. By the time the sausages were finished, the grounds were clear but for them, and even the catering bus and the van of the firework men had heaved up the sloping drive and through the gates into the darkness of the highway.

"Well, that's about it, I think." The Duke had joined them.

Coulson turned to him and to the others, a sausage disappearing into his mouth. "This is the life," he rejoiced. "I've had seven. Remind me tomorrow to give myself a telling-off for sheer greed." He started to hustle the lads towards the van.

The Duke came with him. "I think we'll give you an escort," he said. "Would you like to let me drive? I like vans and buses." It seemed to Raeburn that he spoke like a man with all his plans laid, his baits set.

"Now there is an honour, chaps," declared the headmaster. "Any objections? Speak up, Markland, or for ever hold your peace."

"Can he drive?" asked Prince David. "Or do we need to put up the L-plates?"

They went jollying out of the gates. Cars stood around still, with headlamps full, lighting the scene. Reid and MacFarlane were there; Dale and Sylvester were recognisable shadows; Lord Melfort was even less obtrusive, and near him was what seemed to be the outline of Laidlaw, the head gamekeeper. The car lights were concentrated upon the school van, waiting in the middle of the driveway space and illuminated from all sides. The Duke was ushering the boys into it, along with the detective. To Raeburn he said: "You sit in the front. With me." Raeburn entered. It was a swivel seat, and he turned it so that he could face the school passengers.

The Duke stuffed Coulson and Joan Ker into a jeep driven by Reid. "You'll lead," he told them. The other cars, doors slamming gently, were gulping dark shapes. They dimmed to sidelights as the Duke left them, walking towards the school vehicle.

Raeburn touched the outside of his back pocket, where the now familiar and comfortable shape of the pistol awaited his tap. A quick internal survey of his thoughts, taken like an inventory amid the chaffing and laughter, disclosed to him the three things foremost in his mind at that time. The kidnapping attempt was about to begin, but that was not the first, not the most important. The other two, mingled together, were Joan Ker, and his own death—or life.

The Duke climbed aboard as if he had always driven vans. Switched on the engine, revved up, and in the brief noise while he reached for the gears, nodded sideways to Raeburn to instruct him to lean in that direction.

He said thinly, into the waiting ear: "Ready? Weapon?"

"Self and weapon ready," said Raeburn.

"Very well. See?" He tapped a fingernail on the van side where some sheets of material, solid, newly installed, ran along from below window height to the floor. "Fitted during the celebrations. Bullet-proof. Both sides of the van."

He went on: "I should say somewhere below the Doon." He was fumbling for switches, found one, and turned on the internal lights of the van. Then the headlights. Turned to the passengers: "We're off. Can nobody sing here?"

Under that commanding glower, they wavered into song, but picked it up, and in a moment were in full voice. Like an uncertain carousel, they drove into motion and turned out through the gates, the jeep ahead, and the other cars, falling back, following.

For the want of anything to do that might have more meaning, Raeburn conducted the choir as they swept into the night. A flick ahead showed him that the leading jeep had internal lights on also, illuminating the inhabitants, while the schoolboys were drenched in lights that showed up their tired, shadowed eye-sockets, for it was late now. As he led them from one laboured chorus to another, he saw through the rear windows that the cars had not only fallen back, but their sidelights even were out. He was handicapped by the bright light inside, but he thought that towards the rear window of the nearest following car there might be a shaded gleam, as if someone held a torch to the followers.

They went on. The road was empty. The lamps from the two leading vehicles in the light and dark convoy lit the new spring grass and hedges so that they appeared greener than ever, and at the corners the beams chased their own manufactured shadows among the low branches, or suddenly across immense vistas of the heath.

The Doon came near, and they went slower, offering their bright cargo to the menace that was plotted and waiting. Raeburn marvelled that the boys could not feel in waves the tension from the Duke as he stiffened, certain of the assault but awaiting its unknown shape. Where the road rounded the base of the hill, they made the long swerve at a low pace, and were ready for it when it came. Far back on the road behind he could see the red glow of the brake lights as the other cars eased down, and imagined the cocked guns, the shoulders ready for the butts.

Nothing happened. They drove on. They had to. Below their wheels the road bore them on—no challenge, no movement—and the school gates were there, the jeep entering, their own lights safely following.

As the jeep stopped at the school steps, Coulson was out from it in a skip, trotting for the van with a hand outstretched.

"Tremendous night—simply tremendous, Your Grace. I can't think of a better way of giving the son and heir a send-off, and we were privileged to join in. I'd call for three cheers from our lot if it weren't that the school will be asleep. Good night and thank you. Inside everybody!"

As they disembarked, the Duke was already holding up a hand to arrest the action. It was something more than the gesture of a late host.

They waited for him, wondering at the set smile that moved unexpectedly across the face.

"I wonder—headmaster—" the voice was strange with diffidence. "—I wonder if the party would like to come back with the rest of my guests to Kintalla. Stay the night. Yes, I like the idea—"

"Stay?—The night?"

"Why not? It has been a memorable occasion. They all seem to have enjoyed it. We have beds, enough of everything—late-night supper from the scraps, eh?" It seemed to Raeburn that this hearty man could not be the Duke. And at once he realised that the Duke was essentially thwarted, and wanted to set his trap again.

"Oh, I think it's really too late—Duke, terribly good of you. The lads are tired, and they have an early start. It's been a wonderful time—"

"Oh, wait a bit, Barry—don't be a spoil-sport! A night in the castle would be miraculous; they'd never forget it. We could have you all come in nice and late tomorrow. Say, here by ten. How about it?"—and they bubbled with enthusiasm.

"One small problem only." Coulson searched out the emerging figure of Sergeant Miller, the detective, who was pushing himself forward from his usual background. "Sergeant," said Coulson to him, "what about you? Any problems?"

The Duke said: "Any arrangement you like. Adjoining rooms—communicating doors. We have, as you will have noticed, guards on the entrance."

"Well, in that case, sir, I feel sure it would be all right." The detective glanced quickly towards the prince to detect a withdrawal, seeing there the same anticipation as on the other young faces. "Yes, thank you, sir. Very good indeed, sir."

"Then all aboard, the lot of you, again!" Dr Coulson ushered them. "Do you mind, Duke, if I don't come along this time. I ought not to leave the ship. Anyway, you'll all have more fun if I'm at home. Be good!"

"Same places—same seats." The Duke, withdrawn again, went back to the driver's seat. "Same route back. Singing too."

"Not until we're well away from the school." Raeburn said it in his most schoolmasterly voice, getting the thin, level look from the man at the controls. They waved back to the outline of the headmaster, just visible in the faint porch light. The other cars of the cortège waited outside darkly, only their brake lights showing.

The van droned in a low gear, and the Duke began to lean slightly towards Raeburn, in a signal of talk.

"Not happening," said Raeburn.

The Duke's quiet tones matched his. "You are still confident in your theory that I am mistaken. There is no mistake."

"They could never have expected us to turn and go back."

"Sing!"

Both angry men took a few deep breaths. Raeburn turned then to the vanload. "Singing—by request," and he winked at them. This time they rallied round somewhat more carefree, and he was able to teach them briefly one or two new songs which he had heard in New Zealand, and hardly remembered. Over his shoulder, in the headlamps of the vehicle, he could see the figure of Joan as she swayed beside Reid. On the straight stretches of road behind them he could make out the red glows as the following cars braked occasionally for each other, slowing and slowing as Reid in front held back their journey.

Round the Doon they were almost at a standstill, filling the night and the road with noise and light. A roe deer in the wayside trees stood unmoving, the huge eyes shining, and even the Duke knew there was not an ambush within half a mile of her. But on they went, showing their prize—but with Kintalla nearing, not a hand seemed ready to try the snatch. A mile from the eagle gates, where the road trees were thick, the Duke flashed the jeep in front, and himself stopped. Leaving the engine running, he got out to tap a rear wheel. Distantly, the cars behind him nodded to immobility in a pool of their own rear lights.

Raeburn dismounted to join the Duke where he put off time at the back of the van:

"If you want my view—"

"Not at all."

"It's not on. Or you have no right to stand this party here—"

"No one is at risk—"

"Drive on. Or I shall."

They hissed it under cover of the low, booming engine.

The Duke walked back into the van, leaving Raeburn to follow and shut the door. They drove normally to the gates and through—no singing, no talking. Higgins had the reduced floodlights on for them and the doors opened before they mounted the steps.

"Leave vehicles in front for the night," said the Duke. He was up the steps and inside ahead of them all. Joan Ker was quickly in among the boys, instructing simply. "Not a sound from you lot at this time of night. There's a baby in this house."

"I imagine," said Melfort, "that moderate conversation would be quite in order. It's a sizable place. I was hoping to be offered a nightcap of brandy."

The gamekeepers and other estate staff had come in, to wait just within the door. The sheikh moved away almost at once, and, since the Duke had disappeared to the inner hall, Lord Melfort addressed a question to the prince on the subject of the Balmoral salmon fishing, receiving an adequate and already expert reply. He would soon not be David any more, but a young man facing a lifetime of intrusion.

They waited some moments only, and the Duke was back to them, together with the Duchess and some staff members.

"My dear Edith," Melfort began, in his role as international spokesman.

"No need to worry, anybody," she said. "I had a feeling you would be back, so everything is ready. Wait here for coffee, first, if you like. Some might want a sandwich. Can we have the door closed?"

The trolley followed her. And the drinks. And soon she was sweeping the Markland party upstairs, with some whispered farewells over the staircase.

The Duke beckoned to Raeburn with a circular movement of his brandy glass. "Five minutes," he said. "Dining room."

Upstairs, the Duchess opened a bedroom door, smiling widely to Joan Ker. "Yours," she said, ushering her in. "I'll be back to see you are all right, once I've got the chaps into the dorm."

There were five beds installed in a great back bedroom, and while they waited Walter Fenton, the school captain, allocated them. The detective was installed in a bedroom opening off. He had carried in the bag from Mrs Gibson.

"Any complaints?" The Duchess was enjoying it all. Not many laughs there nowadays, Raeburn was thinking.

They assured her that everything was fine, ma'am, and the door was closed on them. Raeburn briefly caught the eye and the wide grin of young Hewitt.

In the dining room, as at the first council of war, the maps were again out, with Mr Porteous presiding over them. They were like the dead gravestones of a campaign, with no assault, no enemy. They took seats in the same places as before, and waited embarrassed for the Duke's judgment.

He sat at the head of the table, finishing some useless notation in his notebook. And then spoke:

"Some hitch in the plans. *Their* plans. We have no reason whatever to imagine that they have altered their ultimate intention, nor even their timing. They know we are inside. We know they are outside. The final affray may take a slightly altered turn, but all can be certain that the same object, the same methods, are afoot. It would have been impossible, therefore, to put him back into the school. We can protect him here."

"No doubt. He is safer here."

"I may say we should not expect any assault until daybreak. We shall all be aroused shortly before dawn."

"The cars—the jeeps. They should be immobilised. The ones in the drive."

"Not worth doing." The Duke reflected, like one who had solved the problem long since. "We could assemble another fleet in minutes. These are also under surveillance. We are unassailable on the roads."

"The road blocks . . . Are they in place?"

"Of course not. We do not want to impede entry. Leaving is another matter."

The Duke waited for further contributions. His eyes rested upon Raeburn, who had not spoken. He did, now:

"I see that the sheikh is not here. He's probably at his assignment. I believe that if he were here he might be inclined to question the desirability of preparing for an assault while we have a house full of boys, for whom I at least have a measure of responsibility. The proper course—"

Unhurried, with no change of pitch or pace, the Duke cut through: "Since, however, my guest is not here, I shall not presume to speak for him. But you are here. What have you to say? What is it that you would be inclined to question?"

Raeburn looked from him to Lord Melfort. But the second guest did not stir, so Raeburn's answer came undiverted. "Simply that I believe your judgment is wrong on the whole matter. There would be no consideration given to the payment of a ransom for that prince. All these recent kidnappings all over the world would forbid it. This is no more than I have told you before. It is my firm view. And I think that probably the kidnappers are coming to the same conclusion—if they ever thought otherwise."

The Duke's glass moved through a short arc, fending off other talk, closing the subject.

"Any other business?" he concluded, rising. "No? Staff outside will show you to your bedrooms. Turn in soon please. A busy day tomorrow."

For a few minutes Raeburn watched the black landscape from his window. But the bed was comfortable, and he was soon in and falling into sleep, his fingers touching the wooden plaque of the pistol butt under the pillow.

He had expected to wake gently before dawn, as he usually did, or even to hear the awakening tap. What happened was the crashing of the door as it flung full open to its hinges. The light was switched on blindingly, and MacFarlane was shaking him, kneeling over the bed in a panic of words.

"Oh, for Christ's sake, Mr Raeburn—get up! The baby's gone, and the Duke's demented. The wee Earl—they've stolen him."

CHAPTER 14

Raeburn found himself running along the corridor towards the head of the staircase. It had not taken him a minute to dress, since his clothes, with the pistol-weighted pocket, had been almost the only human items in the room. MacFarlane had left him at once, with: "I've to get the rest of them. You go down—"

A door opened, and the skirted and muffled Joan Ker came out. She seized him by the shoulder as he ran, dragging him to a halt:

"Stop running! You've no right to be strenuous in the middle of the night like this—"

"The child! The baby! You've heard—kidnapped—"

"I've heard. The next few hours are going to be hellish. But will you stop sprinting. We have to meet in the dining room."

"Let's hurry."

"Not yet. Is this what it has all been about? Why you're here? All this mystery? The journeys—plannings—whisperings—they were expecting it, and you were to—"

"Almost. Although they didn't expect it to be the child. They were certain—the Duke was—that it was to be the prince."

"That Duke is certain of everything. What about the Duchess—did she know?"

"I don't suppose so."

"The bastards! She would have got the baby out of here fast . . . Did you know somebody is waking the boys? They've to be in on it now. What do you think of that? I say 'No.' "

He thought. "Haven't had much of a chance to . . . Probably best to find something for them to do. We'll have to get the prince out. Away from Markland, too. The whole area is dangerous now. Come on."

The dining room was crowded, but Raeburn pushed them both to drawn-in seats. Most of the servants and staff stood round the walls. Mr Porteous had assembled his maps and was standing by them.

The Duke was at the head of the table, the normal swarthy hue of his face mottled white with hardly held anger and terror; it was the terror of unquestioned authority thwarted, as well as of an endless line pillaged to an end by the taking of the heir. The black eyes burned around, taking in the latecomers, and the bitten lips too were almost white. He had no time or apparent thought for the Duchess, who sat at his side, twisted, her two hands clutching at her mouth. Like all the others, she was waiting for him to put the unbelievable into words.

The room was dominated by a long, dry, whining sob coming from a nursery maid, ill-clad in some sort of overall uniform which she had not managed to put on properly. Instead of standing against the wall where she was no doubt intended to be, she was seated apart, legs useless, on a light chair which someone had pulled in for her, and it gave her an isolation like a prisoner. Her eyes were covered by her hands, for she could not look at the assembly, and her thin body heaved with the paroxysms.

The Duke suddenly lifted his stricken face. It had, to their horror—for there was hardly anyone there who had not thought him invulnerable—the naked look of unexpected human suffering. Raeburn looked to the boys, the five of whom were sitting in an orderly and astounded row at one end of the table, with Miller, the detective, at the wall behind the prince.

"Silence, all!" said the Duke, and as he spoke he reached out to the nursery maid and powerfully flicked her two hands away from her face. They dropped to her lap, and the face hung faint and uncontrolled. She might be fifteen, but the last twenty minutes of her life had struck away all thought of being adult, and she was a child, friendless in that terrible gathering.

"Tell us what you did." The Duke spoke with some more collected authority; not even severely, as if that mattered now. And to the others in the room, looking round he said: "This is all we know."

She drew air into her open mouth, and tried to steady. Began: ". . . I woke two o'clock"—it was a Highland voice—"when Nurse Shaw does the night feed. She always does that one. I heard her getting dressed more than usual—"

"Go on."

"Going to faint," whispered Joan.

The girl was holding on. "I woke again—wee while after three. Something wrong—I thought—Nurse not back to bed—said 'Nurse Shaw—Nurse Shaw' once or twice. I went into the nursery—cot empty —not even warm . . ." The mouth twisted open again in a long moan.

"Go on!"

"And then . . . I didn't know right what to do . . . I ran to tell Her Grace."

The girl drooped, with real sobbing and cries. Joan Ker got up quickly, reaching her as she fell forward. Mr Porteous came to help, and they lifted her back against the wall, laying her out on the floor where the light spared her. She started to talk again:

"Nurse Shaw—will look after him . . . good at babies . . . not harm
. . ." and the voice tailed off at last. They left her lying there and came
back to their seats.

"That is all we know," said the Duke.

The Duchess was able to speak. "Not much to add. He had been fed
and changed. I believe milk enough for some days in the freezer holdall
—it's gone. And changes, blankets, all the creams and things—the
nappy pail; and the carrycot was missing—Oh God! What will they
do!" She had a handkerchief, probably handed to her by the Duke, covering her face.

"Nothing," said the Duke. "We shall hear from them soon.
Straightforward ransom."

"Plan as before." Lord Melfort had already assumed the style of one
who expected to be in charge of operations.

Anger had made the paled face of the Duke look like a gargoyle, and
he trembled, but like a compressed spring. "They will be killed—every
one. Some additional planning and we shall start. None of them could
guess how far we have prepared. The child unhurt—each one of them
dead."

"The road blocks. The three farms," said Raeburn, conscious that
Joan Ker had turned to stare at him. "Get them set."

"The first thing done. All three have reported that they are in place.
Does everyone know where they are? Check your maps." To Raeburn:
"Read them off."

Raeburn had them in mind even without his map out. "Drumragit,
Laigh Torrs and Ben Crocket."

"Correct. It means that no one can leave the peninsula by road."

"The police." The Duchess had raised her head to whisper it.

"Not them!" The Duke was coming back to his cold normality. "This
is all arranged. Our scheme is ready; outsiders would ruin it—miss the
chances. In case anyone needs to be reminded, I say now that it will be
carried out implacably, by all present." In their presence, his shock was
distilling into a thrusting vengeance that put out of mind the cool sentence he had passed earlier upon the kidnappers of the prince.

"Baby!" The Duchess was openly crying. "Oh baby! Where is he?—If
he only had a name."

The Duke was settling to his accustomed pose of dissertation. Joan
Ker rose suddenly from her place beside Raeburn, went round the
table, and took the Duke by the shoulder, whispering into his ear so
that none of them could hear. It was unlikely that he was often whispered at.

When she had finished, he leaned away to look at her, saying: "Yes.
Certainly. That would be helpful." He raised the Duchess by a light

grip on her arm, while Joan Ker took her by elbow and waist and was leading her to the door before she realised she was being led.

"—I have something that will help—something you need—give you strength . . ." Laidlaw opened the door, closing it after them as the Duchess, unresisting, was supported out.

Speaking gently, Joan got her upstairs and into her bedroom.

"The matron, Mrs Gibson—she's a wonderful person—always makes me carry some medicine when I'm out with the boys, in case they fall off the bikes or anything. They're sort of aspirin things. Do please let me give you a couple. Absolutely harmless, but settling. You know?"

While speaking, she had dissolved two in a tumbler. Mrs Gibson had been giving them to the responsible excursion teachers ever since one boy years ago had had to be carried off a mountain, after lying there for hours with a shattered leg. They were a strong barbiturate, and Joan had risked two, knowing how much this woman needed sedation, and how little it would be possible for her or perhaps anyone to understand the work of the next hours.

The Duchess held the tumbler of clouded liquid. "Do you think I should . . . ?"

"Should? You must. Doctor's orders. Well, I'm a kind of nurse anyway. And lie down for a spell. I'm pretty sure they'll be up with good news before long."

"I should be doing something. I may be needed."

"Drink it. If you're needed, you are here. We can go downstairs in a minute."

She drank. "I hope it helps. I can't believe—"

"That's right. Lie down for a moment. It will help the waiting. You are brave."

"I'm not. I'm helpless. What can I do?"

"Just be ready to do it when the Duke asks."

The drug was working fast. She was weeping weakly from closed eyes. "Little boy! Why would they—? A baby . . ."

"It helps so much to know that she is a good nurse. No harm. No harm. He will be well looked after. Of course there must be an explanation. We'll go down and find out." Joan was murmuring now, phrases whose meaning she hardly thought of, but the fine, even note of reassurance which comes authentically to some.

She stopped talking soon, for the other woman was asleep. Joan took a fresh tissue and lightly wiped the tears away, took off the shoes, loosened some of the clothing, and settled her on the bed under a cover.

Going downstairs, she met the white-faced nursery maid being escorted on the way up:

"How are you feeling now?"

"Better a bit, thanks, Miss. I've to lie down."

"Of course. What's your name?"

"Janet, Miss. This is a terrible thing."

"It is indeed. Well, there's something for you to do, Janet." Joan told her about the Duchess and the sleeping draught. "Now, she won't waken for ten hours or more. You go into that bedroom and stretch out on the settee. Put a blanket over yourself. That means Her Grace will have someone she knows with her when she wakes up."

By the time Joan returned to the dining room, the Duke was finishing his planning talk. Staff had come in with packed ration haversacks for issue to each person. There was one at her place.

The Duke looked at her, in question.

"Asleep," she said. "Many hours. Janet is with her."

"Good. Thank you. We are moving now. Someone will put you in the picture. I take it there are no questions."

This time, Miller beat even the ready Lord Melfort to the issue.

"Excuse me, Your Grace, but there is one of great importance. It is within the authority of my duty to state that in no circumstances can His Royal Highness take part in this activity. This means unfortunately that neither can I. I have to request that you convey us both to Prestwick, where I shall ask for an aircraft of the Queen's Flight—"

"I should have thought that, as a necessary part of his education, the prince might be expected to participate in the rescue of one of his subjects who is the victim of an international conspiracy."

"He can't be asked to do that, sir. I'm sure you know that. Also the police must be informed. That is the law."

"I have made other plans. We do not need the police."

"I am sorry, sir, I shall have to make this quite clear. Unless you are prepared to alert the police immediately, I shall do so myself."

The Duke turned more fully towards him. "Do I understand that you are about to take over this operation?"

Miller paused. It was head-on now, and it could not be evaded. The prince stood up:

"May I, sir?" He addressed the Duke. "Sergeant Miller has a difficult job. I don't suppose he likes it very much, but my parents are grateful to him for his faithful service. In this case I should like to make my own decision, which is to join in getting the kidnappers and help to recover the baby. I hope we can do that soon."

"Thank you." The Duke looked briefly to Miller, who was shaking his head, with some words coming—"irregular—dangerous—have to report—"

"There is the question of the boys," Raeburn was saying, but Fenton, the school captain, came in: "Mr Raeburn, we consider ourselves committed. We must join in. We can all shoot. Of course, an exception in the case of young Hewitt here."

"He must be got back to Markland."

"No, please, sir—don't send me away. I can run messages or something—carry bundles . . ."

"Stay," said the Duke. "No one under this roof to drop out. Kill on sight. If they have harmed the child, wound them and leave to me . . . Signals—come on the radio every hour on the hour. Laidlaw will give out arms immediately from the gun room. What else? My own staff to take places now. Others can have two hours' sleep if needed before first light."

Raeburn asked: "Have you covered the possibility of a get-away by sea?"

"Not yet. A good point. I keep a light aircraft with two pilots at Allenhope. They will fly here and patrol the whole coast, looking out for strange craft approaching or leaving."

"They could scout over the moors as well."

"Yes. You see very little that way, but it might be useful. Nothing will substitute for footwork at ground level. That is all. I shall give out first locations. To be changed with circumstances. Check watches."

They started to disperse, Joan Ker moving the boys upstairs. The Duke, his hands suddenly shaking, the face sagging, wiped sweat away from his forehead. Raeburn sat and looked at him, until the Duke took his stare.

"You?" said the Duke, after a time.

"I thought of going to join the sheikh at Talla Head. Now."

"Yes. Do so. Tell him of the latest event. I do not think he will be surprised." The Duke grimaced, catching himself again at once. "The sheikh inclined to your own theory, that the prince might not be the target. See that he knows about the hourly calls." He walked with Raeburn to the door.

"Dr Coulson ought to be told. By telephone?" Raeburn asked.

"I shall do it myself, some time before the party is due to be back at Markland."

Higgins opened the door. "No lights, Higgins. We should go on for as long as possible seeming to have failed to notice anything wrong." He turned to Raeburn as if the man was not there. "Higgins saw and heard nothing. The nurse left the house by a window from the side corridor, where a man was waiting. The window was left open, and their footprints are to be seen in a rose-bed, but they disappear on the gravel and the dry turf beyond. Reid and MacFarlane will look again by day, but I do not think they will find anything more." He took jeep keys from a shelf and handed them over. The door closed.

The jeep was the only thing that moved on the short journey to Talla Head. On the hard, short grass below the road, dipping to where the cliff fell away sheer to its cleft a few yards ahead, was parked the giant open car of the sheikh, who was not in sight. Raeburn braked the jeep off the road, and walked round in front of the headlamps, letting the beams fall full upon him. The sheikh stepped forward from the bedded boulders which perched there.

"What news? What events have been going on since I left the comforts provided by my friend the Duke?"

Raeburn told him. The sheikh made a minimum of interruption, so that the story did not take long.

"Not surprising," he said when it was finished. "Such a chance was in your mind too."

He mounted the driving seat of his superb car, stepping easily over the low door. "Come and see this," he said. Raeburn put out his jeep's lights and got in beside the sheikh, who took his hand in the near darkness and laid it upon a switch at the side of the steering wheel.

"That is the switch of the headlamps. Press down."

The two beams leapt like sunrays down the gully. Moving towards each other, they met and spread more than a hundred yards from the car, and did not become misted with distance before they fell on the sea and the cliff foot four times that distance further on. Raeburn felt almost an excitement as he watched the intrusion of the unwinking flash open the sea to them, when it should have been unseen at that hour. The high cliff walls of the gully, closing in a wedge to the lower level on which the car stood, were white-dotted with nesting birds, some of whom raised their heads so that the eyes sparkled, though none lifted to fly. Nearer to the car, and around it, there was a backward effulgence lighting the boulders and even the start of the land dykes. Standing aside, two car-lengths away, on a tripod firmly bedded, was the rocket-launcher, aimed down, and the sheikh pointed to this:

"Trained on the meeting point of the beams; which is about right, I think. You can see how a helicopter, provided it was piloted to be almost at sea level, could reach the coast here and mount into land, probably with the help of a spotlight, and quite sheltered from radar detection by the cliffs on either side. The weapon swivels as necessary, but I have fixed it in the present position. At the right moment you will switch on the lamps. But I think we shall have them off in the meantime. No point in giving ourselves away."

The night came back to a deeper darkness than ever as the switch went off.

"There is no doubt that you can find the switch? By that time I shall be by the rocket-launcher."

"No. Just below the wheel rim here. I've got it."

"Good. Then we can wait here comfortably. I have enjoyed my night here. It is even like the desert, with which we keep in touch, for we Arabs may perhaps have to go back to it one day. The sea is like the sand. There are even stars."

"We have to make radio contact by walkie-talkie. Every hour on the hour."

"We may have news. It is nearly thirty minutes to pass first."

"I hope they come. We can't miss them from here." Raeburn was aware of a growing hope for action.

"Yes. It requires patience. But a helicopter arrival would remove all doubt. It would demonstrate that the child is still within the territory of the Duke and that they have not succeeded in bringing it out."

It was still dark, with no touch yet of dawn, but their eyes came to see the nearer shapes, and the cliff tops edging the plain of the sky.

"Tell me again," said the sheikh, smiling, "the words which the royal boy used to the Duke."

Raeburn repeated the simple statement by which the prince had made the decision to stay.

"He said well. These are a ruler's words. I am a ruler. I understand. The Duke has much power and riches, but he is not a ruler. He would like to be."

"Our Duke looks as if this will kill him."

The sheikh looked towards him. "Kill him . . . ? Anger, certainly, because of a failure of judgment. Perhaps also because of the death of an heir. But to die of sorrow requires much practice in compassion. In this regard your Duke might be said to be a desert man."

"The Duchess—she's shattered. For her sake alone I'd do anything to get this child back."

There was a faint shrug somewhere in the darkness. Their dialogue had run slowly, with silences, and another lengthy one followed. Then the sheikh added: "We get the child back, safely, because enemies must not prevail. This is virtually a religious matter. Your Bible is vague on this and certain other points."

Some fragments of conversation. Long pauses to listen at the night air. Sheep and moorland birds spoke occasionally from the landward side, but the seabirds were largely silent, and although the small wind kept the waves low, an occasional wandering crest of swell met another in the dark and boomed briefly on the rock headland out of sight.

Both heard it at the same time: a far-off stroking disturbance of the air rather than a sound; fading out entirely for seconds, but each time nearer—faster. They had each other's eyes by now, heads turned to put an ear to the sea and the noise. Soon it was a steady beat, ragged with explosions.

"The switch!" said the sheikh. "Hand on switch. Not on yet! Make no mistake. Switch when I order."

He was out of the car and a mere shadow now behind the weapon, making a click or two with some part of the apparatus.

It was now clearly a helicopter, steering to this part of the coast, and the noise came from low down. For long seconds it made no seeming progress, but beat down there out of sight.

"Feeling his way in," said Raeburn.

"Yes. So I think."

There was suddenly a downward and forward light staring at the sea, looking ahead from some frail cage. They could see the helicopter clearly now, fingering in between the parted cliffs, looking for the sea-ward edge of the shoreline, with its tumbled rocks and weed. So it crept on and up, the engine noise filling the canyon. Will I hear him ask for the lights, Raeburn was saying to himself in a thud of panic.

"Switch!"

It did not appear even to be a shout, but the sheikh's voice bit the air like a blade. The blast of light from the car poured straight down the slope, lifting off the grass to the filled gorge.

It was half again as far away as the meeting points of the headlamps, but still brilliantly lit so that it shone like a moving ornament. The interior could be seen from front to back, like a skeleton, with the long tail and its far rotor openwork like a frail girder. There was one man only inside, open-shirted, and black-haired. He flew on for a second or two, crawling at the cautious first pace over the ground, pushing up a hand to shade his eyes.

They could see the hand on the controls tensing and jerking, and the machine started to lift and surge, coming up to forward speed and try-ing to rise out of the light beam. He had been slightly below the headlamps' full glare, and this new boost brought him to the middle of the point where the beams met—the point to which the sheikh's weapon was aimed and fixed.

Raeburn seemed to hear no more than the rushing whisper of the firing. What he heard and saw was the explosion as the missile hit the helicopter, waist-high at the pilot himself. The man, nearer now, seemed to sit on stoically as the burst of the explosion flashed around him ruinously. It must have killed him at once, but the craft flew on at its new speed.

It had been tilted upward for the climb out of danger, and it was at this angle that it was now making for the low part of the cliff edge where the cars were parked. Raeburn had the swift feeling that it was going to land on the car where he sat, but although his reflexes had never felt more in tune—where had this late sickness and heaviness gone?—he sat there, rather than jumping and running.

Heaved up at an angle of forty-five degrees for the climb which it would never now make, the helicopter laboured in at a straight line for the turf. The engine was whining and racing to extinction, shuddering where two broken blades, sheared halfway down their length by some flying fragments thrown up by the shell burst, threw the craft all out of balance and were about to tear themselves off the hub. So labouring—and it took long—the helicopter squattered slowly to the turf, crossed the edge of the abyss below, and dropped.

Because of the high upward angle at which it had been flying, undirected, the long tail was low, and took the ground first. By the time the tail rotor rested on the grass, screaming itself to twisted decoration, the aircraft was stopped and ready to crash straight down. It stood for a moment on the crumpled tail rotor, then the slender tail bent with the weight and, doubling, let the main body fall forward on to the grass, two car-lengths in front of the men there. For a moment they could see every bolt and rivet of it, and the dead eyes of the man within, while the engine screamed itself to a stop.

"Back!" It was the sheikh's voice. "It may explode."

Leaving the headlights on, Raeburn jumped and ran. They met at the edge of the boulders.

"This is far enough," said the sheikh. "We shall soon know."

They watched. There were no flames or sparks in the wreckage, but they could hear the burst petrol tanks gushing and then dribbling their load over the cliff edge. They waited, the light drenching that concentrated disaster, which like the man within lay dead and cooling, the only sound from it the creaking and snapping of new tensions and loosenings. Even that mainly stopped at last.

"Enough," said the sheikh, stepping forward. "Let us see."

"That was good shooting," said Raeburn. "One shot. All in the preparation, I suppose."

"Yes. You should have left the car. It might have dropped on you."

"It didn't seem to me that you left the gun."

"No, of course not, I had to reload. Always reload. We may have another visitor. If not, remind me to unload."

The wreckage was perched, thinly embedded, so near to the edge of the cliff that they could not walk about it. The cabin seemed empty except for the sundered man and what was probably his kit bundle. Raeburn went to drive the jeep up close, with its headlamps on, too, so that there was as much light as possible.

They opened the door to get at the figure of the pilot, now slumped and weltering. It was the sheikh who reached in to snap off the safety belt, and heave the body out on to the grass. As the pilot came off the seat, the helicopter trembled out of balance, and seemed ready to tip over the edge.

The upper half of the body seemed untouched, but the lower half, from the middle down where the shell had hit, was a fearsome bag of intestines and human frailty, with the legs hardly holding on by shreds of sinew.

The hair was plastered dark, the face Asiatic, close-eyed. It looked at them, all defiance or protest gone.

"What do you think?" the sheikh asked.

"I think I'd say Japanese rather than Chinese," Raeburn thought. "Don't know why—something about the mouth and the teeth."

"Probably. However," said the sheikh, making for his car, "there are some things we can proceed with now." He turned: "How long until the five-o'clock call-up?"

By the light of the car lamps Raeburn read. "About ten minutes."

"That is time."

The sheikh opened lockers, pushed into shelves, and came back with a camera dangling, and a pistol.

"Have we any way," he asked, "of identifying this one?"

"I shouldn't think for sure, although Dale or Sylvester might know which of them had flying qualifications." He had his own notes out. "But this might be the one called Lu Satu. It's the best we can do in the meantime."

"They have a way of measuring heads, ears . . . And of course there's colour of eyes—hand shapes—"

"Quite—all skilled things we can leave to the experts." The sheikh bent to arm's-length of the dead man, his pistol pointing, and shot him through the middle of the forehead. A tremor, almost a frown, seemed to cross the dead face, and the hole was left in the centre above the uninterested eyes.

"This is a very valuable camera, expensive, with flash built in." The sheikh was rigging it. "I think it will do a job as good as can be done by the Duke's people. Let us see."

He leaned over, focusing, and clicked. The flash of the exposure was trifling compared with the car lights. "One or two more, perhaps. We must not leave room for criticism."

In turn, the electronic slave pushed out its piece of pasteboard, three times.

He handed over the small pack to Raeburn. "What do you think?"

They were indeed probably better than Sylvester's. Expertly good enough for identification.

It was moving to five o'clock. They switched off the car lights and waited for the Duke's call.

He came on exactly at the hour:

"Report. Any order. Who has action?"

It was the sheikh who responded at once. "We. At Talla Head. We have the helicopter and the pilot. Both dead."

"Are they on land?"

"Yes."

"Accessible?"

"Yes."

"I shall come. Wait there. Any other action?"

"Four." MacFarlane's deferential voice came over. "There was shooting somewhere near the top of the Doon. A few shots—one way only. I'll go there as soon as it's day."

"Where are you now?"

"Top of Drumdar, Your Grace."

"Report at six. Light enough then. Out. Come in all in order."

He called through his list in order now, but no one had anything to add. Finally: "On my way to Talla Head. Out."

His car lights were soon sweeping the back of the hills that ran down there to the sea, and shortly he drew up and was over to them. They told him what had happened, while he stepped about the ruin of man and machine. It was he who pushed into the mulch of gut and rag to get at the pockets, but there seemed to be nothing identifiable. They held the helicopter steady while he hooked in for the bundle of kit. This he opened in front of the lights, tipping out the contents on the turf. They were items of clothing only, and personal things. He flung them back inside the machine.

"The photographs will be sufficient." He kept them. "We must get this off the cliff and over. It could be seen from the air and the road."

They thrust the dead man back into his command, Raeburn bringing a few of the smaller scattered boulders to drop into the forepart below the instrument panel.

"The jeep. Push it over with the jeep." The Duke looked to Raeburn. "Shall I drive it?"

"No. I'm in charge of this vehicle."

"Careful then. Turf is slippery."

Raeburn edged the jeep on the slant, in the lowest gear, until it touched the battered front of the helicopter with its tough fender. An inch or two at a time, he crept the vehicle into the point of resistance, with the front of the aircraft compressed. It started to slide, and all at once was clear of him, heaving backwards out of sight. They got an impression, by the dropped reflection of the light, of a mangled machine cartwheeling out of sight, until the sea took it with a splash.

"Back off carefully," said the Duke.

Putting the tilting jeep into lowest reverse, Raeburn started to edge away from the cliff side. There was a trick to it, and it was one he didn't know. Taking the power, the car slid suddenly sideways to his left, scooping the skin off the turf like shaving lather. Without a grip, it was helpless. He came out of gear, and they were still going downhill.

"Get out!" It was the Duke.

Raeburn tried it again, gingerly into low gear, and pulled the clutch. The wheels span, searching for a grip, and they were on the edge, the near-side wheels dropping. Raeburn had the door open and stepped out with a thrusting spring behind him, which with the jeep going over left him only upright on the rim of the drop. His feet slipped from under him, and, correcting with arms waving, he leaned forward above the sea, which the vehicle was now hitting, to pause and sink. Toppling after it, he felt a single hand gripping at each ankle, so that he dangled above the sea, but held.

The Duke and the sheikh were lying behind him where they had flung and reached. With hand and toes going, in the flood of the headlamps, they started to press their way back, and were able to stand up.

"No words. No talk." This was the Duke.

"But thanks." Raeburn looked into the Duke's face to say it. The other drew back from him, as if remembering again the small life he could not succour. He looked thinly from Raeburn to the sheikh, and turned from them, saying: "Back to Kintalla. That boy! That boy!"

He turned and left them, and drove away, leaving them both to follow in the sheikh's car. Day was breaking.

CHAPTER 15

Within the gates of Kintalla Castle, at the steps, the Duke was out and waiting for them. Impassive with outrage and hate, he was a pillar of icy revenge. These emotions—the wrong word for him—were somewhere behind that practised face, terrible with the purpose of two score generations. But the briefly overmastering instinct that had made him turn his back on them at the cliff top was not there now, and there was no sign on the features of deprivation, of self-pity.

It seemed natural for him to take a stalking rifle from the rear seat of his car, and sling it from one shoulder. Silently he waited for Raeburn and the sheikh to join him, and they went up the steps together, the door opening as if he exuded a power ray.

Joan Ker stepped out: "The Duchess is still sleeping."

"Yes." He stepped round her, and past Higgins into the hall. Laidlaw was there. The Duke spoke:

"A car for Mr Raeburn. Also rations. I take it yours went over Talla Head in the jeep."

"Yes."

"Later rations for the schoolboys. Tell them to report downstairs at six-thirty."

"What *about* the boys?" Raeburn asked.

"The moor. They shall be posted at any blank spots, once we have seen the dispositions on Mr Porteous's map." The Duke led the way to the dining room, already strewn with reeking breakfast casseroles, and spread also with the maps and instruments of the first meeting there. As the time moved up to six o'clock, the Duke told about the shoot-down at Talla Head, and the sheikh moved busily and quietly among the breakfast pots, eating with some unbelievably huge instinct developed by centuries of intermittent hunger. Others joined him as they listened, standing and eating.

"Forgive me," said the sheikh. "I will return immediately to Talla Head. We may have another visitor—"

". . . so we have accounted certainly for three of the eight: Martinu, Panacz and now Lu Satu, who flew the helicopter. I do not think it likely there will be another helicopter, but it is as well to be ready. The five others are: Nannie Shaw, with outstanding credentials—she is the woman Cove, and she has the baby; Fung has been away for two days from the restaurant near Dumfries where he worked; Konski is also loose somewhere—that is the man Biros of Markland. The head of them, Casio—we must assume he is on Kintalla estate somewhere, probably along with O'Connor. That is all. They cannot get out. The three road blocks are in position, and are being manned, armed, by the farmers concerned. Except in the case of Mr Galloway, whose son is mounting guard at the block while Mr Galloway, of Drumragit, is here, as you can see. As the morning advances the schoolboys will be placed in reasonably protected hides on the moor, covering areas where there are substantial blanks at present. Mr Porteous, please show us these spots. Mr Raeburn at least will want to take a note."

Mr Porteous had the places already marked with prominent blue crosses. "Each is well protected, Your Grace. I shall drop them by car shortly, with food and so on for the day, instructing them as to how to improve the cover. They can be called back in at nightfall—"

"By which time it will be all over. And we can celebrate," Lord Melfort broke in, from the only deep armchair.

"Ah, yes—Melfort." It was the Duke who replied. "You were of course posted to the knoll above Ben Crocket Farm. What brings you here?"

The country's most celebrated diplomat and familiar of the Duke, so far as was known, deliberated for a moment, and then swung to his feet with an obedient salute. "Ready, sir!" he shouted in an unexpectedly bantering tone, to cover the rebuke. "Of course, I'm not amusing anybody, even myself, but we shall finish the job early this day. It is no time for joking. I came here in fact to participate in the hourly round-up—especially to hear about the Doon shooting."

They were all looking at watches, where six o'clock was nearing. The Duke, at the table, pulled a microphone towards himself. It must have been newly connected to an outside transmission aerial, and he did not use walkie-talkie.

MacFarlane from the Doon was the only one with news.

"I'm here on the top, Your Grace. A queer thing this—Miller the detective is here, fair knocked-out. No—he's alive, all right, but he's been creased by a bullet along the side of the skull and he is fair senseless. No sign of anybody—Miller hadn't fired—but it must have been like a club on the head of him. He's not showing any sign of coming round."

"Stay with him." The Duke went the rounds of his scattered team, throwing in the death of Lu Satu and the bringing down of the helicopter. At the end he pushed the microphone back to the wall:

"That's a useful turn-out. The detective fellow was going to be a nuisance. I suppose he went up there before dawn."

"Didn't want anyone to hog his pitch," said Raeburn.

"That must be it."

Raeburn had gathered a fresh haversack of rations and was at the door.

"Where are *you* going?" It was Joan Ker; but the Duke made the same query with his eyebrows.

"I'll start at the Doon—must see this. I suggest you get the four senior schoolboys as their first job to take a stretcher up the Doon and bring back Miller. He'd better lie up here. Somebody can drive them all there—say in the school van."

"Yes—Reid," said the Duke, and turned to other things.

"You will perhaps run me back to Talla Head." It was the sheikh asking. "My own car parked there would perhaps be too noticeable."

"Come on." They were on the way out. Higgins handed Raeburn a set of car keys.

"Take care!" said Joan, following them.

"Yes, of course. Stand by the Duchess. Her name is Edith."

They came to Talla Head, finding the weapon still pointing on a down slope to the sea. The spilled petrol had dried, and the scars were minor where the helicopter and the jeep had finished their landward voyages.

"Yes—this will be adequate." The sheikh had some new contentment within himself, as if he still coiled some far-down spring. "They cannot allow the helicopter to be a mere write-off. I shall have a meeting with someone or another."

He turned to admit Raeburn for a brief moment into a distant affability. "You are fortunate. Not many really sick men have an opportunity to have face-to-face dealings with enemies. Weapons!—war!—" he gestured high. "It is all a gift of fortune. Good luck! God—or Allah—be with you." It was a phrase that Raeburn could see being put together carefully, so that it would not diminish in the future times when the whole tale would be told in some far different setting.

When he reached the Doon, Raeburn was conscious he was climbing the first slopes almost from tree to tree, looking round in the windy low branches, and with his pistol in his hand. The top of the scarped hill had no trees, and, trudging the bare upward turf, Raeburn soon saw that MacFarlane had come to the edge and was looking down at him.

"You're going well, I will say, sir." The man held a hand out and pulled him firmly over the final rim. "Come you and look at what I have here."

Miller the royal detective was laid out no doubt somewhat more tidily than he had been when first struck down. They knelt over him,

MacFarlane lifting the head by the hair, and tilting for Raeburn to see: "What do you make of that, now?"

It was a deep furrow, with the bleeding now stopped, running from above the right ear to the first of the temple. The skull bone, which had not been broken or pierced, showed white here and there among the lifted flesh and hair.

"I left it for somebody to see first; but it should be bandaged. I'll do it now. He was lucky." And MacFarlane gouged some unguent into the wound and firmly bandaged a noble-looking coronet of linen around the forehead and to the back.

"Very professional," said Raeburn.

"Aye. Mind you, it was real handy the way he was the one that got hit. He was going to be a trouble."

"When do you think he will come round?"

"Ach well, do you know, sir—it might be a wee while." MacFarlane was packing his first-aid kit, looking aside. "It's a funny thing you should ask that. I'm not sure he would be terrible useful to us—so—so—"

"So—," Raeburn finished for him, "—so you gave him a double badger."

"You're nearly right, Mr Raeburn." MacFarlane was seriously satisfied. "In fact I gave him a stag—a dart for the likes of a Sutherland royal. They're the hardiest. What day is this? Wednesday? It'll keep him out of mischief until Friday midday at the least."

Raeburn held his peace until he caught the man's straying eye. "You are taking on something, knocking out a royal detective."

MacFarlane was suddenly not evasive. "Mr Raeburn, if he knows what's good for him he'll sleep on. The Duke is his own law and that's the side I'm on. Those that have to do with him, he sees them right."

"Who am I," Raeburn said, "to argue with that? What now?"

"We get this Miller off the mountain."

Raeburn told him then about the stretcher party.

"Man, sir, that was thoughtful of you. Here was I thinking I'd have to heft him down like a hill pony. We'll do it in style."

"Why do you think he got fired at?"

"I would say for sure it was because they were going to land the helicopter here and there was somebody sent up to see that the ground was clear. Right enough, they meant to kill him. Thought they had, maybe."

"He was lucky, then."

"Just what I said."

Raeburn left him to organise the stretcher party of boys, and the last he saw of MacFarlane the gamekeeper had a full telescope out and was sweeping the farthest moor. Others of his kind were doing the same, and hardly a leaf would move on the open face of Kintalla estate without being seen, and also identified. These were men trained to notice and interpret. And they knew sounds, too. Sometime, from some direction, one of them would hear a child's cry.

He took his car southward almost to the lighthouse, to the edge of the fence where the Duke's estate marched with the lands of the Northern Lighthouse Board. On that road, all the way, there would be here and there someone of the Duke's people noting his progress—probably sighting him with a rifle, if only to keep themselves alert. One or two from the other side—from the enemy—might be doing the same thing.

Far south on that road, at the outer edge of a bicycle run from Markland, there was an empty ancient farmhouse dropping into ruin. He had seen it the time they had come here on one of Joan Ker's runs, and it exercised his mind to think there might be a hiding place there, with its flat ground and the smooth straight stretch of road where not only a helicopter but a light aircraft might land and take off. Above, hardly ever out of hearing now, was the private jet aircraft which the Duke had sent to patrol the estate area, circling monotonously round the coast, recording small boat movements, relaying them by some means to the master.

When the seven-o'clock call came, Raeburn was already in place. On the hillside above the ruin was the collapsed walling of a sheep fank, a fold where lambing sheep gathered in the spring to drop their sprawling young, or where, later in the autumn, men and dogs herded them for the separation. There was dry grass inside, and Raeburn built himself a rampart with a loophole through which he could deploy his binoculars as well as the rifle they had given him at the castle. There was a tempting aggressive satisfaction in the completeness that this gave.

Dale came in first on the hourly call, reporting from some spot near a moor loch. He had seen nothing move since daybreak, and had not been at Kintalla for the six-o'clock gathering.

". . . was wondering if the boys are in place, sir . . . would appreciate having the map markings. We ought all to know every pinpoint, in case of stray shooting . . ."

"Not a subject for broadcast. Anyone entitled can have the readings from the castle map by calling. Note everybody, also, there will be no stray shooting. Shoot to kill only. Out."

The Duke called in all his numbers, including those still with him at Kintalla. "Two still here," he said of Sylvester, "Out," and Raeburn could imagine what the secretarial assistant was busy at. Something to do with the final arrangements for Panacz, perhaps even now disinterred from under the leaves and branches near to the Kintalla walls. Reid he used to reinforce MacFarlane, who came in at once on the instruction of "Four."

"Aye. Stretcher party here and away. All in order. Am I moving my position?"

"No. You stay. When Five has finished his present assignment, he will take up duty on the neighbouring height. Are we all familiar with the name and location of the neighbouring height? Out. Come in, Five."

"I'm in," Reid replied. "Have drawn in to roadside along with the bearers and load. Headquarters in two minutes. Otherwise blank."

"Seven has a dispersal duty to do immediately." It was the Duke reminding them that Mr Porteous was due to drop the boys at their moor posts. "He will not be called. Out. Come in, Six."

Raeburn answered: "I have taken up watch at a spot marked number 24 on my original map with references which you have." Heavens, could it be less than four days ago? "An interesting building in the neighbourhood which might be promising."

"Where is this?" It was Lord Melfort's voice, out of turn, and anxious that he might be missing something.

"Wait." It was the Duke. Over the air they could hear the rustle among his maps, even a whispering—probably with Mr Porteous. He seemed to turn aside from this to say offhandedly: "Conversation with six only, please." Shortly:

"Yes. Location found and understood. And agreed. If nothing there, you may be asked to move north by mid-morning. Out."

He reached the sheikh on the Eleven call, and was told: "Do not think I am running out of patience, but I am growing troubled at the lack of action. We miss an opportunity."

"Explain."

"They ought by now to have made an attempt to reach the helicopter entry point surreptitiously. At least some of them must have heard the rocket shot. There is good ground cover here—enough to make the trial possible."

"Quite. But there may not be enough ground cover from their present main point. Still, I agree. A move may have to be forced. Please wait."

"Naturally."

"Out. Thirteen."

"It becomes more clear all the time." Lord Melfort was losing no time. "There can be no remaining doubt that information is leaking from our group. These current signals are being tapped. Nothing else explains the situation just described by Sheikh Ibn." Raeburn wondered if this was the sheikh's real name. It was one of the many things he might have to find out if the trivia of life were to extend for him beyond tomorrow night. "We are probably at the stage when an intricate code is required to deal with even the simplest messages. I was reluctant to develop this idea too far on an earlier occasion—"

"I am sure most of us remember your contribution most clearly. You may be right. It will have been noticed that much of the information we have just passed is phrased in somewhat less precise terms. Also that many of the items, in any case, are of such a nature that they might as well be in clear. Have you any immediate solution?"

"Perhaps not in precise terms. I shall give it some thought. In the meantime I thought it necessary to remind—"

"Of course. All are glad to have the warning repeated. Are you in position?"

"Certainly. I am on the hillside above Ben Crocket."

"Thank you. We have all—including any intruders—heard of that with deep interest. Out."

There was little difference in the pattern of the next two hourly exchanges. Laidlaw had fired at a moving shadow in the heather, and the Duke had opened the radio-call system to probe this. The head gamekeeper was certain there had been something there, on the high ridge of land that ran down the peninsula of Kintalla, but there were no traces of a hit, and the thing had gone. Otherwise, the morning was still.

For his part, Raeburn had memorised every stone of the ruined cottage where he felt at first there might be shelter for what they sought. His ears were stretched to listen for a baby sound, but only the week-old lambs were speaking, and there reached to him from the stones of the ruin an undeniable emptiness that persuaded him at last there could be nobody there.

He said this to the Duke on one of the late-morning round-ups, and it was agreed he should go to relieve Melfort. It was not said what new task Lord Melfort would be assigned to. Raeburn's last act on leaving his stance was to walk direct to the cottage and push into the ruins through the old splintered entrance door. No human was there, but among the ruins of floorboards and shelving, the crushed tangle of bedsteads tumbled by roof slates, an old ewe stood staring dully at a dead lamb that had not survived a day. And she looked up at him, almost without fear, almost hopefully, as a member of that two-legged race that mostly interrupted such lives as hers to bring both aid and terror.

He came cautiously and slowing to the farm of Ben Crocket. It was past midday now and the farm lay on the southward slope of the hill above, facing the sun, seeming a blessed place of peace and content, probably with a long, quiet record of small harvests and herds sheltered against the hard days of that place, and always gathered in. Raeburn parked his car and watched the farm for a time through his glasses. He could see the heavy truckload which formed the road block, drawn across at a place opposite the entrance to the farm where the road narrowed between dykes and there was no way round for another vehicle moving on the highway. Beside it, in the sun, a man—it would be Hislop, the farmer—sat on a chair dragged out into the middle of the road. A heavy coat was loose about his shoulders, there was a rifle across his knees, and he was reading a book. Raeburn suddenly ached to know what book it was.

He scanned the high slope of the hill, searching for Lord Melfort. No doubt Melfort was seeing him, and taking his time about coming down. He would be expecting to be relieved. So Raeburn went back to the car, round a bend where a small wood cut out the farm, to collect his gear. His food haversack was there, and so was the rifle, and even the pistol which he had slipped out of his hip pocket, where it was taking bites out of him. Before he opened the door, he took another sweep of the landscape with his binoculars, this time towards the other side of the valley, where lower moor and brae ran lumpily towards Kintalla.

Across the moor there was a figure running, a skirted figure, bright with wool to the neck, and he realised with a stound of pleasure that it was Joan Ker.

She had seen him, probably by recognising the car, and she was waving arms as she ran. He kept the glasses on her, not waving yet, but holding the view, when he felt the presence of someone else. He was dropping the glasses from his face as the voice said: "Raeburn."

Biros was there, stepping out from behind the low hedge that outlined the wood.

"Konski," said Raeburn.

His weapons were in the car, but he slung off the glasses quickly, for their dangling would hamper him, and moved out to the centre of the road. If Konski had a weapon he made no move to use it. Instead, coming forward on the capable legs, there was something professional and destructive in the way he advanced, raised off his heels, and stepping that way rather than walking. His hands were already in front of him, flat-palmed, chopping and weaving as if to try not only the muscles that made them scythe and move, but the thickness of the air, the resistance they would have to meet before they reached and broke bones. His face was not so much inscrutable as quite without expression, as if even the small effort required to grimace with hate was better drained off by the explosive force he was now visibly gathering in to his shoulders and hips.

He stopped for a second, half crouching, in one of the karate-style poses which had always seemed to Raeburn to be pretentious and over-decorative for a fighting man—the hands with the fingers too far forward, leaving, for a start, the wrists too exposed to an opponent of the same art. Still, it was clear that this was how they were to come together, and Raeburn marvelled briefly at the unwise arrogance of bearing that brought Konski forward again, the outside edges of his hands moving suddenly in axe-like sweeps to break or paralyse his forearms. Certainly they moved fast, these arms with their palm blades.

The early chops were easy to avoid, and Raeburn was conscious as the combat developed that he was probably moving too far out of reach for every group of strokes. At the height of his playing heyday he had found himself on great occasions, twice most years, against the two Welshmen who were the fastest and hardest flank forwards in the world, and having to avoid them both at once. And, in addition, to win a ball and get it away, himself unscathed. Willie Guthrie, the wee Hawick man who served him the ball from the base of the scrum—Hawick almost never had international scrum halves, so Willie had had to be specially good—could put it out (some university chap had calculated) at nearly seventy miles an hour, and Raeburn's job was to pick this missile out of the air safely, and do something substantial with it, while keeping a tail of the eye open for Evans and Roberts (they were always called Evans or Roberts. He had more than once, in parties after the big games, ventured to express sorrow for the Welsh predicament, of never having had nearly enough clans, though otherwise so adequate a people).

These lightly inconsequential thoughts were going through Raeburn's head as he swayed in front of the man who was trying to kill him. After a time Konski abandoned the arm chops and started with the legs, swivelling fast on his well-planted feet and making a great sweep sideways with one or other of his legs, stiff at the knee, the sole of the foot flattened to break a knee joint, or even, very improbable with a weaving opponent, to get into the groin.

To Raeburn, it seemed unbelievable. But he watched it with interest for a few moves, moving now nearer to Konski and swaying off no farther than was needed. He had never seen this fighting art except in films, and had dismissed it as some sort of badly photographed trick, for it was inconceivable that any combatant would for so comparatively long a swerve actually turn his back upon a lively opponent. But here was this fellow—at least he wasn't shouting "Hoi!"—swinging round repeatedly, a long leg stretched towards him, when of course he wasn't there—and for a fraction of a second losing sight of Raeburn altogether.

It made Raeburn move in and in. Always nearer to the death-dealing, swinging foot. There seemed quite a long period during which he was out of sight. As the foot swung to break him, he let the movement go on, trying one or two very brief but menacing gestures in that interregnum to which the unsighted Konski never even reacted. By this time Raeburn knew that, when he surely won this fight, it would not be by any of the graceful avoidances for which he had been renowned.

There came a series of foot attacks when even Konski was more concerned with the ritual of his own movements than with their effect. There was first, as the foot swung, a swift glance under the armpit at Raeburn, but immediately the swinging body blotted out the target, Raeburn saw his chance and quickly took it.

Here was the striking foot, swinging round again. He plucked the foot out of the air, moving in, took it safely and suddenly in his two hands, and broke it off. Every bone on both sides of the ankle snapped and crumbled, and Konski would never again walk on that foot, attached now only by a sock of skin. As he bent on the other leg with the terrible pain, a bubble of anguish seething through his almost closed lips, Raeburn slid his hands further up the leg, took the limb from ankle to knee, and broke it like a dry stick across his own leg. He let the broken man fall upon the ground. Raeburn stood back.

Konski, murmuring with the agony and the unbelievable fact of it, scrabbled upon the ground. He got his hands under him, and heaved himself upright upon the one good leg.

He hardly had time to look at Raeburn, wondering with defiance, before he fell again. A whine had come from the trees, and only Raeburn was near enough to see the scoop that the bullet took out of the base of the skull. Konski went down gently this time, and he was dead.

Lord Melfort was stepping forward from the trees.

"I must say," he said to Raeburn, "I enjoyed that. Thank you for setting him up for me." He bent over, pointing the pistol and silencer down at the dead man. "We'd better finish this, in tidy fashion."

"Not more! Not more!" And Joan Ker, stricken, ran from the dyke where she had watched. But, even knowing she was there, Melfort found no difficulty in concluding his share in the ritual. He leaned casually over and shot Konski precisely through the middle of the forehead.

"There—I should have done that the first time—that's what the Duke wants. Of course, small arms are not my weapons." He straightened up, with his stalking rifle still slung upon a shoulder. "I thought we had better use the silencer. We didn't want the good farmer Hislop coming upon us like the wrath of God. I stopped to have a word with him on the way down. A severe man—reading Bacon's *Essays.*"

Melfort was busying himself about the car, while Raeburn looked round for Joan. She was sitting, back turned to them, on a low boulder which had fallen from the dry dyke, and she had her head buried in her hands. He left her for the moment.

His gear had been lifted out of the car and was now stacked at the hedge, carried there by Melfort—the rations haversack, two duffle coats, binoculars, the pistol, the rifle which had been issued the night before at Kintalla and he had never used yet.

"Is that all?" Melfort was saying. "I'll take this car now. You won't need it. I'll get Hislop to let me through. By the way, have you noticed about your radio—it's smashed. It fell out of your pocket during the scuffle, and I think you tramped on it." He stooped to pick up the trampled ruin, springing with wires and broken plastic. "Finished!" He flung it into the trees.

"We ought to get this fellow off the road," said Raeburn.

"Of course. Help me to lift him. We'll shove him into the boot. When I get back to Kintalla he can be given the works by Dale or Sylvester."

They stuffed him in, and Melfort slammed the lid down. He paused to point at Joan Ker:

"What about her?"

"I don't know. She might want to stay with me."

Melfort raised his voice: "Do you want a lift back to Kintalla, or the school or somewhere?"

The head stayed down. Melfort said: "Apparently not." He got into the driving seat, slammed the door; started the engine, looked out.

"Good show," he said to Raeburn, in a voice more of approval than cordiality, as if talking to a forester who had neatly felled a small tree. He drove quickly out of sight.

CHAPTER 16

Raeburn went and stood beside Joan, and after a time, knowing he was there, she stood up and leaned against him, holding. He gathered her.

"Sorry you had to see that," he said.

"You don't need to talk—for a minute—but, oh yes, I want you to. That was awful—but I wouldn't have missed it. I knew he wasn't going to get you. You're strong—you're terrible!" Long gaps between the phrases.

"How is Duchess Edith?"

"Not awake yet. But she looks peaceful."

"I suppose there is just a chance of good news for her when she wakes."

"Hope so. No sign yet. The Duke keeps on the move, visiting all the people out on the moor. Most of the houses have been checked. But he is certain the main kidnappers and the baby itself are still within the estate."

"No word from them? No ransom demand?"

"No."

"It'll come. What about our boys?"

"I asked the Duke to let me visit them, and then come here. Reid drove me. They're all in good cover, I should say."

"You walked the last stage. I saw you coming."

"Where are you going now?"

"To the farm here. Coming?"

"Of course."

They gathered the stuff from where Melfort had dumped it, and walked up the road to where Hislop still sat in the sun. He scanned them with his glasses, and let them come on, not moving the rifle across his knees. They were all nodding in recognition at one another before they came together.

"Miss Ker, is it?" asked Hislop; and to Raeburn: "Of course I know you fine, even before you came to this part. We used always to be seeing you on the television. We could do with you in that team nowadays."

"Everybody says that," Joan told him.

"It's the God's truth. You could manage a wee drop of hospitality, the two of you?" He waved towards his flowered kitchen window, and his wife came out with a tray, glasses and a bottle.

They had their dram there, passing the time of day.

"It's a terrible thing this," said the farmer's wife. "Is there no word yet? That wee baby, stolen! You feel it's as if it was one of your own."

Hislop pointed out to them the third shooting butt up the hillside, which was the outlook point where Melfort had been, and they got ready to go.

"One thing," said Raeburn. "I've broken my radio. At the next contact on the hour will you please tell the Duke. He might ask you to pass a message."

"I'll do that," the farmer said. "And I won't go indoors until dark. I'm my own master here, but in considerations like this I'll do everything exactly the way the Duke wants. He knows about things—big things."

When they were installed in the butt—a weathered unroofed three-sided shelter of planks and turf, he scanned the immense roll of the empty landscape, with the binoculars, picking out individual sheep in the far distance, and lingering on any movement until the lenses explained it to him. He was at his sweeping of the land practically all the time; she took a spell occasionally. The light was brilliant, and they even got to know the habits of the sheep, most of them restless with their expected lambs. But no sign of a human movement.

They talked, occasionally. She said:

"This time tomorrow, and you should be flying to that hospital."

"I doubt it. The Duke has too much on his mind. How could he think of breaking off to indulge his medical hobby?"

"You're wrong. I asked him."

"You asked him!"

"He said: 'The entire matter is arranged. It goes forward as planned.' I think he was a bit offended I asked, if somebody like me could possibly offend somebody like him. Where is the helicopter landing?"

"Not a clue."

"Can I come?"

"You can not. No place for you. Time to think about jaunts after it's over . . . successfully, if that's the word."

"Well—how are you feeling?"

"To tell the truth, I'm feeling just fine. Don't quote me, but that encounter with Mr Biros, or Konski, did me a world of good."

"I wonder what version Lord Melfort will be giving, at this moment. There's a chancer, if you ask me."

"I didn't. And, well, you know that's no way to talk about the darling of the pro-consular scene."

"What a bastard! They're a pair—he and the Duke."

"Like to like. But at the moment, I have no complaints."

"Even fewer with me. And then there's Markland, maybe, ahead."

"One move at a time . . . you know?"

On other themes, as the afternoon went by, they had each other laughing at odd teaching adventures, the common experiences that arise out of meeting and matching the young. Or she told him the outrageous gossip of women's colleges, in exchange for his memories of blundering back-stage inoffensiveness at great masculine sporting occasions. There is a purely verbal intimacy that can often span temperaments, make a grossness of closer contact, and even enhance the unspoken, and they were refreshed and restored as they waited on that slope of Ben Crocket.

"Wait a minute—" Raeburn had the glasses up, pointing at the farm. "I think I see Hislop waving . . . Yes, he's signalling us to come down." They gathered their stuff and strode and bounded down the firm slope.

"There has been nothing to report until now," said Hislop, in his carrying hill voice as soon as they were in earshot. "But I've just had Mr Dale on the walkie-talkie, speaking for the Duke, and you have to go to another point for the night watch. I'll show you—I know the place well, although it's not on my hirsel."

When they joined him, he had his own map out, and Raeburn spread his.

"Here it is. It's a place called Hewson Dod, a small hill peak across the moor about three miles from here. See here, on the map.

"I suppose it's a very good place for a look-out, because the Dod lies at the south end of a long straight stretch of road, which runs to the foot of the hill and then bends round it. There is good cover among stones on the north slope, from where you can look back up the whole length of the road. The best way to get there is to go through that glen you see across from this road, climb up the burn side—there's a wee loch at the top—skirt that, come down into the next valley, and you'll see the road on the far side, running south. Before you get on to it you'll see Hewson Dod standing out from the landscape. You'll be there in not much more than an hour. I hope between the lot of us we can get all this over by night."

They were quickly across the highway, and into the glen which cut through the hill ridge. The burn spouted from the granite heart of the hill. They would have gladly lingered by its pools, but they went up a turfy stairway, found the little loch, pitted with the spreading ripples of rising trout, and were across the watershed perhaps before the Ben Crocket farmer would have guessed. As the hills fell away from them to their right, the south, they saw and recognised easily the small cone of Hewson Dod. It would have been tempting to make straight for it across the wild moor, but instead, as Hislop had advised, they went due east towards the road, knowing it would be quicker.

As they went, they talked and laughed, as if unclouded by the several sorrows which hung upon them and those they knew: not only the lost baby, but Raeburn's own fate, that death-sentence spelled out by the best experts which somehow, momentarily, was to be put in abeyance by the whim of an aristocrat whose judgment could be not only faulty, but could put even those nearest to him in peril. They felt these small shudders of the soul and, human, quickly put them aside.

It seemed likely that they had found, coming late to each of them, another eccentricity of the human predicament that lifted the moment beyond the bleak limits of mortality. Raeburn noticed that as they went, stepping high-legged among the heaths and bog grass, they were often holding hands, reaching naturally to the other, not for support or aid, but for association; for a joint ease.

Soon they stepped on the firm black undulation of the road and went strongly south, until the Hewson Dod was coming towards them, rising towards the sky. The last stretch of the road, on the straight, before it began to round the base of the little hill leftwards, was across a ridge like a man-made viaduct, except that it was a furrow carved by some earthy violence before man had seen this place at all, and now worn until it could carry the traffic of mankind along a flattened summit. To their left it plunged into a grass gully, then went heaving up to the hill ridges behind. On their right, it fell away in a long slope to the valley floor they had just crossed, thick with bushes of gorse and brakes of juniper.

Looking ahead as they walked, Raeburn was identifying the cluster of handy boulders, perhaps two thirds of the way up the Dod slope, where they would make their entrenchment. There would be concealment, and even a man with a car, and binoculars, edging along the road, would not be likely to pick out a figure lying there. He had his eye on the place, when from that very spot there flickered a little flame, and he heard the whistle of the bullet near his head a fraction before the rifle cracked. He had his arms round Joan at once, bundling her and himself heaving and rolling over the gully edge on the left, where they sprawled to the bottom.

They were still tumbling when the second shot came, and Raeburn realised that most of the gully bottom was commanded from the firing post on the hill. He crammed the two of them in against the bank below the raised road, seeing that this cut off the view from the hill. He had only to edge out an arm's-length or two and the boulders were in sight, which meant that the marksman could see them too. There were two more shots, but beyond them into the clear, and one splintered the edge of a loose stone.

She hadn't said anything, leaving it to him. But now: "Sorry. I was a bit slow in catching on to what was happening."

"That was brisk work, but you did well. Do you mind if I mention that you are marginally heavier than a football?"

"Who's shooting?"

"How do I know? It might be Casio, or O'Connor, or Miss Cove, or Fung. Or any two, three or four of them."

"No," said Joan. "They aren't all there. That's sure. Probably only one. The rest of them, and the most important one, will be somewhere else with the baby. And they wouldn't have brought the baby here."

"You're probably right."

"What do we do now?"

"I think we should have some grub. There's no radio, which would have been useful, but there are a few sandwiches. Fall to!"

He doled them out from his haversack, and they ate with their backs leaning against the grass bank of the road, with their legs tucked in out of sight. An hour passed, and the sun was moving now strongly to the west. But it was still full afternoon.

They edged further along the deepest part of the gully, to where a concrete pipe had been embedded to carry flood water under the road. There they wedged again. There were two more shots at long intervals.

"A good thing we moved," said Raeburn. "He has worked his way round the hill. The shots are getting a better angle in towards us. Sit quiet."

She laughed lightly at him, and he knew she would remember this.

In the later quiet, suddenly there was the sound of a voice—an urgent, eager treble, a forced small whistle; words: "Hi! Hsst! I say, sir!"

They both looked to the spot at the same time. Crouched behind a thick gorse bush on the last ridge above the gully, out of sight of the Dod, his eyes sparkling with awareness of accomplishment, and expecting rebuke, was Anthony Biggs Hewitt.

"Hewitt! Biggs!" Raeburn stretched a warning hand. "In heaven's name, what are you doing there? Keep down!"

"I brought you some things, sir. And for Miss Ker."

"Keep down! This is dangerous. Can you see what's happening?"

"I think so, sir. That's how I found you. I heard the shots. Somebody is trying to shoot you."

"Yes. They're in the middle of the front of that hill to your left. Keep out of sight of it."

"Can I come down, sir?"

"That's going to be difficult, Biggs—but we'd better get you out of there. Wait—let me . . ."

"I could roll down, sir—fast—head over heels, you know."

Joan said urgently: "No! Too risky!"

"I might be able to make a diversion. We've got to get him off that ridge. There may be somebody else looking. Listen, Biggs! Is it clear grass ahead of you all the way to the bottom?"

"Yes."

"No loose stones? I can't see any from here."

"No, none, sir."

"Well, see this. I'm going to throw this duffle coat up on to the road. As soon as I do that, thingummy is going to have a shot at it. The moment you hear the shot, start down. Go fast. I'll stop you. Can you do that?"

"Of course."

"Stand by, then." Raeburn took some time, adjusting the big garment, stuffing grass into the shoulders and hood, shaping it to something that might at a distance look like a human shape. He bent it over slightly:

"Ready?"

"Yes."

Raeburn launched it across the edge of the road, so that for a mere deceiving fraction of a second the coat might look, to a man at the trigger, like a figure starting a crouching run. It was enough. The marksman got in two shots, each of which struck the duffle coat, before it collapsed like a flat skin in the middle of the road.

Hewitt had come off the ridge like a whirling ball, his knees at his ears, his hands gathered into his midriff, and Raeburn was reaching for him, scooping him into the shelter of the embankment, almost at the same time as the second shot was echoing. There was a third, a reaction shot, into the halfway slope of the ridge to show that the man with the rifle had seen some action there.

"Good old Biggs!" They straightened him out. "Are you hurt?"

"No—kind of winded maybe." Raeburn rubbed the flat stomach with a practised circular hand. The boy's knees were bleeding a little where he had scraped some concealed gravel.

"Well, now—" Joan was severe. "Would you mind telling us what you are doing here?"

"I brought you this, Miss Ker." He had a squashed haversack, which he now dangled by its sling. "I heard you hadn't got one. And I got Mr Dale to give me this for you, sir." He fished inside his shirt and pulled out a walkie-talkie radio.

"Great!" whooped Raeburn, snatching it. "No time to lose. We'll whistle up Reid or MacFarlane to deal with our friend here." He switched, and pressed, but the whole circuit seemed to be dead.

"Not manned. I thought 'he' would be standing by all the time."

"Open it up," said Joan.

Raeburn weighed the instrument in his hand, looking at her. "You

could be right," he said. "It feels light." He opened it at the catch.
There were no batteries.

"Oh, that's awful," Hewitt moaned.

"Not your fault, Biggs. How did you know I needed one?"

"It was when I heard Lord Melfort tell how he had shot the man
who was a cook at Markland, and you bust up your radio. The Duke
asked him if he hadn't thought of giving you his, and that's when
I . . ."

"The Duke thinks of everything," murmured Joan. "Anyway, you
did brilliantly, Biggs. Thanks for the haversack." She laughed. "I bet
you looked inside to see if the food was there."

"Yes, I did. I say, can I . . . ?"

"Yes, what is it?"

"Sir. I think I could get through that pipe—"

"What? Impossible. Far too narrow."

"And then I could easily get down the other slope—plenty of bushes
to hide behind—and get back to Kintalla for help."

Raeburn held an arm to the aqueduct opening. It was the width of
wrist to elbow. "See?"

"Let me try, sir." He had his jacket off, and was shoving inside, and
wriggling. Cocking one shoulder up and the other down, he made a
lop-sided shape of himself, and got in to the waist before coming to a
halt.

"Pull me out. I think I know how to do it."

Raeburn hauled him scraping back by the legs, and the boy at once
had his shirt off:

"This will make all the difference . . ."

"It will take the skin off you."

"And if I turn a bit sideways—it's slightly wider that way." He was
in again.

Joan Ker made to stop him, but Raeburn waved her back. He tried
to say something, stumbling, no flow to the words, no coherence:
"—All in danger—lives—who are we to say what is right for him to
do—?" and she left them to it.

The boy's feet were now level with the entrance, and he was
developing some wave of effort and leverage along his body which
seemed to let him grip the raw sides of the concrete and work himself
in and in. His voice boomed thinly now along the tube, which also
caught his gasps of effort.

He said: "If you could put your hands against the end, sir, I might
be able to push against them and move better." So Raeburn braced his
open palms at the end of the pipe, tensing himself into the ground by
the knees and stiffened along bent arms. The feet pressed, the man's
arms straightening and pushing, and the thin body went forward.

There were times when the boy stopped altogether, and Raeburn eased back, waiting for the small strength to gather again. At last the feet moved an inch or two beyond the reach of Raeburn's arms.

"You're on your own now, Biggs."

"OK." Another inch, and then a long pause.

"All right, are you, Biggs?"

The boy was gasping heavily. "I—I think I'm stuck. It's got narrow." They could see him relax, spent with the effort.

"Oh Christ!" It was Joan Ker, in a sob that was a whine. "He's stuck. He'll never get out. He is going to be stuck there for ever!"

"Quiet!" She saw the mask of bone that framed the man's face, now with the skin drawn across it like paper—a face desperate with resolve. "He'll get out of there if I have to batter the pipe to grit with a sledge-hammer," he hissed at her. But he put a smile along the pipe to the boy.

"Hold on there, Biggs. Another trick coming up." Raeburn stood up, stripping off his trousers. He stepped out of them, and swung on his back, with a leg lying up the grass bank, the other reaching into the hole, and his hands white on the cast outside rim.

"Get that, Biggs, my lad. That's a leg. Keep going now."

The soles of the boy's feet braced again, and he made a move forward. "Great, sir! We're away again." Raeburn slowly straightened out his own leg.

They moved through all that was available of the leg, and then the tip-stretched toes. "I think it's getting a little wider," said Hewitt.

"Here!" Joan was at Raeburn's side, with a football-sized round stone she had pawed cautiously from the near slope. "Add this."

"Another trick soon, Biggs." He was out, they rolled the stone in, and he pushed it forward with his toes.

"Oh, that's super." He was making headway, had a lithe roll about his forward movement. They added another small boulder, and all at once he was moving freely.

"I'm nearly there. I have a hold of the outside rim."

"Stay there for a minute—have a breather. I want to look." Raeburn backed out, scooping the boulders out with his toes. He turned to put his head in, looking through.

"You could put your trousers on, if you think there's time," her voice said behind him.

"If you insist." He wriggled into them.

"OK, now, Biggs—remember there is a man with a gun waiting out there. Can you have a peep out?"

"It's all thick bushes round the entrance, and there is a kind of path where the water has been running, with bushes on either side. I'm pretty sure I won't be seen."

"Fine. Well, slip out in your own time, and lie low. I have to get your shirt and things to you—and a letter."

When the boy looked back in towards them, they could see the lifted skin on his shoulders and the bottom of the rib cage, the blood seeping heavily.

"Oh, my God, look at him! Torn to bits." Joan mouthed it with her hands trying to seal her lips.

"No. But painful. Talk to him." Raeburn had a note pad out and was already writing.

She was talking. "Can I call you Biggs, too? I mean not only just now, but for keeps?" The light voices surged back and forth in the tunnel, distorted, and Raeburn, concentrating on his writing, nevertheless felt a sweep of happiness to have these two with him.

He had finished the note, and folded it now, putting it into the inside pocket of Hewitt's jacket, which had a zipper to close it. He bundled the shirt and jacket tightly, tied the bundle by the sleeves, and got ready to throw. Two small hands waited at the other end of the pipe.

"Catch!" He launched the missile and it went straight through, with Hewitt fielding it.

"Well held!" Raeburn added. "Nobody's asking you to drop a goal. Undo the bundle and get the things on. Your sore bits will feel better when they are covered . . . They'll feel worse," he said aside to Joan Ker. "What a liar I am!"

"Clothes on," came from the end of the tunnel.

"Good! Now listen to me carefully. There is a written message in your inside jacket pocket. Make sure it's there—and zip up again. Right? Now, that has to go into the Duke's own hands. Nobody else. Say it's from me. Right? Now, how do you get to the Duke? Look round behind you. Straight across the valley, do you see a glen—a gap in the hills—point to it; I can see it from here myself. That's it. You go down through the bushes, and once you are across the river you will be out of sight of that hill where the chap is with the gun. Go through that glen. It climbs up gently, and at the top there is a small loch. Go round that. A burn flows out of the other end. Follow that, and you'll see how the hill slopes down to another valley with a road. The only house in sight is a farm called Ben Crocket. Go up there—you'll see a big truck blocking the road—and you will find the farmer, whose name is Mr Hislop. Tell him who you are, where you come from, and ask him from me to run you in the car to Kintalla Castle. Ask him please not to use the walkie-talkie. Then of course you give the note to the Duke. Have you got all that?"

The boy waited, rehearsing it. Then: "Yes, I have. I can see it all from here. I'll run all the way."

"Don't exhaust yourself. There's time enough. You can run downhill. Keep an eye on the Hewson Dod—that's the hill to your left—for the first bit. The gunman is there. Keep out of sight."

"I think I can do that, sir. There is a lot of bushy stuff. I'll be able to run most of the way, I'm sure. I'm kind of glad to get out of that pipe. Can I go now?"

"Yes. And good luck." Joan echoed it at his side.

Hewitt was out of sight at once, and they sat back, by an immediate mutual pact without a word spoken. And so they sat for about twenty minutes, silent, tucked in, gathering what strength might still be left and needed.

At the end of that time, he spoke the unspeakable. He had to declare it.

"Twenty minutes. No shooting. He's through."

She looked straight ahead—no agreement, no nodding. He had to speak beyond this.

"—Unless he's been seen and followed. And caught. That might be worse." As she sat with a face of stone, not seeing him, Raeburn gathered up the other duffle coat and threw it, shaped, forward on to the grass. Before it rested limply, it had bounced with the two leaping bullets that came at it out of the face of Hewson Dod.

"That's a relief," he said. "We've still got the sniper all to ourselves. And wee Biggs is pelting round that loch, brave wee character."

They were silent then together for a long time. For an hour or more. There had to be, even at the best, the long sloping journey down to the far Crocket road; the encounter with Hislop and the many questions there to be answered; the journey to the castle; that ordeal of debriefing (and the boy was only nine, without even Mrs Gibson there to look after him); the despatch of Reid or MacFarlane, or whoever it might be; the problem of even such an adequate performer as one of these getting within range and to grips with the man on the face of the Dod; the long tiresome explanations afterwards; and still, the main disaster, the lost baby, as the time moved on to the second night.

It was almost a relief when the shooting started. Surprisingly soon. There were three shots, as they looked at each other. To Raeburn, at once, they sounded deeper in note, with more authority somehow, than the shooting they had heard up to now. It was a close sequence of shots, and for a long time they stayed braced for more before realising finally that this seemed to be all.

He waited, taking no initiative, for fully two minutes. So that it was she who had to say: "What do we do now?"

"Nothing. Absolutely nothing. We don't know what has happened, although we can hope for the best. It might be no more than another feint, to draw us from cover. This is one we sit out."

It was fully fifteen minutes before they heard the car, a heavy jeep by the sound of it, moving ponderously up the road from the direction of Hewson Dod. It seemed to slow at the sight of the fallen duffle coat in the roadway, then crawled along, a voice shouting: "Reid. Reid from Kintalla. Are ye there, Mr Raeburn?"

They were glad to stretch legs up on to the road.

"You again, Mr Reid. Second time for me. Well, who talks first?"

Reid, his cap off, his hard eyes unshaded, showed the wisps of hair sweated on to his mostly bald skull. He put the cap back on, to show he was in no lingering mood.

"I was to tell you from His Grace that he would be obliged if you would take the night watch as arranged on Hewson Dod."

"Certainly. What about the man who was there?"

"Ach—he's dead."

"How?"

"It didn't take long. There is a track round the back, to the coast side of the Dod, and I drove there and went in over the top. He hadn't thought of protecting his back. You would hear the shots, I suppose."

"Yes. Who is he? Do you know?"

"I don't. A kind of Chinese sort of a chap, I would think. But he'll not worry you at the Dod tonight. He's in the back there"—and Reid gave a nod over his shoulder towards the canvas-shrouded rear seats of his vehicle—"if you would like to have a look at him."

"I think not. Thanks, though. Sounds like Fung."

"Like enough. Have you all you need? I have some blankets, a torch, flasks of tea and things . . ." He was out, stuffing these into a kitbag.

"What about the boy?"

"Oh—he did fine. He's in his bed already."

"There are no batteries in my radio. Can you give me yours?"

"Of course. Give me your one and I'll get new batteries when I get in. Is the lady staying?"

"Yes," she said.

"That's fine, then. You'll have all you need." He mounted the jeep, put it into gear, and was moving forward. "The Duke will come on the air every hour. Will you, he says, come in until midnight, and start again at six. He'll be up all night, calling on the hour, in case there is anything."

"Understood."

"And, Mr Raeburn, you've to be ready to fly out at three o'clock tomorrow. Details later."

"If the job's done—"

"Whether or no, His Grace said. I'm off then." The jeep swept into the dusk, the red lights already showing.

They laughed him out of sight, thinking of one phrase in particular and with general relief at the stage reached.

"Efficient mob," said Raeburn, as they shouldered the kit towards the Dod. "Life or death, it's all the same to the Duke. I hope he gets his problem solved, though, before I have to be off."

"Hewitt—Biggs—he did it."

"Of course he did it. He'll never forget he did it. He'll never forget there's almost nothing he can't do."

Among the boulders against the brae face, there was no sign of occupation. An overhang of the cliff rock itself made almost a cave towards the back of the enclosure, and from the front boulders they could see, unseen, the long road north, and especially the naked gully where they had been. The night was falling as they made their hide ready. There were loose candles among the debris of comforts Reid had flung together, and these lit the recesses of their den.

The nine-o'clock call revealed that only the gamekeepers, the professionals, the sheikh at Talla Head and the two at Hewson Dod were still outside, with the Duke roaming the countryside at will, but mainly sitting in the castle at his maps. The Duke was not now specifying the individual situations. Instead he was saying: "at the agreed spot" or "your special map reference" with a number. And the death of Fung was not being mentioned.

On Hewson Dod they had a hot supper, noticing that a late moon would give some light about the countryside, and certainly show up the road. Between nine and ten o'clock, for most of the time, Raeburn pored over his maps, spreading them all over the covered floor of the back part of the cave, while Joan kept watch on the night that held nothing. He identified all the country they had covered that day, and the approaches to their present hide. This was interrupted by the ten-o'clock call, a short routine one with nothing new.

At the end of the sequence the Duke called him back in:

"Six."

"Here."

The Duke waited for a time, then said: "The Duchess wants to talk. Over."

Her voice said: "Barry. It's Edith."

"You! How are you? How do you feel?"

"Oh, you know . . . not much to say really about that—I wanted to thank you so much for all you have done."

"Joan Ker insists on saying again—he'll be well looked after. That's the whole point of the affair."

"Look after her . . . Has anybody told you all the boys are here indoors, none the worse for their day out."

"Thanks. May I say—there is one boy, young, called Hewitt—"

"I know about him. I saw him to bed. He is in my special care"—there was a catch, a gulp—"I'm looking after him. We have another friend of yours here. Your Dr Grant. Ready for you for tomorrow. He bandaged up our young Biggs . . ." She went off shortly.

Joan said: "They say, so long as you have somebody to mother . . ."

Raeburn said nothing.

He was busy with the maps, and he exclaimed to her: "Here is something—you remember the day we met Duchess Edith on the hill, and she pointed out that high hill farm Binnanee? Well, Binnanee is just over the ridge to the east of us. It's even nearer than Ben Crocket."

"Interesting. I suppose if you knew the countryside well, you would find that all Kintalla ground didn't amount to so very much."

"No—I dare say—I suppose not—still, funny thing that—something funny—I don't know what . . ."

He was silent for a long time, in thought, so she did not trouble him with words. He looked up and down at the maps, read his notes, came back to the maps, made a few remarks when it seemed he had abandoned her.

At last: "I think I've got it. I have something. Can I try it on you?"

"Too late. Try it on himself. It's time for the radio call. I'll hear anyway."

So when the Duke came on, seconds later, and it was Raeburn's turn, he said: "Routine only, but I have something important. Will you come back to me?"

The round went on, and the Duke said at the end: "Six. You again."

"Six here. I think I can tell you where the baby is."

"What! You can tell—"

"First, have all the Kintalla houses been called upon?"

"Most of them. All but the farthest. Where—"

"Has Binnanee?"

"I don't think so. Mr Porteous?"

"No, sir," a voice said faintly in the background.

"Does Mr Porteous or anybody with you know the appearance of John Noble the shepherd who lives there? Is he a tall man with a black beard?"

"No." It was the Duke's voice. "I know him. He is short and clean-shaven."

"Then he is probably being kept prisoner in his own house, by the man I describe, and others. Almost certainly with the baby. You remember when the minister at the party said Noble hadn't been at church—never absent before—"

"Yes—yes—I remember—go on—Noble wasn't at the party . . ."

Raeburn told briefly how he had seen that tall, bearded man stooping through the door, that day on the hill with Joan, when they had met the Duchess. "If the Duchess were there, she could tell you . . ."

Faintly, strident, at the back, came the voice: "But I *am* here. Of course I remember. He means there were other people there."

"Yes. Tell me if it's feasible. That was the rendezvous. They could gather there and make preparations—Noble wouldn't be missed for days. The helicopter could have landed easily and got out again. It probably got there at least once already—"

"Stop!" The Duke held them up, waiting while he thrashed at it in his mind. Then: "This seems very likely. Melfort? Mr Porteous? Laidlaw?" They must have nodded. "Attention all! At the foot of the first Binnanee slope there is a flat piece of ground, with an old building in ruins, some fallen rocks and a clump of trees. We gather there at first light tomorrow morning—everybody. All arms—all equipment. Say seven-fifteen. Until then, no radio call before six o'clock. I shall open the circuit hourly so that anyone with a message may speak. Otherwise, silence. Out!—No, hold!—Six? Thank you. Out."

Raeburn looked at Joan. "What do you think?"

"I think it's very likely. Well worth trying anyway. She will have an awful night of it. At least none of them knew of any other explanation for the strangers at Binnanee."

He held to his maps for a time yet, while she crouched in the den watching him, but saying nothing. At last he folded them all, put them away in his haversack, and made the nightly preparations.

There was a waterproof sheet, which he spread on the flat floor drift of dead pine needles and leaves, in against the rock face and roofed by the overhang. He put the two duffle coats down, and a blanket; gathered filled haversacks for pillows, and spread the remaining blankets for the top. She watched as he worked, her own tidying done; when he seemed ready, he loosened his tie, and took off his shoes, laying them to hand at the outside of the double bed.

"We'll have to lie close. It will be cold in the small hours. We have to sleep well for a busy day tomorrow."

"Yes," she said.

He left an inch or two of one of the candles within arm's length, so that the lighting of the cave dwindled to dimness. She laid her own shoes beside his, seemed to loosen some garments, and so they stretched together, bedded.

Almost at once, they turned to each other, and were close, clasped, twined. It was at first merely the full-stretch length of them, hands firmly held, even the kisses late in beginning, since that would interrupt and punctuate the long need to be one. They did not speak, for the limbs can articulate the great experience better than words. Soon—

or it might be not so soon—he loosed one of her hands and twined his into her hair at the back of the head, pressing the skull and the neck sinews to force them to familiarity; and in a while the other hand too went roving blindly and becoming wise.

The touching, the gentle holding, the searching, the discovering. "Yes!"—the whisper of completion, the unbearable but true gratefulness.

They would never remember how long the silence lasted then, the stillness. At last, softly, she was speaking again:—"Something of you!" —like a Fate intimating some endless continuity of life. —A prisoner briefly visited, he acknowledged her with his arms.

The candle guttered low, and they drowsed away with it.

CHAPTER 17

"Hi! You! Wake up!" The voice stirred him at last, and Raeburn slowly stretched to alertness, opening his eyes. Joan Ker was up and trim, patted into tidy freshness, and she was pouring two mugs of coffee from one of the flasks. Two lit candle stumps deepened the darkness, but the morning was coming fast, holding the chill whose frost sparkled the rocks.

"Well, what have you been doing that made you so sleepy?" she quizzed blithely, while he stared in wonder at her. Better even than unending rapture would be the unpredictable variety. She was holding out a mug, handle turned towards him.

"We have to be on our way at once," she said busily. "That's the breakfast."

"I'm a slow starter," he mouthed, and oiled his throat with coffee. "What's the idea of the lack of solids in the diet? There were sandwiches left. Have you scoffed them?"

"No sandwiches for you. No solids. You have a big medical day, so not a thing until that's over. Nurse's orders."

"What about you?"

"Nothing for me either. I'm very happy."

"Oh good! I'm delighted to hear it. Me too." But she was in no way abashed.

She showed him the spring dripping from the mossy rock where she had sluiced her face and hands, and he took time there to shave off his growth of beard. Coming back to the cave, he hardly needed the torch.

It was going to be a bracing day with the cold sun, so they left the blankets and the duffles, plunging to the road below and pitching to the slope beyond, which soon carried them higher than the small peak of Hewson Dod, and the sky reddened to the lit east.

The rim of the sun, struggling to heave out of some faraway range of black, chased them down the far slope, overtaking them finally to burst up, spreading from a streamer to a section, as the ball, climbing clear, moved and brightened into yellow, and they watched it dissolve the last traces of shadow and revealing the whole new valley.

Raeburn took his glasses, sweeping the horizon and the nearer ground, pausing on features, moving on and back. At last he handed them to her, pointing out what he had been identifying.

"That's Binnanee, to the left of where the sun is now. Don't look at the sun directly. The house is facing us, so that we are looking at it straight on. The last time, we saw it at a far greater distance, and we were looking more from the north, at the gable on the left-hand side where the peats are stacked. Tell me if you see any sign of life. They have still got the fire going. You can see the smoke, going straight up. Pale blue . . . There is the place where we meet the others, down the slope from the house and to the right—see the trees? Some of our people are already there. They're standing in cover, so I don't think I can make them out, with this direct sunlight . . . Two cars are parked; one of them is the sheikh's. Not much doubt he would be there . . ."

"I think I can see the Duchess."

"Very likely." He took the glasses briefly from her, looking. "Yes," he said, handing them back, "that's the road up to Binnanee—pretty rough —and it comes down to meet a better road running along the bottom of this valley. Come on, we'd better join them."

They were soon on the road, and then on the hill track. Coming up to the meeting place, they kept behind the shield of the rocks and the tumbled walls, out of the line of fire from the cottage, but calmly in the middle of the road was the sheikh, fitting his rocket-launcher on its tripod, and sighting.

Laidlaw and his two gamekeepers were there; Mr Porteous; the Duke, with Dale and Sylvester manipulating maps and instruments for him; the Duchess; none of the schoolboys. The Duke's welcome was a mere glance as they came up the last stretch. Joan went forward to take the Duchess by the elbows, and they went aside.

"I have come to the conclusion," said the Duke, walking off with Raeburn so that they both were slanted off to stand beneath the largest of the tattered trees, "that there is little likelihood of firing from the house at this stage, although that may come later. There is no doubt that they have the child in the cottage, certainly with more than one of them." He looked at Raeburn direct, with the distaste of his own failure. "I am bound to concede that several of your judgments in this whole matter have been correct. Worse still, mine have been wrong— an improper situation for me. However, in view of what is at stake . . ." He paused, and with a frozen movement which in any one else might have been a shrug, as if the safety of his heir might even override the importance of his accuracy, walked back to his tasks, passing Joan on the way without a sign.

She came up to Raeburn, saying: "I've persuaded her to go and sit in the car. Might try and slip her another pill, later, if necessary. She says Biggs is still sleeping."

"Where are the boys?"

"Coming later. Get your glasses. Do you see something hanging in front of the house?"

He focused on Binnanee. There was a limp blue flag dangling from a pole on the grass near the door.

"She says that's one of the baby's shawls. They guess it's meant to be a sign the baby's there. It seems to have cheered her up a bit."

An approaching vehicle making its way along the low valley road started to reveal itself from behind the knolls as the school van. It took the rough track road, bumping and swaying, to draw up near them. Walter Fenton, the school captain, was driving. He came out, with the prince, Van Moubray and Murdoch, the junior captain.

"Drive over here," said the Duke, coming forward. "Out of sight of the house," and Fenton took it over. "And gather round me here."

They lost sight of Binnanee as they circled him, all with their weapons. As they settled, a shot, violent in explosion, came from the house, and the bullet spurted stones and dust from among the spread legs of the tripod where the sheikh's weapon was mounted on the road.

The sheikh, back at the roadside, looked for a moment through the wind-torn trees that straggled there; then walked to the tripod, lifted it and the weapon, and brought them to shelter.

The Duke waited for them to quieten again, beckoning them in to him.

"Nevertheless," he said, "I do not expect any further casual shooting at this point. The tripod gun was perhaps a little obvious." He allowed the pause to linger, and continued:

"Therefore, no shooting from us unless it is certain that, firstly, the target can be killed; and secondly, that the child will remain unharmed.

"In that cottage on the hill"—he waved an arm in the direction of the concealed Binnanee—"my son is being held a prisoner. In due course we can expect to hear of a ransom demand. The people involved appear to be as follows: there is first a man called Casio, who is the leader; I imagine he arrived by the helicopter which many of us heard two nights ago, and which could easily land near the house. By that time Binnanee, as it is called, was almost certainly occupied by the second head of the gang, whose name is O'Connor, well known to the Irish authorities, but involved also in Central Europe. He probably came by land, and occupied the house as long ago as last week, making a captive of the only occupant—a shepherd called John Noble—or even murdering him. It was there, it can be certainly assumed, that the baby was taken by his nurse, a woman whose real name appears to be Cove, during the night before last. She was joined beside the castle by a man from the East known as Fung, who has already been disposed of. They no doubt made their way on foot across the moor to this place. Accordingly, so far, we can make two assumptions: we are dealing with no more than three participants—two men and a woman; and the baby is safe and alive. However, these are determined people." He spoke this with assurance, as one who knew what determination could be. "Their obvious ruse will be to try to get what they want, and escape by threatening the child's life. They will have no hesitation at all in killing him."

The Duchess's face looked blankly at the ground. Round her shoulders was the arm of Joan Ker.

The Duke went on: "For reasons that are attributable to experience and judgment"—he deliberately took Raeburn's eye, and looked away indifferently—"I have come to the conclusion that the crisis will not come until at least midday. This gives us time to make our dispositions. Laidlaw will take these"—he pointed to Murdoch and Van Moubray of the boys, and Dale—"and go round the back of the cottage, covering an attempt on that side. The rest of us will spread from here along the front of the slope, and be ready to act. There is good cover on most of the ground.

"We shall revert to the radio calls each hour on the hour. Incidentally, the man shot last night, Fung, was carrying this." He held up a walkie-talkie set, larger than the instruments they had been using, and red in colour. "This set, like ours, is sealed to a waveband which does not happen to be near to ours, and is not adjustable. It would appear that at least those in their inner circle have been able to communicate, and they may be able to make contact across a wider range than we can, but not much.

"First, Laidlaw's party will move out. Take the school van and go round by the south road into Glen Dorrim, which is over the hill behind Binnanee. There is a track to within about half a mile of the cottage at the back, and the three of you will then string out, find an emplacement each. Be vigilant with your guns, and simply wait for further instructions." Thus he hustled them on the road and away.

The others he spread in a wide half-circle on the down side of the slope below the cottage. Close together, nearest to the base point at the ruins, were Raeburn, with Reid and MacFarlane, grouped like a strong firing point in the same huddle of rocks, with a clear command of the cottage. The prince was pointed to a place within the walls, but Fenton, the senior, was strung at the farthest end of the arc, and went readily to his post, hoping for glory. The women sat in the closed car, and the sheikh, screened by a straggle of branches, set up his weapon again.

Raeburn, before going into his place, had time to say to the sheikh:

"I saw the shot fired, that nearly hit the rocket gun. It came from a roof skylight window, set in between the two attic windows. If you try your binoculars there I think you'll see a man lurking, ready to stretch out and fire."

The sheikh studied it at leisure. "Yes, I see. That is my target." Laidlaw's group were not in place in time for the eight-o'clock call, but the others had a round-up. There was good cover on the down side of the hill, and shortly before nine o'clock the Duke moved across and among them, visiting. On the lower ground it was not difficult for a hill man to move like this unseen, but the cover was thinner in the neighbourhood of the cottage.

Another vehicle moved on the glen road, and one of the farmers came in a truck, carrying Dr Grant as a passenger. He put the doctor down in the cover of the walls, and would have stayed to talk to him, but the Duke at once waved him away.

As the truck bumped downwards, a shot took a splinter from its dashboard, and the driver doubled the speed, hammering along the road to safety as another shot came, this time wide.

"I could see him that time," Reid said calmly, sighting through his telescopic lens. "Could have taken the face off him. But of course, the Duke said 'No shooting, unless the baby would be safe' . . ."

Grant went into the women's car. He had a large bag of impedimenta, but in his pockets a flask and tablets. He gave a sedative to the reluctant Duchess.

"Take these," he said. "I'm telling you they're what you need. Doctor's orders. I should maybe have been here before." In a moment he came out and, seeing Raeburn, who was nearest to the wall, spoke across to him: "Your Hewitt is fine. A grand wee chap. Up and about. Wanted to come."

"Tell Miss Ker."

"I did."

It was in this almost picnic atmosphere that the first of the hours passed. But there were frequent shots now, well aimed, from the shaded internal recesses of the cottage, through the open windows, as the marksmen behind tried to find their targets in the heather and gorse clumps. They lay low. "Wait," the Duke was still saying.

In the midst of this, they saw a figure suddenly reach an outhouse wall at the cottage, and stand up against it. A young figure, looking downhill, with his back against the shed wall. He stood there, out of sight of the cottage windows, and after a time waved towards the ruins and the trees.

"My soul!" said Reid, not using his binoculars, and skilled in observation. "Do you see who that is? How did he get there?"

"It's the prince," said MacFarlane. "I wouldn't have said it was possible, in that cover. He'll be hard put to it to get out of there."

As they spoke, the lad ducked down from the wall and was out of sight, stooping into the bush. A banked rise ran slanting for a small distance away from the crest where the cottage stood, and by this time the Duke and all the others had their binoculars on the hillside, where nothing seemed to move, and waited tensely for the sound of a rifle. The minutes passed, and there was nothing.

The Duke was back again, shrunk with anger, when the prince slipped out of a bush clump at the wall, low-doubled, and stood and stretched on the shaded grass.

He went forward to the Duke, who spoke with the thin strain that all of them knew by now: "That was foolish, prince. I disapprove. This must be said. There are too many handicaps already. You imperil us."

"I'm sorry, sir—last thing I'd want is to worry you at this time. I think it might help you to know I'm fairly sure Mr Noble is alive—he seems to be a prisoner in that shed: tied up, I expect, and probably gagged. I gave a tap like this"—he made a signal with his knuckles on a dyke stone—"and there was a reply like this"—his shut mouth hummed out a wordless reply, with changing notes as if muffled in a gag. "It might help the tactics to know he is alive."

"It might!" The Duke wheeled about and walked away from him.

After a silence, MacFarlane spoke across the gap: "That was a fine stalk, prince. Who taught you to do that?"

David smiled politely. "Malcolm Sinclair, at Balmoral."

"Oh, him!" It was quietly acknowledged—the quietness of one master hill man's tribute to another. Reid and MacFarlane nodded at each other, in full understanding, and went back to their sighting vigil.

"He'll be at the church next Sunday," said MacFarlane slowly in the ample quiet.

Raeburn said: "We'll all be at the church next Sunday."

"Not you, Barry." Dr Grant had joined the conversation. "You'll be busy."

When the Duke made the one-o'clock call, it was again the unchanging check-over. Nothing to report, all alert, no movement, no sign. When it was over, Raeburn was idling relaxed behind the wall, while the Duke called in another number."

"Everyone out, except Higgins at Fourteen"—the spare number.

"Your Grace," came the response at once.

"Higgins. Phone your Prestwick number at once. Tell them to have the helicopter here at two o'clock precisely, for Mr Raeburn and Dr Grant. Here is the map reference"—and he read off the spot where he was himself standing in an eight-letter number from the Ordnance Survey map. Higgins repeated it, and was signalled out.

The Duke said nothing, and Raeburn, pondering this fresh sign of the man's ability to take so many bountiful decisions amid his own strains, turned away.

Lying on the top of the dyke wall, where the Duke had put it down after the morning briefing, was the red walkie-talkie which had been in the possession of Fung, and Raeburn lifted it idly, switching on.

Immediately it was talking, a clear coherent voice: a voice he knew. It was saying, calmly, urgently: "He has signalled up the helicopter. Due to be here at two o'clock. Make your move now." The voice, which had lately become so familiar, was Dale's. The reply came, in the same instrument: "Going now."

Raeburn took perhaps five seconds to set it all together—to come to the conclusion—and he turned at once, darting to the side of the Duke a few footsteps away and back at his vigil; taking him fiercely by the shoulder; pouring out the words:

"Duke!" He waved the red instrument in the man's face. "It's Dale! He's talking to them—telling about the helicopter—your own message. Dale is the man who—"

"Yes. Quiet!" The Duke was pointing to the door of the cottage of Binnanee, which was opening. Out stepped a thick man, touched with grey about the head, not armed visibly. And after him, a woman, carrying a tiny white-wrapped bundle. The door stood open behind them. In the middle of the sloping roof above, the skylight window was flung back and a rifle came forward, with a hint of a black-bearded face intent behind.

Every eye was on the two in front of the house, where they stood on the cobblestones, in a move clearly rehearsed. The man was slightly in front and had a loud-hailer, which he was not hastening to use. The girl, in denims much at odds with her decorous uniform, was a pace behind him and to the side. She now held up the baby, which was only lightly swaddled; and she had him by a hand round each leg, so that he hung downward, with that vulnerable head toward the stones. Those with binoculars or telescopic sights could see the detail.

"Jesus!" said someone—it might be Mr Porteous—"She'll drop him."

"Not yet." Raeburn said it, hoping he saw the move ahead. His glasses were sweeping the cottage front.

The loud-hailer was now at the man's lips. He started to talk.

"Duke! I am Casio. We know each other.

"If your friends shoot me, the nurse will drop the baby by its head on the stones. No escape. No one can reach in time. We do not mind to die, if what we plan does not succeed. If you want the son, you will help. Some have died already, but we are not softened.

"Here is what is to happen, and you will give the necessary orders. You have a helicopter arriving soon. When it comes, you will give or-

ders for it to take us to where we want to go. No questions. There will
be four of us, adult people, and the baby."

"Oh no! Oh no!" The Duchess moaned, covering her eyes.

Raeburn had squirmed his way into the heather, coming up between
MacFarlane and Reid.

The hailer went on: "In the house here, after our departure, you
find a letter—a long letter, Duke—address to you. It describes a series
of transactions by which you make sure the return of your son. Complicated, but of course with your wealth and facilities it should not occupy
much time. Sums of money and other negotiables valuable to be made
available to me in certain places of the world. I describe at some length
the methods by which you will accomplish. I believe you know that I
am also expert at these procedures. You are not dealing with the normal
impulsives who attempt such matters.

"I can say that the total concerned is more than twenty million ster-
ling, which I have assured you can realise in the time. The plan has
been some years in the preparation, and it is not probable that you will
circumvent it.

"I shall now remain here for one minute—with child in sight. At the
end of that time, I think, you will accept the conditions and we can
proceed to details.

"When all is complete, the values transferred, the son will be safely
returned. Otherwise not. That is all. One minute. Acknowledge."

The Duke stood up, waved. He remained standing.

"Four adults—" Reid was starting to say.

"Listen! Listen to me!" Raeburn lay between them, and they kept the
sighted rifles to their eyes, not looking round at him. "Listen—could
you shoot them from here? These two?"

"Easy. I could pick off his ears from here . . . But the baby—"

"Trust me." Raeburn spoke with his glasses firm into his eyes. "If
Casio died with a shot, how long would it take the woman to know he
had been shot?"

They thought about this. Then: "I would say hardly two seconds at
the most. From where she stands she would see the bullet coming out
of his back. Aye, two seconds at the most. Maybe a fraction less. She'll
be fast at the thinking."

They could hear the thin thread of sound as the baby rocked and
wailed with his discomfort.

"Then that will probably do. Trust me, please—no time to talk, even
to the Duke—this is the only way—"

"Oh—I think we trust you right enough—"

"There isn't time to explain. Reid, you kill Casio when I say the
word. And, MacFarlane, kill the girl a bare two seconds after. Can you
do that?"

"Aye—the heart—it's exposed. She's got the baby high up."

"Sight!" said Reid; and they were still. "When I say," said Raeburn. "Now!"

The two shots were like one and a quick echo. Casio died without a backward stagger, so clean did the shot go through him, and he seemed to take a long time to crumple. The girl was driven back an inch or two by her shot and, as Raeburn had expected and prayed, her first reaction in death, before she started to go down, was to grip tightly, for only moments, at the tiny ankles.

But it might be enough. Raeburn had seen, and now they could all see, the prince as he leaped and ran from the bush cover at the end of the shed wall. He had got back there, and was crouching, hearing Casio's declaration, and ready for what might be done. There were only fourteen paces of hard running between his post and the dead and falling girl, whose last grip had probably made the time long enough.

He got there as the baby fell, and took it low like a rugby ball on his outstretched forearm, gathered it to his chest, and kept racing in a sharp turn towards the downhill shade. Weaving fiercely into the sparse bushes of the top slope, he was another score of paces away when the first shot came from O'Connor. He crouched lower, still running, the child's head now cupped into his open hand, the puny body lying along his forearm so that the whole arm could swing free and help him balance. He began to be out of sight of the man at the skylight window, who put in two more shots. The boy ran on, seemingly untouched, not checking, to where the cover was heavier as he came down the hill and neared them.

Above his head, suddenly, the straight rumble of the sheikh's rocket soared, crashing the roof, picking out the middle section and the whole skylight and surrounding slates as if with a scoop. Bare timbers were suddenly there, and what might be paint dripping. The firing ceased from Binnanee. The prince, seeing nothing of this, ran on, still crouched, gasping now with the strain.

"Take your time, man," Walter Fenton shouted from the line, standing. "Slow up! It's finished."

David, grateful, grasped at what they were saying and slowed. Looked back, and understood. He trotted the last distance to the wall where they were, pulling and tidying at the bundle, diffidently, as he came.

The Duchess, white, pinched, had her arms out, saying nothing. He handed her the bundle, where the small cry was fading, and the eyes were looking round in wonder.

The boy said: "I didn't realise how small they were." She put her arms round, concealing the bundle, and Joan Ker enveloped them both.

The Duke called over Dr Grant. "Examine please," he said. Grant took the huddle of women and child towards the sheikh's car. To Sylvester, the Duke said: "Call in the others. Same way as they went." In the background they heard Sylvester at the walkie-talkie: "It's all over. Come in—to here. The school van."

They were gathered now at the rendezvous, the Duke still instructing: "Reid and MacFarlane, see to Noble. Tidy up at the cottage. Take Sylvester—photographs." They went up the hill, still with their guns, out of habit.

Grant came from the car, holding out to the Duke the rewrapped child. "Nothing wrong. A fine boy, Duke. None the worse. Well fed, too. He needs to sleep."

The Duke said: "Sheikh, oblige me please by taking the Duchess and the baby back to the castle. Mr Porteous will go too. I shall be a little longer."

As they started, Joan stepped out of the car. The Duchess leaned, silent, to the prince, but could not speak, and they were away. By this time the Duke was already speaking to the prince:

"A great deal has to be said, Prince—"

"If you will excuse me, sir, no! We're not supposed to be good at this sort of thing."

"We?"

"Us royals. I shall have to make a report to the family, of course, but it is likely to be decided that nothing should be said in public."

"Or even in private. I think you are right."

"This is not my decision, of course, sir, but it seems that a great deal is owed to yourself and others—"

"Nothing to be said. I hope that is the decision. Not even in confidence. What would you want to do? If you could agree to tell the minimum, I should be happy with that."

"Where is Sergeant Miller?"

"Dumfries Hospital. Quite comfortable. Probably out on Sunday."

"Then if you will permit me, Duke, I ought to go back to Markland and report first to the headmaster. I shall then have to telephone the family. I am sure"—he smiled—"they will be sensible. May I tell Dr Coulson that you will phone him later?"

"Say I shall call on him at Markland in the evening. I have other things to discuss. I see the school van coming. If Mr Fenton is able to drive—he is?—the school party can leave at once. Mr Fenton, pass my thanks to all concerned as you travel."

The van fussed up to a stop. They were soon away again, adding the prince and leaving the two Kintalla men, Dale and Laidlaw, behind.

"This I must see," Dale was saying, staring up the hill. "We only heard it from the back. All over?" Others were telling him.

Raeburn was at the Duke's elbow. "Duke—about Dale—"

"Leave Dale to me." He was the implacable, no-feeling Duke again, restored to chill and control, and he said, in the voice that carried: "Dale!"

Dale turned, looked, and started down the hill again towards him. "Sir?"

"This." The Duke held it up. He had taken it from a pocket. It was a blackened zip length, burned by fire, to which adhered fragments of wizened red plastic. "This," he said again. "It belonged to one of our company zip folders, private to the secretariat such as yourself, and I took it from the burned-out Iglietti in which you had tried to destroy Raeburn, to say nothing of MacFarlane, who I am glad to see is moving down the hill towards you, with his rifle ready. And you have been with the organisation long enough to know that few have ever been more ready than MacFarlane with the rifle."

Dale, his eyes wide with urbane astonishment, looked with polite attention at the Duke and prepared himself to speak.

"If people would only pay heed to the experience which can be gathered in a career like mine"—it was Lord Melfort, inevitably, who was speaking—"as I have said many times to you, Duke, in this very context, there is always a flaw within. One who, somehow, sometimes, if not in this case, succeeds in betraying the whole matter. Here we have a typical incident—"

Dale interrupted: "Sir—this is monstrous. Who is accusing me? These years of faithful service—my own contribution, well authenticated—deaths to convenience you—this is—"

"It needs little further proof." The Duke was thinly businesslike. "This is a period when I have had to accustom myself to admitting faulty judgment. Demonstrated finally by the fact that you have in your pocket, as well as our instrument, an alien walkie-talkie . . . Stupid name, I confess." He was back to normal, as the pedantry showed. "Take it out, Dale. Show it to us."

The Duke had in his hand the one that had been taken from Fung. He held it up.

"Dale. Show it to us. Let us see it."

No one felt a need to hurry. Least of all Dale. He looked around at the diminished gathering. And was calm; impassive. He reached into a pocket and pulled out the instrument which was a match for the one Fung had carried. Holding it in his hand, defiantly, it spoke again, metallically, the words which the Duke was speaking softly into the red object in his own hand.

"Dale—you are the one who kept them informed from inside. Cleverly done—long familiar with our methods—our weaknesses, if we have any. You are dead."

Dale threw the radio on the ground; had his pistol out, and pointing —not at the Duke, so that those with guns did not kill him at once, but at Raeburn. He raised the other hand to point:

"That's the man who spoiled it. Saw too much. Cared too little. No time to find his weaknesses."

He fired, and the bullet took Raeburn at the middle of the waist. It seemed to him a spread blow, not the sharp piercing he would have expected. And it seemed to him that he took a long time to fall, and not senseless, but the legs unusable, for the first time he could ever remember. Joan and Grant ran to him.

It was Reid who fired first, at once after Dale's gun had gone off. And there was no need for another shot. The rifle bullet shattered Dale's hand, took the pistol sweeping away in a frail ruin of metal.

The traitor, the betrayer—Dale stood, letting his ruined hand dangle; speaking: "It was worth it. It nearly succeeded. The next time yes! If not by me—I spent six years on it. Never suspected . . ."

"Dale!" The Duke had his own pistol out now. "Look to me. Direct."

He held the pistol up, aiming levelly and steadily. Dale turned the face full to him, head up, so that when the shot went off the black-red hole sprang clear in the middle of the forehead. He went down.

With Raeburn stretched out, Joan was helping, unspeaking, and Grant, absorbed, medical, had the clothes up and down, so that the pale belly and groin were exposed. Others came to watch. "Back, everybody," said Grant, and they went.

The hole was to the right of the thin waist, little blood flowing from it, and Grant first explored round the back.

"Still inside," he said. "That's good. It went through two folds of belt." And he started to press gently round the fresh fleshly crater. Raeburn watched, not able to lift and see the wound.

"Will he—?" Joan tried to speak. "Is it—?"

"Curtains?" asked Raeburn.

"Don't know yet." Grant sounded almost casual. It was his training. He felt round, pressed deeper until the man groaned.

"You're hurting him," she said, no tears yet.

"Have to," he said. "Won't be long. Get me the bag."

When she was away for the moment, he said to Raeburn: "If we're lucky, it might be in a bit that's expendable . . . I'm going to give you a wee jag—take away the pain. You'll sleep."

"Sooner the better . . . watch her—she'll worry."

Grant opened the bag as she laid it down, filled a syringe, and pressed a great quantity into the arm. "That'll work soon. Shut your eyes."

From the north, humming only and then louder, came the buzz of an approaching aircraft. The doctor said to Joan: "I need your help. Hold this pad quite firmly on the wound. I have to shave him. It's for the operating theatre."

There was a flask of warm water, some lather, and a blade which he plied around the low abdomen, clearing the milky skin so that the patient, losing feeling, yet felt the cold chill on the area long covered.

The helicopter was overhead, thrusting its loud and sustaining engine down towards the land. A door opened, and men came with a stretcher. As they lifted him on to it, now blanket-covered, he struggled to open the eyes, saw her face, and mustered the force to say—"Joan."

They lifted him in, Grant alongside. Joan Ker also thrust towards the steps. Dr Grant looked at her in query. "Are you coming?"

"I'm going to stay with him to the end."

He drew her in, a hand on her shoulders, and told her: "Watch what you say, girl. It might take forty years."

Now, he was far away. He remembered her—the face, the voice, and beyond that a muddle of great events, some of which had been the peak of his life. He was in a dark tunnel, ready to go out into the light and the conflict. There were those at his side to be trusted, to share and uphold, and the bright green beyond waited for their appearance. His hands felt dimly for the new yellow leather that someone would hand him before they ran on. The helicopter lifted out, and the extra surge of roar and scream might be a human cheering to greet the sight of the colours. He seemed to run forward towards the sound and the battle.

Alastair Dunnett, who was editor of *The Scotsman* for seventeen years, has been Chairman of one of the largest oil businesses in the United Kingdom since 1972 and Director of Scottish Television since 1975. He is the author of three previous novels and several non-fiction books about Scotland. He is married to the novelist Dorothy Dunnett, has two sons, and lives in Edinburgh.